THE PRISM FILES BOOK THREE

PRIDEFALL

BRENDAN NOBLE

For my awesome alpha and beta readers: Andrea, Breana, Mom, Dad, Lauren, Rachel, and Ross. Without all of you, this series wouldn't be possible.

Also by Brendan Noble

The Prism Files, Book One:
The Fractured Prism

The Prism Files, Book Two:
Crimson Reigns

Contents

Chapter 1

Smoke ruled the air. Ash conquered the ground. The screams surrounded me. Someone shook me awake. My vision blurred. I blinked up at the figure above me. They yelled something, but a shrieking tore through my eardrums. Panic flooded my senses. I screamed.

My vision slowly returned. I groaned and looked to the side. Ashes covered the statue of Law, and a halo of flames crowned its decapitated head. My hand trembled as I tried to raise my arm, and my lungs struggled for air. *I should be dead.*

Beyond the fallen statue, I saw the destruction laid out before me. Four craters filled the mall in front of the capitol building, where thousands of Reds, both Fracture and Militia members, had stood just moments before. Bodies were everywhere: a sea of crimson stained the turf and ash. Everywhere I looked, there were more people dead or bleeding out, their screams piercing into the late afternoon sky.

The figure shook me again. I groaned and squinted, trying to make sense of what was happening. A boy was yelling at me with panic in his eyes, "Ivan! Look at me! Ivan, we've gotta get out of here!"

"What happened?" I mumbled as the boy's face came into focus. *Where have I seen him before?*

He grabbed my arm, trying to pull me to my feet. "The Front

bombed us. You got hit pretty hard. Consider this repayment for saving my life."

Oliver. He was the boy I'd saved during the Fracture meeting after Princess Helena's death. *How did he get here?*

"Snapback just heard over the radio that the military is coming," he continued. "We've gotta go."

"The military?" The Front had pulled the army out, did that change? A cough forced itself from my lungs as I pulled on his arm and hoisted myself to my feet. A sharp pain ran down my spine when I stood. My legs felt like they'd been smacked by a hammer. But, I was alive. When I'd gained my footing, my mind began to clear. *The UPF bombed us. Where's Delaware?*

My chest seized as I scanned the bodies laid out before me and stumbled down the stairs. *Please be alive.* Oliver attempted to pull me back, but I pushed on. All I knew was that I needed to find her. Nothing else mattered.

The rank smell of death smothered me as I climbed through the bodies. I gagged. I couldn't find her. Delaware had been near the blast that hit me, but she could have ended up anywhere. Flashbacks of her stepping out of the Militia's unarmed lines and raising her gun at Max ran through my head as I stood in the field of death, turning over bodies in a desperate search. Unrelenting, Oliver continued his calls for me to run. *Where is she?*

I turned back towards the capitol building. Snapback stood yards away, tears streaming down his face. My body froze. His hands shook as they held his ripped and battered cap. My eyes met his. He shook his head.

I panicked and sprinted towards him, choking on tears. I

2

couldn't stop myself from screaming her name, the name I'd given her. "Delaware!" Snapback tried to stop me from running past him, but I pushed him out of the way as he pled with me to stop. I didn't. I couldn't. I had to see her. My best friend. My little sister.

My legs gave up when I saw Delaware, a blanket of crimson ash wrapping her lifeless body. The bomb had burned her face almost beyond recognition, but there was no doubt it was her. I yelled in pain as I trembled by her side. *Why'd you do it Del? Why'd you have to do it?*

Delaware was never one to give up on a fight, and that sparked her end. When she'd stepped out of the Militia's lines and raised that pistol, she changed everything. Our moment of unity vanished with that shot. She wanted revenge on Max as much as anything. She got it. *I hope it was worth leaving us behind.*

As I knelt there, a million emotions hit me at once: rage against the UPF, anger at Delaware, sadness at the loss of my best friend, fear at what would come next, and hopelessness at the slaughter around me. It was too much. All I could do was shake and cry as Snapback and Oliver tried to pull me to my feet. *What a hero I am.*

After an eternity of crying next to her, I gave in to my friends' attempts and limped to my feet with their help. My eyes met Snapback's, and I grabbed him in a tight hug. He'd just lost his girlfriend. If he could push through and survive for her, so could I.

I swallowed and forced myself to mutter, "Where do we go now?"

He scanned the destruction around us, his eyes lost. "We need to help everyone we can, get them to safety. She... she's gone. It's my job now." He placed his tattered hat on his head. A few brown strands of hair pushed their way through the holes. "The army will be here soon."

I tried to shake the panic from my mind, but I couldn't stop it from moving at a hundred miles an hour. "It was a damn trap! Shit! They knew something like this would happen, and we made ourselves perfect targets." My stomach flipped. I fell back to my knees and vomited. "Damn it!"

He took a raspy breath and gripped my shoulder. "I know, but we don't have time. We need to get everyone out of here."

"We're surrounded," I spat as I struggled to my feet. "We can't hide." I wondered what Julia thought as she watched her boyfriend be bombed on live TV. *Does she think I'm dead? This was supposed to be a happy day for her.*

Oliver cut in. "We don't need to, probably. The Front really only cares about the Fracture, right?"

I stared into the ashen sky and muttered, "I hope you're right, but we can't take any more risks. Get everyone back to Payne-Phalen. Snap, your fighters were away from the blast, right?"

He nodded before pointing at the state of his cap. "Mostly."

"Good. If they come for us, we have the walls and gates to make a stand."

Snap ran his hand along the brim of his hat, contemplating the plan. "It's all we've got, so it'll do. We need to hurry. Go. I'll take Oliver with me. Grab anyone you can and meet back at HQ."

I glanced towards where I'd parked the Minutemen car and sighed in relief. It had been far enough away from the blast. *At least something survived.*

The bodies of dead Militia members littered the path to the car. If I hadn't vomited already, I would have again. Guts covered the pavement. From the look of it, most of those still alive had already fled back towards Payne-Phalen. *How long was I out?*

There were a few remaining survivors, and as I started pushing my way towards the car, I heard a cry to my right. Two Reds, about my age, were limping towards me. My legs protested with each step as I closed the distance. The taller, lankier one was trying to avoid putting any weight on one of his legs and had his arm wrapped around the other's shoulder for support. Crimson coated his pale skin, and his eyes were full of desperation. His shorter, Hispanic friend wasn't in much better shape, though, and one of his arms hung uselessly by his side.

When I approached, the shorter one spoke, "Oh, thank God. I thought we were gonna... Holy shit you're Coyote!"

His shock forced me to chuckle. It felt wrong. "C'mon. The army's closing in." I nodded towards the car. "Let's do introductions on the way."

I could tell he was trying to smile through the pain. "Thank you. I... I didn't know how we were going to get back. The bombs..."

"We'll be fine if we hurry. Follow me." I replaced him alongside his limping friend and started the walk towards the car, groaning with the extra weight pushing down on my back. "We'll get you guys home. Hopefully, we still have some of our doctors. After this shit, we're gonna need them."

After only a couple of yards of progress, we stopped as a girl's wailing came from near a downed tree. I nodded to the Red that could walk, handed his friend back over to him, and limped as fast as I could towards the sound. Each step sent another shock up my spine, but if there was a chance to save more of the survivors, I had to take it.

An Orange girl was bent down next to the tree, screaming for help as I arrived. "My friend... Her leg."

The tree trapped the Yellow girl's leg just above her knee. Her eyes were wild, and she flailed her other leg at the tree in a fruitless attempt to move it. I held my hands out in front of me, trying to speak calmly, but I wasn't in any better shape. "Stop moving. Can you do that?"

The Yellow girl shuddered but nodded.

"Good. You'll be okay." I waved to her friend. "Help me lift it!"

The Orange girl trembled but followed my instructions. She lined up on the other side of the tree, and I counted down. On one, we lifted it together, just enough for the trapped girl to slide her leg out. My back screamed as she slid free, and I dropped my end with a *thump.* I winced and tried to help up the girl who had been trapped, but she shook her head. "I... I can't walk. My leg won't move."

Shit. If she'd broken her leg, there wasn't much we could do at Payne-Phalen. But we needed to survive. There weren't any other safe places. "I'll carry you, c'mon."

Her dark brown eyes were full of fear as I picked her up in my arms. She shivered. *She's going into shock. We need to hurry.* My muscles burned, but I ignored the pain and pushed towards the car. Her friend clutched her ribs and followed close behind.

Each step I took was over a body or through another puddle of crimson. My insides flipped inside out, but there was no escaping the sights. No matter where I looked, the horrors followed. *Is this what war looks like?*

We'd tried to stop a civil war. We'd failed. The rioters had destroyed so much of the city and murdered hundreds of innocent people, but that didn't excuse the actions of the UPF. Nothing could do that. They knew they were firing on both the Fracture rioters and unarmed Militia marchers. They didn't care.

Thinking about it won't help. I looked down at the girl. "What's your name?"

Her breathing was raspy, but her eyes focused on me as she brushed a strand of her brunette hair from her face. "Lillian. I... I know you."

I forced a smile. "Ivan. I was the guy on the statue."

She winced as I stumbled over a body, and her response was more a squeak, "The Red King himself."

I chuckled, but the pain from the laughter forced me to stop. "The what?"

Her friend fixed her cornrows as her own distraction. The grey ash was streaked across her black hair and skin, but she didn't seem to mind. "You *are* going to be the king, aren't you?"

"Do I... ack... Do I look like a king to you?" I replied as we closed in on the car.

She smirked cheekily and raised an eyebrow. "You did up there."

The Reds caught up, and the limping one started gesturing wildly. "What is he doing?" I asked the shorter one.

"He can't talk. It's sign language," he replied. "Tyler says a real king would have run instead of helping us escape."

"Harsh, but not wrong," I said as we reached the car. The Orange girl opened the door for me to put Lillian in the passenger seat. After I had her in, I took off my jacket and threw it over her to try to keep her warm. She was still shaking, and her face was pale. I glanced at the Orange girl. "What was your name?"

She half-smiled. "Kaja, *your highness.*"

I shook my head. "I am and never will be okay with being called 'your highness.'"

The translator Red loaded Tyler into the car before holding his good arm out at an upward angle for an old Red handshake. "Emmanuel, but you can call me Manny."

I completed my half of the handshake and nodded. "Glad you and Tyler are alright."

Tyler signed something that looked like he was gesturing from me to him. I didn't need to translation to know what he meant, and I forced myself to smile at him as Manny slid in next to him.

I rounded the car to the driver's side, but something froze me as I placed my hand on the door handle. Hesitant, I stared back at the field, taking in every detail. It was the last thing I wanted to do, but I needed to remember it: the sights, the smells, the way the ash coated the world like a corrupted snowfall, all of it. I needed that moment to never leave my memory. I needed it to drive me forward, into the darkness. *Rage, rage against the dying of the light.*

With a deep breath, I yanked open the door and threw myself into the driver's seat. Lillian was clutching the jacket, trying to be brave through the pain. I tried to smile at her, but it was too difficult to fight the weight that hung over me. Everything happened so fast. Julia's birthday party felt like it had been days ago, not hours. Now, we sat in the middle of a mass slaughter, not knowing why we were the ones lucky enough to survive. Delaware's charred face flashed in my mind, and my hands shook as I turned the key. *Stay strong.*

The gear lever wouldn't move. I grunted, trying to force the car into drive. It still didn't budge. Anger took over as I yelled and slammed my fist into the steering wheel before trying again.

"You okay?" Kaja asked from the back.

Finally, it slid into gear, and we rolled back toward Payne-Phalen. I shook my head. "No."

I wanted to say that everything was fine, but I couldn't. In one minute, we'd gone from preventing a slaughter to being at the center of one. I wasn't ready for this, no one was, but seeing so many people dead less than a week after our raid on the New Ulm camp was horrific. We'd rescued over a thousand Reds and pre-Prism Black Tags from the United People's Front's concentration camps that night, but now, they got their revenge.

My best friend was gone, and hundreds of Militia marchers were dead because I asked them to stand in the line of fire. We were yet again caught in a fight so much bigger than us, and people died because of it. Silence hung over the car as I gunned it down the street. My blood was on fire. *We'll make them pay.*

Manny's voice came from the back after a minute. "Tyler says Delaware was a good leader. She held us together."

Was. The road was blurry through my tear-filled eyes as I

gripped the steering wheel so hard it hurt. "She was more than that. She did the impossible. The Militia was destroyed, people were starving, and the Enclave was gone, but she kept things together and made Payne-Phalen a home for everyone. She thought she wasn't ready to be captain, but she did what none of us could have." I choked for a moment before finishing, "And now she's gone."

Lillian looked at me with concern. "Did you know her well?"

I scoffed through the tears and bit my lip. "You could say that. I... I recruited her into the Militia after we saved her from one of the work orphanages. She was like my little sister, the last family I had left."

Kaja muttered from the back, "Shit. That sucks."

With a grimace, I replied, "She made her choice when she raised that gun." I paused and whispered to myself, "She made her choice." *Do you actually believe that?*

Manny spoke again, "She sacrificed herself to stop Max. I dunno, but that sound pretty heroic to me."

My heart was in a knot, and this discussion was just making it worse. I looked at him in the mirror, my eyes narrow. "It doesn't matter if it was reckless or heroic. In the end, she's gone, and we have to figure out how to pick up the pieces."

Lillian screamed. I snapped my gaze to the road just as a black jeep pulled in front of us and the first shot flew through the windshield.

Chapter 2

Worst day ever. I flicked the steering wheel to the right, sending the car skidding across the battered and broken pavement and onto the sidewalk. "Get your heads down!" I yelled.

My heart raced and the engine revved as I slammed my foot on the gas. We flew around the corner as a barrage of bullets flew into the side of the car. Manny cried out, but I didn't have time to see what happened as three more jeeps appeared and joined the pursuit.

Kaja yelled from the back, "They're coming!"

"No shit! I couldn't tell!" I called back as we screeched onto the next street. Just ahead of us was the highway. On the other side was the gate to Payne-Phalen. *Almost there.*

My ears rang as more bullets smacked against the back of the car. I swerved back and forth to avoid the fire, but they were unrelenting. Even with the car's speed advantage, we were pulling away too slowly. It was only a matter of time until a stray bullet popped a tire. We were sitting ducks.

I pulled my pistol. Lillian's eyes widened. "What are you doing? Are you crazy?"

Probably. I flicked off the safety and stuck my arm backwards out the shattered window, using the rearview window to aim. I'd never tried anything like that before, but we needed to fire back if we wanted to survive. "Yeah, I guess I am." The shots deflected off the closest jeep's fender. They charged on.

Kaja scoffed from the back. "That did a hell of a lot."

It wasn't easy splitting my attention between the road ahead of me and the jeeps behind, but I still had a couple shots left. *If I can just hit one tire...*

A bullet flew through our back windshield and whizzed by my ear. I jolted in shock, sending the car swerving. The smell of burning rubber filled my nose as we drifted to a stop under the highway overpass. Without thinking, I got out of the car and raised my gun. *Four jeeps, three bullets.* My passengers screamed at me to get back in the car. I didn't listen.

I fired at the closest jeep's tire. It popped, sending the jeep spinning into the one trailing behind it. The loud *crunch* of metal smashing metal filled the air as the jeeps collided. I smiled to myself, but I didn't have time to celebrate. *Two more.*

I raised my gun again. My hands shook. *C'mon. Not now.* The second shot missed and drew sparks against the pavement. "Shit!" Before I could aim again, a bullet skimmed my left shoulder, and I winced in pain as my companions screamed from the car.

Ignoring their cries, I took a quick breath and raised my gun for the last shot. *You've got this.* My finger gripped the trigger. This time, I didn't miss. The bullet pierced the tire, forcing the jeep to hobble to a stop. But there was no time to celebrate. The soldiers stormed out and aimed at me. I yelped and jumped back in the car, ducking as bullets peppered the door.

"Go!" Kaja yelled as I threw the car back in drive. The last jeep was closing in fast. I gunned it just as it was about to crash into us. It flew through where I'd stood just seconds before.

They tried to sweep us from behind. I swerved back and forth, trying to avoid their attacks. In the mirror, I could see Tyler was signing, but Manny was too busy whimpering to translate.

Without ammo, there was no way to take the last jeep out. *Speed it is.* We flew down the road, and soon, the Payne-Phalen gate came into view. *Come on, come on.* The car groaned as the spray of bullets had done their damage. It didn't matter. All we needed was a hundred more yards out of it.

Kaja screamed from the back as another round of bullets shattered what was left of the back window. I gripped the steering wheel and pushed the car for everything it could give me. "We're going to make it!" I shouted, more to reassure myself than any of them. It wasn't working. My heart felt like it was seizing as we flew towards the gate. *I want to go home.*

The Militia fighters at the gate opened it just wide enough for our car and opened fire on the jeep. We slid through the gap, and the fighters on the other side pushed it shut. Only seconds later, the jeep smashed into it, sending metal and glass shards flying, but the gate held. *Maybe the Front can build some things right.*

I breathed a sigh of relief as we drove through the old neighborhood. In the rearview mirror, I could see the fighters holding the gate against the soldiers. *We did it.*

The car sputtered to a stop as we reached the Militia HQ. Injured people lying on old sheets, tarps, or whatever they could find covered the whole street in front of us. A few Orange and Yellow doctors were helping everyone they could, but there were hundreds of people there. They needed help.

My whole body ached as I opened the door and stepped back into the world. The sun was setting now, and with it, the temperature. The cold should have burned against my exposed skin, but I felt nothing.

As the others tried to get out of the car, Manny cried out. I looked back to see the blood seeping through his shirt. *No.* I pointed to an open spot on the grass. "Get him down and cover the wound. Now! I'll get the doctor."

Kaja and Tyler helped Manny to the ground as I tripped more than ran towards the doctor. *No one else dies today.* The Orange doctor was bent over an injured Red when I showed up, panting and pointing. He looked up at me. "What's wrong?"

"My friend. They shot him. He's bleeding out."

He took a sharp breath and looked back down at his patient. "Try not to move it until I get back." He stood and scanned the street. "Where?"

I waved for him to follow me, and we made our way back towards Manny. Tyler had wrapped his shirt around his friend's stomach, but the blood kept seeping through. The doctor gestured for him to move from Manny's side. I took a breath before remembering Lillian was still in the car, unable to leave with her injured leg.

"I was wondering if you'd forgotten me," she said as I opened her door and lifted her out.

"Sorry about that."

Concern filled her eyes as I carried her towards Manny. "Is he going to be okay?"

I shook my head. "We can only hope."

When we reached the others, I set Lillian down. The doctor could take a look at her once he finished with Manny. With that bullet wound, he was the priority. There was no way these doctors would be able to fix Lillian's leg, but she needed it checked out by somebody who had a clue what they were talking about.

My damaged earpiece crackled as Snapback's voice came through. "Ivan, you there?"

I touched my ear. "Yeah."

His voice forced its way through the static. "I've been trying to get in touch with you for the last ten minutes. The military's here. They're shooting on sight."

I sighed and looked up at the HQ. "Sorry, I think my radio is damaged. Probably why I haven't heard from Jonah. And I know. We barely escaped them ourselves. I've got a group here with some pretty serious injuries, and there's definitely not enough doctors."

"We never have enough, but with this shit? I don't know what we're going to do."

I groaned. "We need to get these people to the Royal Hospital."

Kaja raised her eyebrow at me as Snap responded, "That'd be great, but how the hell do you expect to do that? The military is about to retake the city, and the Fracture is all but dead. They're not going to distract the UPF anymore. All eyes are on us."

"But they can't attack ambulances from the Royal Hospital. The UPF has enough to deal with. They wouldn't risk pissing off the royals now."

"That might work." He hesitated. "Fine, try it. What the hell do we have to lose anymore?"

I closed my eyes. "A lot."

Kaja studied me as she tried to help Lillian stay out of the snow. "You want to do *what*?"

"I don't *want* to do anything, trust me, but we need to get people help. There's hundreds of people injured. The Royal Hospital can shuttle people into royal territory." I huffed. The last thing I needed right now was more questions.

Tyler signed aggressively, but with Manny injured, none of us knew what he was saying. He slumped his shoulders and sighed before returning his attention to his friend. I felt bad for him, but there were bigger concerns.

Kaja knelt next to Lillian and took out a knife. I put my hand on her arm. "We should wait for the doctor to finish with Manny."

She shrugged me off. "We don't have time for that." She sliced off Lillian's pant leg just above the wound. When she pulled away the fabric, my heart dropped.

Lillian screamed and covered her eyes. Kaja scrambled to her side and stroked her head, whispering, "You're okay. You're going to be okay."

Everything below where the tree had fallen on her leg was a deep purple. I winced just looking at it. There was no doubt in my mind that it had to be amputated.

Tyler signed something again. This time, Manny groaned before translating, "He says you trust the royals too much."

"I probably do, but do you have a better idea?" I replied.

Tyler shrugged as I looked to Kaja before back at him. Their friends were desperate. *I need to call Julia.* I pulled out my cell phone and sighed. *She's going to be frantic.* The phone rang for a couple seconds before she picked up. I could tell she'd been crying as her voice shook. "Ivan?"

I bit my lip and smiled. "It's me."

She broke into tears. "I saw the video. I... I thought you were dead. They cut out the stream right after the strike."

"I'm okay. Not great, but I'm alive. A lot of others, though... They need your help."

"Is Delaware..."

I paused and fought against the hole I felt in my chest. *Now isn't the time.* I couldn't find the words to answer. There was silence on the other end, and I knew she didn't know what to say either. Eventually, I mustered up the strength to speak, "Others are alive and need doctors. We need to get them to the Royal Hospital. The few doctors we have can't treat everyone."

"How many are there?"

I scanned the scene in front of me. Reds, Oranges, and Yellows were scattered everywhere. "At least fifty need a hospital, maybe more."

There was a pause as she thought. "I will do everything I can. Mother won't support us transporting them into royal territory, but maybe we can send doctors to set up stations there?"

"Okay, but some of these people need real surgery. We have to save everyone we can. It's time for the royals to put some skin in the game unless they want to sit back and watch the Front slaughter us again."

She sighed. "I know, but I can only do so much, Ivan."

She's doing everything she can. I took a deep breath and tried to soften my tone. "Thank you, Julia. And I'm sorry. I didn't mean to be so intense. It's just insane over here..."

"Shh, it's okay. I understand. Just give me a bit to figure all of this out." She paused. "I'm just happy you're alive. I was so scared."

I bit my cheek. "I'm sorry you had to see it. We'll talk later. I love you."

"I love you too. Please be safe."

I smiled softly to myself, "I will," before the tension gripped my heart again. When I hung up, an array of smirks from my new companions greeted me. I shrugged. "What?"

Tyler looked up from Manny and made a heart symbol while Kaja exclaimed, "Ha! So, it is true."

I'd forgotten that beyond the royals, our relationship was still a rumor at best. People knew something was going on, but they didn't know how serious we were. I snapped back, "We're under attack, and you're worried about my relationship?"

Lillian smiled, but with her pain, it came out more like a wince. "That's so adorable."

I felt my cheeks flush, pissing me off even more. "Unfortunately, most people don't think that."

Tyler signed something, and Manny groaned. "He says most people are dumbasses."

"There's more important things than my relationship," I replied. Manny coughed, and I looked over at him. "Doc, what's the report?"

The doctor sighed. "He's stable, but he needs surgery. That bullet is still lodged in his body and could do serious damage if it isn't removed. Better hope the royals follow through."

Shit. We were betting a lot of the Royal Council sending ambulances. But if anyone could convince them, it was Julia.

Kaja nodded before squeezing Lillian's hand. "How're you feeling?"

Lillian winced. "It burns. I... I don't want to lose my leg."

I crossed my arms. "I hope you won't have to, but for now, stay still. Julia is trying to get ambulances."

Manny scrunched his nose, unconvinced. "You think it'll work? I mean, the royals never help us."

"The royals have been the ones supplying the food to keep this place going. There's some terrible people behind those walls, but they have hearts too."

The doctor knelt next to Lillian and examined her leg. "I wish I could do something for you, but they're going to have to operate if you want to keep your leg. I wish you all the best, and for all of our sakes, I hope those royal doctors get here soon."

The doctor's words sounded distant as I scanned the crowd of injured people scattered across the street. *Why would they do this?* My eyes fell on the entrance of the HQ. It looked like people had piled up all the spare sheets and blankets they could find from the nearby houses and apartments. Delaware had built a community out of these people. They were doing everything they could to help one another, but so many were injured or dead. There weren't enough of us left standing to fight the Front and care for the wounded. *Why'd you have to leave, Del? These people need you. I need you.*

With the aftermath of the strike and the car chase, everything had been moving so quickly. I tried to ignore the void in my chest, but now I had time to think, to feel. Under my frosty shell, all I felt was loss. Delaware wasn't coming back. I'd never see my best friend again. All I wanted was to go home, hug Julia, and cry. The world was falling apart, and I didn't know how to stop it.

Shots beyond the wall pulled me from my daze. *They're coming for us.*

There was no way to know if the UPF had the guts to bomb us again. I thought that they only sent the airstrikes because of the Fracture, but if they were desperate, they would do it again. To them, the Militia was nothing more than a terrorist group. St. Paul was in chaos, and our elimination would make a clean slate for them to build on. I hoped that at the very least, having Yellows and Oranges with us would make them more cautious. The elites didn't care about the deaths of Reds, but killing those from higher colors would turn some heads at the very least.

Lillian craned her head towards the walls. "Do you think they'll get us?"

Kaja cracked her knuckles. "We'll hold them off. We always have."

I sighed. "I think they'd risk losing the support they have left among the Greens and Yellows if they assaulted the neighborhood. The Front is on edge, but there's a reason they've ruled for a hundred years. They're not stupid. They'll kill anyone outside the Payne-Phalen walls and claim that they were Fracture rioters that escaped, but they can only go so far."

We all looked up as a van skidded to a stop at the other end of the block. Snapback and Oliver jumped out and slid open the side door, revealing yet another group of wounded. I took a deep breath. "That explains the shots. You guys good? I need to talk to Snapback."

Lillian tried to force a smile. "Yeah, we'll be fine. Thanks, Ivan."

Manny just groaned and held his thumb up.

I nodded. "I'll be back, hopefully with an ambulance."

Snapback was carrying a Red to an open spot when I approached. He looked tired, but I doubted that he would admit it. Just like me, the work kept his mind off Delaware. He set the Red down and turned towards me. "Any news?"

I shook my head. "Julia is going to do what she can, but she's skeptical we can bring people to the hospital. She's trying to get them to at least send some doctors over."

He closed his eyes and rubbed the back of his neck, wincing. "Sending a couple docs isn't going to do it. We need a whole damn hospital!"

"She's doing everything she can."

He clenched his fists. "It's not enough, Ivan! Look around you. We're dying here, and the royals can't spare a damn ambulance? What use are they if they're going to leave us hanging when we're being slaughtered? If Julia's going to be queen, doesn't she have some power?" He ripped off his hat and squeezed it.

I grabbed his arm. "Nothing is that simple with the royals," I snarled. "I don't like it either, but what options do we have Snap? We never had royal support before, but now, because of her, we have *something*. The Whites are corrupt and selfish, but we need them."

He stared down at his tattered hat, his hands shaking. "When this is all over, Ivan, you get to go back to your fancy palace and girlfriend. Just remember, for some of us, this is all we have."

I bit my cheek and released him. He'd stabbed my open wound. *How do I reconcile my two lives?* After a few seconds, I finally snapped back, "You're right! I'm lucky. I'm not one of you any-more, but I'll never be a royal either. I don't belong anywhere. Like it or not, I'm trying to use my position to help save this damn country, but I don't know how. Delaware's gone. It's just us, and we need to figure it out."

He grabbed me in a hug, catching me off guard. After a moment of shock, I hugged him back. Snapback was always one to try and hide his emotions, but he'd lost everything. He was a good guy. He deserved better.

When we stepped back from each other, he looked ready to say something again, but gunshots echoed beyond the wall. His eyes widened. "C'mon, they need our help holding the gate."

I glanced back towards my group before running with him. I may have been stuck in-between worlds, but the Militia still needed me. There wasn't much left to defend in Payne-Phalen, but we would protect everything we could for as long as possible.

When we reached the wall, one of the Militia fighters tossed us each a rifle. "They're trying to take out the main gate."

The wall towered before us as I felt the weight of the rifle in my trembling hands. All the pent-up rage I'd felt towards the UPF was ready to burst. Every inch of me burned in hatred at every-thing they'd done, at how they'd slaughtered my best friend. *They're going to pay.*

I gazed up at the about seven-foot-tall wooden platform the

Militia had built along the back of the wall, allowing our fighters some cover while they shot down at the attacking Front troops. It wasn't much, but it was emblematic of what the Militia did best: making do with what we had. I nodded to Snapback. "Ready?"

He gripped his rifle and started towards the ladder up to the platform. *I'll take that as a yes.*

A few steps behind him, I bolted up the ladder as quickly as my bruised muscles would allow. Each step sent another shot down my spine, but I ignored the pain as my rage burned on. The ladder's creaking was barely audible over the persistent pounding of gunfire against my ears. *How long can we hold them off?*

We reached the top and scrambled behind the wall, which rose just three feet above the platform. It wasn't enough protection to stand, even with the military shooting from an upward angle, and the splintered boards tore into my exposed knees as we waited for our moment to return fire. My bodyguard outfit from Julia's birthday party was shredded from the bombing, not that its thin fabric would have provided much protection anyway.

As Snap silently counted down, I tested my throbbing shoulder. I was lucky the bullet hadn't done more than draw a little blood. On one, we sprung to our feet and rained bullets down on the soldiers. Each shot sent a deafening roar through my eardrums and jabbed at my shoulder. It felt good fighting back against the people that felt no shame for enslaving and bombing innocent people. In the ashes of the airstrike, something had ignited inside me; I was on fire.

Each time I rose to fire off a couple more shots, I watched as my bullets ripped through the soldiers. In the moment, any guilt

I'd felt before when I killed was gone. I was fighting for everything I had left and for those I'd lost... for Delaware.

A fighter next to me screamed as a bullet tore through his chest. He collapsed and fell off the back of the platform. I winced when I heard him smack into the ground below.

The rage was gone. Panic choked me again. The rifle's cold grip suddenly felt alien in my hands. I sat against the wall, shivering in the cold late-winter air. Rage, fear, and sorrow battled for my heart. Screams echoed from both sides of the wall, piercing through my clouded mind. It was too much. *This is war.*

Snapback shook me, "Ivan! We need you."

I took a shaky breath and snapped my eyes to his. Unable to bring myself to speak, I just nodded and readied my rifle. *We win, or we die.* With a yell, I popped up and aimed at the next wave of soldiers. They hid behind jeeps, trees, and buildings as we fired down at them. It was impossible to know how long we would be able to hold the wall, but that didn't matter. This was survival.

My sights focused on the head of an advancing soldier and tightened my finger around the trigger. Before I could fire, approaching siren interrupted me. Snap turned towards me, and our eyes met in surprise as we thought the same thing. *Ambulances. Julia did it.*

A shot broke through the sirens' rings. Pain stabbed through my left arm. I cried out and fell to my knees. "Damn it!" Blood gushed from a wound a few inches above my elbow, but from the look of it, the bullet only grazed me.

Snapback pulled me towards the ladder. "C'mon. At least you had good timing."

"Screw you." I ripped off my sleeve and tied it around the wound to act as a make-shift gauze.

"Wait a sec," he said.

"What?"

"Look." Snapback pointed towards the ambulances.

I blocked the sun with my hand as I analyzed the situation. A line of soldiers blocked the ambulances. *It's not gonna work.* Doctors argued with the soldiers, but they weren't budging. "Shit. They're stopping ambulances now?"

"Apparently."

Oliver called from the bottom of the ladder. "Snapback! Ivan! You guys need to hear this."

Snap and I exchanged glances before he headed down. I followed, using my good arm to climb down the ladder. When I hopped to the bottom, I was disoriented and stumbled before Snapback swooped under my arm to catch me.

"Remember when I was the one panicking under fire?" he said.

I chuckled, but before I could respond, Oliver held up Snap's radio. A soldier's voice was repeating a message over it. "...demand surrender in exchange for allowing the ambulances through. I repeat. We will not permit the ambulances to pass through without immediate surrender."

Snap's wide eyes met mine as my stomach turned over. *What now?*

Chapter 3

"We can't surrender! What do we have left?" Snap said, pacing in a circle.

"Do we have a choice?" Oliver replied.

Snapback ripped off his hat. "Shit! Can't we just get one break?"

I groaned and grabbed my injured arm. Between the shoulder shot and this one, it did little more than hang there, useless. "Not when you're a Red." My mind spun. Beyond the gate were the ambulances we needed to save dozens of lives. But if we surrendered, more could die. "We're screwed either way, but I think we have to do it."

"Are you nuts?" Snap spat. "Where are we gonna go?"

"Why don't you ask them?" I nodded to the radio.

He snatched it from Oliver's grasp. "This is Snapback. What are the terms?"

The voice came back. "The residents of the Militia will be relocated back to the place you call the Enclave and placed under military occupation. All weapons and other contraband will be seized, but no one will be harmed. We will allow the ambulances to transport those patients that require hospitalization."

Snapback fixed his eyes on me. *He wants me to make the decision.* A few months ago, I had been his lieutenant, so he wasn't used to leading yet. It was understandable, but I wasn't the captain of the Militia. It shouldn't have been my call to make. But should didn't matter. I took a deep breath. "We don't have a choice. If we don't surrender, they'll beat us down anyway and we won't get the ambulances."

He crossed his arms and shook his head. "Fine. I hate it, but I trust you."

My chest was in a vice. I whispered, more to myself than to him, "Glad someone does."

Snapback didn't hear me and started barking orders, "Oliver, get everyone you can ready for when the ambulances come. We won't have much time."

I watched Oliver go before saying, "I should stay and help. Without Del..."

"No. Without Naomi, we need you in the palace even more. They're going to take everything. You're all we got with the Whites. Get Julia on the throne and fix this."

As I turned to leave, he raised the radio to give them our answer. The pain on his face was the same one I felt in my heart. For a hundred years, the Militia never surrendered to the UPF. We just did. Beyond the remnants in other cities, we were all that was left of the group. Letting them win this battle went against my instincts, but this was bigger than one battle. We needed to survive and save as many lives as possible. That's all that mattered.

My arm and shoulder screamed at me as I limped back towards the HQ. If either of the shots had more than grazed me, I could've been dead. I cursed at the pain, but that fact shocked me to my core. Right now, though, Manny and Lillian were a much higher priority. The gates crawled open behind me as the ambulances rolled through. Five of them flew by me, enough to hopefully cover the worst off.

When I reached the ambulances, the Blue doctor that seemed in charge was talking to Oliver. His eyes wandered to my arm, but I waved him off. "I'm not the priority."

He struggled to make eye contact when he responded, "Show us those that need urgent surgery. The rest, I'm afraid, we cannot admit. I will leave a few of my nurses and doctors to assist with the lower priority cases."

I nodded. "Thank you. You have no idea how much this means to us."

He didn't smile. "Thank Princess Julia. She convinced the Council to send us over Queen Vera's objections."

Has the black widow lost her venom? I turned to Oliver. "You got this? I've got at least two that need to go."

He nodded. "Grab them and take one of the ambulances. Snapback and I will handle things here."

My new friends were all gazing at the ambulances and doctors scrambling through the crowd when I returned. Lillian had a worried look on her face. I smiled at her. "You're going to be okay, I promise."

Her breaths were raspy. "You're bleeding..."

"Don't worry about me. I've had worse." I groaned as I knelt next to her.

She didn't seem convinced but let it go. "What if the Front knocks me down a color? I don't want to be a Red."

Tyler gave her a middle finger as I chuckled. "Believe me, it's better to be Red than dead. Besides, they know you're with the Militia now. Color doesn't matter when you're a terrorist."

Her eyes widened. "Was that supposed to help?"

"No, it was supposed to make you laugh," I replied.

Kaja studied the situation. "They just let them through?"

My fists clenched. "No, they didn't."

"What happened then?"

"We surrendered." My tongue felt dirty just saying it.

"We can't just abandon Payne-Phalen!" Kaja shouted, her brows furrowed. "This is our home now."

I sighed. "I'm sorry. We didn't have a choice if we wanted to save the injured people. The military will relocate the Militia to the Enclave. It'll suck, but they'll live. And speaking of living..." I nodded towards Lillian and Manny. "We need to get them to the hospital."

Kaja huffed but complied. With my arm in awful shape, I couldn't hold Lillian, but Tyler stepped in for me. She winced as he picked her up. From the coloring of her skin, her leg was getting worse. We were lucky that the doctors came when they did.

I shuffled over to Manny. "Can you walk?"

"I can make it to the ambulance," he replied, struggling to sit up.

I raised an eyebrow. "You sure?"

He struggled to his feet, his injured arm hanging limply by his side. Kaja threw his good arm over her shoulder and tried to help him. "We're all coming," she said, her eyes narrow.

"There's only enough beds for those who need surgery."

She shook her head. "Hell no. We're a team now. You weren't

the only one getting shot at!"

"Fine," I groaned. "You can come, but we'll have to stand in the ambulance. Tyler might be able to sit, but we're getting everyone we can into one trip."

As Tyler scrunched his face, Manny laughed and said, "He's no wimp."

Tyler nodded and shuffled towards the ambulance with Lillian in his arms. *What have I gotten myself into with these guys?*

As we walked, the doctors worked their way through the crowd and grabbed those that Snapback and Oliver set as high priority. It looked like the help would be enough, but for so many people, it came too late. Those airstrikes had killed hundreds of people instantly and hundreds more in the following minutes as we struggled to save the ones we could. I never thought I could hate the UPF more than I did before, but now, every bit of me wanted revenge. The gunfight by the gate had let out my rage, but I was still steaming.

We reached the ambulance, and a Green nurse helped Kaja and Tyler set Manny and Lillian down on two of the beds they'd prepared. The rest of the group piled into the back while the nurse pulled me to the side. "We're going to do everything we can, but there is a good chance we can't save her leg." She glanced at my arm.

I nodded, ignoring her worried glance. "I know, but thanks for being here."

"There are some things more important than a tag."

She climbed into the front while I joined the others in the back. While we had been talking, a couple of the doctors had loaded two Reds onto the other beds. One of them was wrapped around his stomach and chest, and from the look of the blood splattered across the gauze, he had been shot multiple times. The other was unconscious and wheezing. I wondered if it was just lung damage from the blast or something else. Regardless, I was glad they would have a chance to get the care they needed.

The nurse in the driver's seat yelled something back to us, but before I could respond, he gunned it. I lost my balance and stumbled into Kaja, who kindly stepped to the side instead of trying to help. My shoulder smacked into the back door with a *bang*. I groaned as I fell to the floor. "Thanks for that. It's not like my arm wasn't injured already."

Kaja gave me a wry smile as the nurse asked, "Everything alright?"

I called back, "Yeah, just lost my balance."

With a laugh, Kaja offered me a hand. "Good thing we're going to the hospital. Just don't die before then."

After she pulled me up, I tested out my arm. It was sore but worked: just another pain to deal with. "You're just a ray of sunshine, aren't you?"

Lillian giggled. "That's my Kaja."

"One of us needs to be realistic." Kaja smirked and squeezed her hand.

Lillian smiled back. "One of us needs to have hope."

Tyler steadied himself nearer to the front of the ambulance before flashing a few signs at Manny, who weakly translated for him, "That's easy for a Yellow to say."

"Is it easy for the girl who is about to lose her leg?" Lillian said, wincing as we hit a bump.

Tyler bobbed his head side to side as if he was considering her comeback. Manny shrugged. "This stuff sucks, but what are we without hope?"

Kaja scoffed and leaned her back on the doors next to me. "Living in the real world. We just surrendered!"

Lillian replied, "We've made it this far. I see no reason to believe we can't end this. I mean, the Red King himself is right here."

Don't put your hope in me. I rested my head against the back door. "Please don't call me that."

"Why do you resist the nickname so much?" Lillian said.

I swept my arm at my ripped clothes. "Look at me. Do I look like a damn king to you?"

Kaja raised her eyebrow and analyzed my face. "What don't you like about it, the 'Red' part, or the 'King?'"

"I've been a Red my whole life. I have no shame in that, but I will never be king." I scoffed at the idea. Even considering the possibility of getting married or being king still made me squirm. I hated war, but it seemed easier than that.

Tyler signed, and Manny nodded. "Once a Red, always a Red."

The shot Red in the corner moaned. I walked over. "You alright?"

"Waddya think?"

I put my hand on his shoulder. "We'll be there soon."

"Not gonna make it." He shook his head and coughed.

My chest locked up. *I can't watch another person die today.* I grabbed his hand and squeezed. "You're going to make it. These guys can help you. Stay with us." I yelled up to the front, "How far we got left? This guy's in bad shape back here."

The second nurse climbed back and crouched next to the sputtering man, inspecting his wounds. "He has lost a lot of blood, but we just passed through the gates. He'll make it." *Almost home.* She placed the back of her hand on his forehead. "Fever… The wound is likely infected. With something this bad, though, I can't risk doing anything more until we arrive. I'll stay back here until then. Thank you for calling up to us."

I nodded and turned back to the group. "How are you feeling, Lillian?"

"I can make it," she said through gritted teeth.

Kaja patted her head and whispered, "You're doing great." I raised an eyebrow, and she glared back. "I can be supportive when I want to."

We all chuckled as the ambulance ground to a halt. The nurse flipped open the back door and slid the shot man out the back on his gurney as the driver grabbed the other end. She spoke to me as they started wheeling the man through the snow, "We'll send someone for the others."

I nodded and motioned to Kaja to grab the other end of Manny's gurney. Even with one arm, I could lift him enough, and we carried him out the back. As we stepped into the snow, two Green nurses appeared from the hospital entrance across from us. They grabbed the gurney for us, and I nodded my head towards the ambulance. "There's two more in there. We'll grab one of them."

They nodded and began carrying Manny towards the hospital doors as Kaja and I went back for Lillian. Soon, they would be in surgery, and I could see Julia. *This nightmare of a day is almost over.*

Inside the hospital, doctors and nurses scurried in preparation for the surgeries. We weren't the only group that needed help, and the ambulances likely would need at least another trip to bring everyone. It was a high-tech and elite hospital, but it wasn't massive. With only the royalty to care for, they had never dealt with this many people. I was thankful, though, that they were doing what they could. We had nobody else.

Lillian scrunched her face as we handed her to a set of nurses. While they carried her off, she looked back at Kaja, her eyes full of worry. Kaja's face shared that pain. I understood how she felt: useless as someone she cared about suffered. I put a hand on her shoulder. "It's going to be alright, I promise."

Her fists clenched. "How do you know?"

"Because I've stood where you've stood, and I can tell you that it sucks. But no matter what happens, it's going to be okay. Leg or no leg, we'll make sure she's cared for."

She whipped around to glare up at me. "Why do you care? Why aren't you running off to see your princess?"

I stared down the hall towards where Lillian and Manny would be in surgery. "You said it. We're a team now, and I'm not letting anyone else die on my watch."

Chapter 4

"You need to be more careful." The nurse finished tying up the gauze around my arm and shoulder as she gave me a stern glare. I had my shirt off, and she'd seen the scars scattered across my body. When she saw the wounds, she'd wanted to put my arm in a sling for the time being to hold my shoulder still, but I refused.

I scowled at her. "Tell that to the Front assholes that shot me."

Her eyes widened. "How many of them did you shoot?"

My chest tightened, and I grabbed her arm. Fear filled her eyes. Shocked with myself, I let go and stared down at my hands as they shook. *What is wrong with me?* I took a raspy breath. "I'm sorry. It's been an insane day, but that isn't your fault."

The nurse held her nose high. "I hope you don't treat *her* like that."

My heart sunk with guilt as I wondered what Julia would think of what I'd done over the past few hours. *I'm no king.*

"Your arm will heal in time. Let us know if something feels off. Until then, we need this room for other patients," the nurse said before racing out the door.

"Still a Red," I whispered to myself before throwing my shirt back on and following her into the busy hallway, where Kaja was gawking at me.

"What?" I asked.

"How did you get all those scars?"

I chuckled. Spying on me was a dangerous game, but Kaja didn't seem scared of taking risks. "Peeking at me?"

"No..." Crossing her arms, she paced back to one of the benches and mumbled to herself.

The pain in my back stabbed at me as I sat across from her. "I've been in the Militia most of my life. That life comes with a cost."

Her orange tag spun as she flicked it. "Does Princess Julia know that?"

I nodded. "She does, and I need to call her."

Kaja tapped her feet and stared down the hall as I called Julia. The phone rang for a few seconds before she picked up. "Ivan! What happened at Payne-Phalen? Are you safe?"

"Thanks to you, yes."

"And the others? I tried to send the ambulances as swiftly as possible, but the Council was slow to act. We had to get creative."

I glanced at Kaja before staring down at my feet. "They're getting cared for, but a lot of people were in bad shape. We had to surrender Payne-Phalen to the UPF to get the ambulances through."

She scoffed. "Those tyrants will regret that. The Council won't accept the Front defying a royal order." She paused before finishing, "What does that mean for Snapback and the others?"

"We didn't have a choice. With the Fracture gone, they would have beaten us eventually. The Militia will be dragged back to the Enclave and lose their weapons, but it's better than slaughter. At least we could save the injured. One of the people I picked up was shot; another had a tree fall on their leg. They're both in surgery."

"It gives them a chance to fight another day. You were brave to know when to surrender, but there's something you aren't telling me."

How'd she know? I hesitated. "Between the escape and defending the walls… I got shot, twice."

"Oh my gosh. Ivan! Are you alright?"

My arm complained as I shifted. "I'm beat up from the airstrike, but the bullets only grazed me. I'll be okay." My mind replayed the sight of the fighter next to me screaming as he collapsed off the platform. I was lucky to be alive, but she was worried enough already.

The concern didn't fade from her voice. "When will your friends be out of surgery?"

"Soon. I'm sorry it's been so long."

She sighed. "It's alright. I understand why you want to stay with them. Perhaps I should stop by the hospital? I would like to meet those impacted in the blast, and their stories may push the Council to act."

I smiled. "They would probably appreciate it too. You're kind of an icon with some of these guys."

"Am I?" She sounded surprised.

"Come on over and see for yourself. I know at least one person who is excited to meet you," I said. Kaja grinned at that comment. I knew she didn't want to show her excitement, but it bled through every part of her face.

Julia responded, "I will be over in a few minutes." A voice crackled on her end of the call. "Alex seems interested in coming as well."

"Guess it's going to be a party at the Royal Hospital," I spat before softening my tone. "See you in a bit."

Kaja beamed at me before glancing down the hall again. She couldn't wait to see her friend but waited patiently. Tyler, on the other hand, had shuffled down the hall a few minutes ago to find out how Manny was doing. Without any hope of getting Delaware back, it was hard to remember how desperate I would have been in their situation.

Worry was better than hopelessness, and the image of Delaware's body crept back into my head. *She's gone now.* I shut my eyes and leaned my head back against the wall. *Why'd you leave me Del? Why'd you leave Snap? I wasn't ready. I'm not ready.*

Tyler snapped in front of my face, jolting me back to the real world. He pointed down the hall. I wasn't sure what he meant. "Are they out?"

He nodded before waving his arm at his injured leg. From the look of it, he must have just damaged his ankle, as the doctors had given him a walking boot while I was busy talking with Julia.

I smiled at him. "Good as new."

With a shrug, he shuffled down the hall towards our friends, determined to ignore the boot as he waddled. I chuckled and walked with Kaja behind him. After getting lost, we found a nurse who directed us down a couple of hallways to Lillian and Manny's room, the familiar smell of antiseptics filling my lungs the whole way. *I'm never going to escape this damn hospital.*

When we reached the room, Kaja threw open the door and rushed to Lillian's side. She was awake, but it looked like the drugs hadn't worn off yet as she gave us a lost look. Tyler paced over to Manny and tried to stop him from messing with the machine that was hooked up to him. Manny's eyes wandered, and Tyler glared at his friend as he pinned his arms to the bed.

I walked over to the window, trying to give the friends their space as the TV in the room blared the UPF's reports of the attack. Lillian raised a shaky finger and pointed at it. Pictures of both Delaware and Max appeared on the screen, and I had to look away as the newscaster spoke, "Military generals have confirmed that the strike eliminated the leaders of two terrorist organizations: Max 853902 of the Fracture and Militia Captain Naomi 233942, codenamed 'Delaware.' General Secretary Bachton spoke minutes ago regarding the strike, which he described as a 'necessary measure to ensure the safety of the residents of St. Paul.' More details are still to come, but I, for one, am thankful for the military's swift action to end the destruction caused by these terrorists."

Tyler snatched the remote from the foot of Lillian's bed and flipped off the TV, ending the stream of noise. Emphatically, he signed towards Manny, who groaned before laughing. Tyler rolled his eyes and signed it again. This time, Manny translated, slurring his speech, "He says they're full of shit."

I huffed. "Nothing's changed there. You doing okay?"

"I feel funny," he said with another laugh, causing him to wince in pain.

He is high as hell. With a smirk, I quipped back, "As long as you don't feel dead."

"I'll be good to go soon," he replied. "It was just a tiny piece of metal, right?"

Lillian scoffed. "You were shot."

"Yeah, but they got it out. I'm good," Manny said, beaming.

He really doesn't get it. I shook my head. "Rest." I looked towards Lillian. With how the blankets covered her, it was hard to tell if they had to amputate. "How are you?"

Struggling against the drugs, she sat up and flicked the covers off of her to reveal her wrapped leg. There was no stump. *We made it in time.* Her smile stretched from ear to ear. "They said I won't be able to walk for a couple days, but look, it's still there!"

For the first time since the airstrike, I felt at ease. There was finally some good news: they both were fine. Lillian and Kaja couldn't have passed through the Prism that long ago. It would have been a disaster for her to lose a leg at such a young age, even as a Yellow.

Kaja squeezed her and exclaimed, "I won't have to push a wheelchair forever! You have no idea how happy that makes me."

Lillian giggled. "I'm *so* happy for you. How are your ribs?"

Groaning, Kaja released her. "Not great, but I'd been ignoring them until you said that."

I nodded towards the door. "Get them checked while you have the chance. We'll keep an eye on her."

She rolled her eyes but complied and sauntered out the door. I felt like a hypocrite, telling her to get her ribs checked while only reluctantly getting my arm wrapped myself.

As the others took a few minutes to rest, I looked out towards the descending sun. The last few slivers of light warmed my body before slipping under the horizon, leaving me with a shiver. Winters in the Twin Cities never seemed to end, and this one had already felt like an eternity of dark days and darker nights. Part of me wished none of the last eight or so months had ever happened. My old life was awful, but I had my best friend, people weren't being killed in airstrikes, and it didn't feel like the world was on my shoulders. The rest of me, though, remembered that if all this hadn't happened, Julia could have been killed on that street corner, the Preus family could have seized the throne, and I could have been dragged off to the work camps instead of saving people from them.

My head throbbed. I wanted Julia to be there already. I wanted this all to be over. I wanted… I didn't know what I wanted. Everything had been moving so quickly before, but now, I couldn't keep up. Our problems with the Fracture seemed to have appeared and disappeared in a flash. They were gone, but they took so much with them: St. Paul was in ruins, Delaware was gone, hundreds, if not thousands, of Yellows, Oranges, and Reds had been massacred during their crimson reign of the West 7th neighborhood, and any chance at a peaceful end to the conflict was in tatters.

"Ivan!!"

I shook myself out of my daze. "What?"

Lillian smiled and nodded towards the door. "Your princess is here."

I couldn't hold back my smile as my heart raced. Tyler made another mocking heart as I sprinted for the door, flipping him off as I passed by. In the hall, an excited Kaja had Julia pinned to the wall and was blabbering questions faster than Julia could answer. She'd changed out of her gown from the party and switched to a flowery coral colored skirt with a white blouse. Just the sight of her washed away my stress.

Alex could only stand to the side and laugh at Kaja's enthusiasm. We made eye contact, and she just shrugged.

Julia's eyes lit up as she saw me, and we both rushed to each other, meeting in a hug as she said, "I'm so glad you're alright."

I stroked the back of her head, holding her tight to me as she shook in my arms. "I'm alive. It's okay." Kaja made a face from behind her. "Shut up, Kaja."

Releasing me, Julia raised an eyebrow, warning me as always to behave. "Kaja was just telling me about your adventures and asking a lot of questions about us."

Alex leaned against the wall and crossed her arms. "Too many questions."

I laughed. "Of course she did."

Julia took my hand, and we shared a smile before concern returned to her face. "How are things in St. Paul?"

"Terrible. Between the Fracture attacking everyone and the airstrike, there are so many people dead or injured. The ambulances helped, though. How'd you do it?"

"With a bit of negotiation," she looked at her sister with a grin, "and some *intricate* persuasion."

Alex shrugged. "Some people in high places like to kiss and tell."

"The Council members sleeping around? Shocker," I replied.

"Even Mom's pressure can't outweigh the exposure of their secrets," Alex said.

I squeezed Julia's hand. "I'm surprised you let her."

She wrinkled her nose. "It was either do nothing, and let more people die, or play dirty." She eyed Alex. "Luckily, one of us is good at that."

Alex put her fingers to the shaved side of her head, where the burn from Cockroach's attack still emblazoned her scalp. "Someone needs to know the secrets and how to use them. How else do we ensure our queen is unchallenged?"

Julia gave her the glare that I was all too familiar with and sighed before glancing towards Lillian's room. "How are they?"

I followed her gaze. "They're both alive, and Lillian still has both legs. She's pretty excited to meet you. They all are."

Kaja grabbed her arm, pulling her towards the room. "C'mon! You can talk with your boyfriend later."

Julia giggled as she passed by, and I could only watch as Kaja yanked her away. I started to follow before glancing back at Alex, who hadn't budged. "You coming?"

She took a sharp breath and almost whispered, "Yeah."

"Everything alright?"

She passed me before pausing with her hand on the door. "You're not the only one who lost someone in that strike."

I wanted to respond, but she slid into the room before I could. *Who did she know?* I shrugged and joined them. Inside, Julia was engaged in a conversation with the group. She smiled at me as I walked in, and Tyler signed something that I assumed was sarcastic.

Julia raised an eyebrow at him and signed something back. He blushed as his eyes filled with shock. We all laughed. *He didn't realize the princesses are fluent in basically everything.* She signed something else, and he nodded before she spoke, "What happened?"

Tyler looked down and rubbed his foot along the floor. Alex stepped closer to him to draw his attention before signing. He smiled softly before responding. *I'm so lost here.*

Manny translated for the rest of us. "His owner cut out his tongue after the Prism. They couldn't do it to a Black Tag, but once he was a Red…"

Quickly, Tyler signed something back. Alex nodded. "They're lucky you didn't kill them."

"Alex…" Julia warned.

"Fine, I'll be good." Alex raised her arms in surrender.

Julia smiled at her before turning back to Lillian. "We will make sure you are taken care of." She swept her arm towards the rest of the group. "All of you have been through so much, even before today. We won't abandon you, not again."

Nobody said anything for a few moments. It was hard to know what that meant. As she wasn't queen yet, she couldn't make them royal servants, and with the current state of St. Paul, it would be nearly impossible to ensure supplies reached the Militia. I wasn't going to question her in front of the group, though.

Lillian winced as she shifted in the bed. "You guys don't need to stay here if you don't want to."

Manny laughed. "Where do you think we're gonna go? The palace?"

Julia straightened her skirt and smiled. "That sounds like a wonderful idea."

Chapter 5

*T**his is a terrible idea.* The splendor of the palace's entrance met us as Julia led the group into the Great Hall. As we walked, I couldn't help but question whether we should be poking the lioness even more after Vera attempted to murder me.

We had convinced the nurses to let Lillian and Manny go. While it was obvious they still felt the pain post-surgery, I was happy they were able to come. Lillian needed a wheelchair, and Manny struggled to walk, but if this was their only chance to see the palace, then they had to take it.

Both of them gawked with the others as we made our way through the Great Hall and towards the throne room. Smiling at their reactions, I remembered the awe of entering the palace for the first time. I'd been stripped down, humiliated, and taunted, but there was something about the place that separated it from the cold, broken world in which we lived.

I caught up to Julia and nudged her, prompting a smirk as she said, "You can take the rebel out of the Militia, but you can't take the Militia out of the rebel."

"You can try," I replied. "Is this how you expected your birthday to go?"

"Not at all." She glanced over her shoulder and whispered, "Alex and Tyler seem to be getting along."

I copied her move, catching a glimpse of Alex laughing and signing with Tyler. "Princesses dating Reds is all the rage I hear."

She chuckled before sighing. "How are you doing, you know, with Delaware?"

My chest seized again, and I hesitated before saying anything. I didn't want to think about it, let alone talk about it. *I'm doing a great job ignoring my feelings.* "Later. I'd rather focus on surviving our current problem with Vera and the Council first."

"Do you not trust me?"

I scoffed. "Oh, I trust you, but I also trust your mom to ruin everything if she gets the chance. What, exactly, is the plan? We can't just walk in there and say, 'Hey, we brought a bunch of people who almost died. I know you hated letting Ivan in here, but can we allow these guys and some others to work as servants?'"

She furrowed her brow and squared her icy blue gaze at me. "Trust me."

"Fine." I took a deep breath. "I'd just rather not be hit by another bomb or shot today."

"Since when are you the cautious one? I thought you would be happy about this."

Running my fingers along the marble wall as we walked, I bit my cheek. "You know that I would love for them to be able to stay. I've missed my team, and the last few hours, I felt like I had a new one. I'm just afraid to lose them, you know? My friends, my family, they're all gone. I don't want to give myself hope for it just to be snuffed out again."

She tapped her hand against mine as we walked along. I wished we could hold hands, but even though basically everyone in the palace knew about our relationship, everything was secretive still. I hated it. "I'm sorry, Ivan. There is hope, though. Remember that. Everything you've done, everyone you've lost, there's a reason. I am sure of it."

Am I? We reached the doors to the throne room, and the rest of the group caught up as I replied, "If this goes well, I'll believe you."

She smiled. "It will, my love."

Alex put her arm around her sister. "Ready?"

Julia stood taller and took a deep breath. "Yes. Though, you don't have to be a part of this if you don't want to be."

Alex chuckled. "There's no way I'm missing mom's face when these guys walk in."

"Your assurances are appreciated," Julia replied before turning to the Blue guarding the door and nodding. He bowed, and I watched the lion on the doors' face split as he pushed them open.

Here we go. Together, Julia and I led the way into the throne room, decorated with its familiar ice-blue accents. Greeting us were the chilled stares of Vera, Natasha, and the Royal Council. While I was busy being enraged at the UPF, I hadn't forgotten what Vera's plot to kill me in Chicago. The Fracture was all but defeated, but enemies still lurked around every corner. Inside the palace or beyond, it was impossible to know where I was safe anymore.

Vera glared at us from the throne, sending a shiver down my spine. With Helena's death just two months before, she'd shed much of the veil that had covered her schemes. Still, I had no idea what else she was planning. With Natasha's chances of becoming queen in jeopardy and her own power waning, it was only a matter of time before she acted.

Demonstrating to the others, I knelt in front of Vera. My instincts screamed at me not to, but this battle was about more than my pride. I would never be loyal to the Council, Vera, or the Whites in general. I knelt so Julia could be the one to sit on that throne. If she didn't become queen, yet another generation was doomed to suffer under the Prism.

Vera drummed her fingers on the throne's armrests as the rest of the group knelt beside me, even Manny, who moaned in pain as he did so. Lillian could only bow her head from the wheelchair.

Along with her sister, Julia stayed standing, though she curtsied before Vera spoke, "I do hope, my daughters, there is a pertinent reason that you brought these people into our home."

Julia held her head high, speaking to both the Council and her mother, "It is my belief that we should speak with those impacted by the airstrike and its aftermath. Ivan saved this group from the military, and the Royal Hospital has treated their injuries." She gestured towards them. "Lillian would have lost her leg and perhaps died from her wounds, but because we were willing to help, she will be able to walk again. Emmanuel would have bled out in Payne-Phalen from his gunshot wound, but our surgeons were able to remove the bullet. The strike hit more than just the Fracture. We all saw the nonviolent marchers before the bombing. They are suffering as well."

George Foster, the head of the Royal Council, crossed his arms. "What are you suggesting?"

Julia held her hands together in front of her as she walked

slowly towards him. "The Treaty of Minneapolis separated us from the Prism, but the People's Front has failed in their responsibilities to protect the people. We must argue that their actions are a direct violation of the treaty, and therefore the monarchy is free to assert its status as the protector of those people against the government. The first step towards that would be bringing those injured in the strikes into the royal service."

Foster scowled. "You are proposing treason!"

She stepped forward again, her voice gaining intensity. "Is it treasonous to oppose a government that feels no shame in slaughtering its people in the streets and bombing unarmed protestors? What are we as royals if not the protectors of something greater than ourselves? We cannot sit behind our walls as the country burns. This is our land too. These are our people too."

Vera swiped her arm across her body and snapped, "That's enough! I have heard far too many of your lectures in recent months. We understand the gravity of the situation, but our role is to ensure *our* people are safe. Your suggestion places all of our lives unnecessarily at risk."

Alex scoffed. "So, what is *your* plan?"

Vera stood and strode towards her daughters. "After extensive discussions, the General Secretary and I have reached an agreement."

She's been negotiating with the UPF? For how long? There's no way this is good.

She stopped in front of Julia and whisked a hair from in front of her daughter's face. There was no way that Julia liked that, but she held her poise as Vera continued with narrowed eyes, "In an effort to avoid the current situation escalating into another civil war, we have agreed on a set of compromises that will be beneficial for us all. The most important of which is the returning of royal lands and businesses formerly seized by the Front in exchange for the Front retaining a share of the profits. They have also agreed to exempt the royalty from the embargoes and tariffs currently placed on many foreign nations, allowing us access to the goods we need once again."

I replied, "What's the catch?"

Vera shot me a disconcerting look before responding, "There are only two conditions. First, the royal military is to be dissolved and replaced by a small, defensive garrison to protect royal territory. Second, the election shall be canceled."

Shit.

Julia took a step back, flustered. "Who would serve as monarch?"

Isn't it obvious?

A grin crept over her mother's face as she paced back to the throne and took her place on it. "Royal law must be amended, but the agreement requires that I serve as queen."

I clenched my fist and pressed it against the floor, trying to resist yelling and giving her exactly what she wanted. My breathing was heavy as my body rejected what my ears heard. *We're doomed. The royals get special perks while our only hope for change is destroyed.*

Kaja shouted, "You don't deserve to be queen!"

I grinned. Kaja didn't have my control, but Vera deserved the verbal assault.

Vera raised her chin, looking down upon Kaja, whose eyes were now wide in realization of what she just did. "Stand, girl. What is your name?"

Kaja whimpered, shaking as she did. "My name is Kaja, Kaja Owens."

"What makes you believe that you should decide who wears the White Crown, Kaja Owens?" She waited for a response, but nothing came as we all silently glared at her in rage. "Well?"

Kaja swallowed before responding, "A queen shouldn't be surprised when her poorest subjects come to her. How she treats the least of her people says the most about her, and I already know everything I need to know about you."

Vera was visibly surprised by her ferocity in response. "You have a fire to you, Kaja, but when it comes to ruling, sometimes you are left without a real choice. Do all of you wish for another crippling conflict that will only end in the monarchy's destruction and all of our deaths? Pah! Of course not." She waved her hand as if swatting away a bug, and her gaze narrowed as she closed the space between them. "Tensions are rising in this country, and in a time like this, radical change is not practical. These St. Paul Accords will allow for my people to prosper once again. *That* is my responsibility as the queen."

I swallowed in fear. We'd walked into another trap. As Julia and I made eye contact, that same fear filled her eyes. Vera beat us. Alex had used her gossip cards on the Council already. They would go with Vera's plan, and there was nothing we could do to stop her.

After her shock passed, Julia spoke, "Do you not wonder,

Mother, why the Front demanded that you sit on the throne instead of Natasha or myself?"

"Are you truly that concerned, my daughter, about your own personal power so much that you would reject the Front's once in a century offer to restore our lands and businesses?"

Julia looked towards her oldest sister. "Natasha, you are okay with this? You care about the traditions. Do you not fear an end to the free selection of the monarch?"

Natasha stared at her feet. "I am sorry, Julia. I wish it were not the best option, but I do not see another way."

Julia shook her head and pled, instead, to the Council members, "We cannot allow ourselves to become nothing more than the Front's puppets. There is a peaceful solution; this is not it. Abandoning our principles will only hurt us."

Foster cleared his throat. "It is an *unusual* request, but I do believe, given the gravity of the situation, that it is within the power of the Royal Council to create a one-time exception to the rule."

Alex groaned. "You know this creates a precedent for the future, and you're doing it anyway. Don't you ever get sick of abusing your power, Mother?"

Julia stepped forward. "The royalty will be forever fractured by this. Duke Bilgram's coalition will only get stronger, and I doubt my supporters will accept the destruction of the coronation process. If we lose what has held us together for so long, the Front will destroy what's left of us. They are using you, Mother. I'm sorry, but this deal is a trap."

Rage simmered in Vera's face. "Enough! Both of you are out of line. The decision has already been made unanimously by the

Council, and the St. Paul Accords will be signed. I am truly sorry that this is how the election must end. Since I understand your discontent, though, I am willing to allow you to bring your visitors into your service. I hope that will allow you to see that I wish to make this work."

Gasps came from the group as Julia nodded to her mom. She was still shaking from the surprise. "While I object to the Accords, the gesture is appreciated. If the Council has decided, then I understand there is nothing I can do."

Why are you letting her get away with this?

Vera grinned. "I am glad to hear your understanding. Now, please show your new servants to their quarters."

My heart raced, and anxiety consumed me as the others stood and began towards the doors. *She is a master manipulator.* I was happy my new friends would be able to stay, but Vera was using this as additional cover for her plan. I wasn't going to let her get away with it. *If Julia doesn't become queen, she can't arrest Vera. She's going to come for me.*

Julia looked back at me as I remained kneeling. "Come, Ivan. It's over."

I glanced over my shoulder at her before meeting the glare of Vera and whispering to myself, "No, it's not."

Chapter 6

Alex groaned as we walked through the halls. "What do we do now?"

I clenched and unclenched my fists as I thought. "We need to find a way to take her down. Maybe find evidence that she was the one that hired those guys to kill me in Chicago. If she's found guilty of attempted murder, she can't be queen."

She scoffed. "Right, piece of cake considering they're dead."

"You got a better idea?"

Julia turned in front of us and held up her hands. "We will figure out a plan of action. For now, let's get our new friends settled in, shall we?"

Ever the diplomat.

Lillian smiled. "What will we be doing?"

Julia returned the smile. "We have plenty of opportunities for the four of you, and I think we both have specific roles in mind." She glanced at her sister.

Alex turned around to face us as she walked backwards. "Once Tyler's ankle has recovered, I could use him as a footman. Unfortunately, I'm not sure you can be a bodyguard without being able to talk into the earpiece."

Tyler cocked his head to his side. I leaned over to him and whispered, "It means you'll go with her places, holding her doors and carrying heavy stuff."

He made a face that said, "Ah," and signed something to Alex.

"Yes, you can come to the parties," she replied.

Tyler beamed, and Manny looked ready to jump out of shoes. "What about me?"

Julia responded, "How do you like horses?"

"They're... tall?"

Julia chuckled. "Would you be interested in being a stable hand? You would still be able to see Tyler and your other friends. Obviously, you'll need to take time to recover from your wound, but..."

Manny cut her off, "That sounds fun!"

Alex laughed. "Yeah, if you like horse manure."

"Do I get to ride them?"

Julia responded, "Of course! Though, you'll have to learn."

Bumping into Manny, Kaja said, "I can't wait to see you with *two* injured arms after you fall off."

Lillian frowned. "Kaja, don't ruin his fun."

"Don't worry," Manny said. "I've always wanted to ride a horse. Never thought I'd have the chance."

We'd reached the Great Hall again, and Julia gazed at the ceiling, her lips parted in awe. I knew she loved the beautiful architecture of the palace, even after living her whole life within its walls. "We will ensure you learn. Now, Lillian and Kaja, you're not eighteen yet, so you cannot be handmaidens, but we both could use you as our personal maids. You would be maintaining our rooms and helping us prepare ourselves for various events. Think of it as being a handmaiden-in-training. We will allow you both to choose who you want to work with."

The girls glanced at each other. "I'll go with Julia," Lillian chirped.

Alex gasped. "Not me? Fine, I guess Kaja is stuck with me then."

Kaja faked a bow. "It's an honor to serve you, m'lady."

Smiling, Alex looked at her sister. "Looks like I don't even need to train her."

"I doubt you could train her if you tried," I replied, sliding next to Julia. "Do you want me to show them around the palace?"

"It's late," Julia said with a yawn. "Why don't you show them to their rooms? They can pair up in the two open ones on your hall. Meet me upstairs when you are done." Julia's eyes met mine when she finished.

I smiled at her. While I was excited to have a new team, I was exhausted. Time alone with her sounded amazing after that crappy day. She nodded to the rest of the group, telling me to go as the corners of her mouth curling in amusement.

"Right," I said before turning back to them. "Let's go see the Red King's suite, shall we?"

The princesses went upstairs while the rest of us headed towards the southern end of the palace. I led the group through the winding maze that was the servants' wing, our footsteps echoing through the stone halls as we went. The whole way, I remembered my first days in the palace. My entire life changed on that street corner in St. Paul, and now, those four had the same thing happen to them just because they ended up in that car with me. *The world works in strange ways.*

As much as Vera's reveal stressed me out, I welcomed the distraction of getting the group settled in. Anything to keep my mind off the horrors I'd experienced in St. Paul.

Thinking beyond the present made my head throb. I was lost on what to do next. Everything had relied on Julia becoming queen and using the royal military. Now, those hopes were gone if we couldn't find evidence of Vera's attack, and with the Militia waving the white flag, our list of available allies was short.

We passed by my room first, and I swung open the door to show them the tiny place. "I told you it was the king's suite."

Kaja peeked inside. "It's like a closet, and you still can't keep it clean."

I rolled my eyes and slammed the door. It popped open. *Some things never change.* I forced it shut again, and, only after I heard it *click*, guided them towards their rooms. The first was for the boys, and Tyler shuffled into it, a wide smile on his face. Manny translated as Tyler signed something towards me. "He says thank you."

"No need to thank me. This was all Julia."

Lillian touched my arm, and I looked down at her as she said, "Then thank her for us. I still can't believe this is happening."

I sighed and scanned the stone walls of the servants' wing. "It took me a while to get used to it. Hell, I *still* am getting used to it. There's something about this place, though, that makes it feel like home."

Tyler flashed a heart at me and raised his eyebrows.

"I didn't mean love, but that sure helps." Manny was too busy climbing into his bed to translate Tyler's response, so I just shrugged. "Let me know if you two need anything. Julia should have some maids bringing uniforms and stuff to you soon. Just a warning, though, we may be servants just like them, but they don't ignore the color of your tag. Status means everything around here."

Now solidly cocooned in his blanket, Manny responded, "Thanks for everything, Ivan."

I nodded to him. Tyler seemed about my age, and Manny couldn't have been more than two or three years younger than me, but after everything I'd been through, I felt ancient compared to their child-like wonder. I missed that feeling.

With the boys settled in, I waved for the girls to follow me next door. After I opened the room and Lillian rolled into it, I said, "Unfortunately, there's not much when it comes to help with wheelchairs around here, but I'm *sure* Kaja will be more than happy to help you get around. Right, Kaja?"

She beamed as she skipped into the room. "This is going to be awesome."

"I thought Lillian was the positive one?" I asked with a chuckle.

Kaja turned back towards me. "I'm not negative, just realistic, and this is a dream."

I knocked on the door frame. "Glad to hear you're excited, but remember that the palace has its own dangers. A lot of people don't want us here." It was weird giving the lecture I'd heard from Julia and Jonah a hundred times. *Funny how things change.*

Lillian smiled. "Thank you so much, Ivan. If it wasn't for you..."

I raised my hand to stop her. "We've all suffered enough today. It won't help thinking about what could have happened. You're alive, and you're safe. That's what matters." Her face drooped, and I sighed. "Get some rest. Like I said, if you ever need anything,

I'm two doors down. Don't hesitate to ask."

They nodded, and I made my way back to my room. My clothes were destroyed, and I was badly in need of a shower. After grabbing a set of jeans and a t-shirt, I headed to the bathrooms.

My skin felt like it'd been replaced by ash. As the water ran down my face and chest, I winced. The blast had burned my skin, and I hadn't noticed with everything that had happened. It was nothing serious, but even the water felt like pinpricks. To make matters worse, the water seared at my wounded arm and shoulder, and I had to bite my tongue to stop myself from screaming. *I hate everything.*

After a couple minutes of the pain, I turned the water off and just stood there, my mind blank and exhausted. So many people had died, but we had to live on like nothing had changed. I was a bodyguard again, trying to protect the life of the one person I had left. *How can I protect her when I failed everyone else?*

It felt wrong going from a warzone to the safety of the palace, but Snapback was right. I was needed here. If there was any hope for the Militia, we needed what little royal support we had left.

When I finished, I changed and headed towards the Great Hall. With nothing but the sound of my footsteps against the stone floor to distract me, my thoughts wandered. My mind went back to the scenes after the strike: the crimson painted grass, the endless sea of bodies, the screams that pierced my soul, and Delaware's charred body resting in a blanket of ash. Anxiety squeezed my brain as rage fueled my heart.

The door was shut when I reached Julia's room, so I knocked. There was no reply for a couple of seconds before Alex opened the door. Her eyes were red, catching me off guard. I'd never seen her cry before. *Who did she lose in that strike?*

She glanced towards Julia, who was walking towards us, before making her way towards the couch. I shut the door and embraced Julia. We both shook. Finally, away from the world, I felt the weight of the day hit me, and I started to cry. She whispered, "I'm so sorry, Ivan. She didn't deserve it."

I couldn't muster a response and shut my eyes as Julia's hand cradled the back of my head. My body felt distant. I wished the chaos of the day was a nightmare that I could wake up from, that I could have my best friend back. Instead, she was gone forever.

The pain from the blast still throbbed in my back, and I tried to focus on the feeling of Julia's hand running along it. My rage receded, but what replaced it was worse: loss. Everyone I'd cared about was dead: Delaware, Poseidon, El Capitan, Zeus, Blitzkrieg, Penn, Bobcat, Southpaw, the list went on and on, and that didn't even include my acquaintances from the Enclave that had starved to death or been executed in the camps. I loved Julia more than anything, but the deaths had torn a hole in my heart that I didn't know how to fill.

I eventually forced myself to step out of the hug. "She got the revenge she wanted. She didn't care about the consequences, and I don't know how to go on knowing that."

Julia nodded her head towards the couch, and we sat across from Alex, who stared blankly at the coffee table. Julia held my hands as she responded, "I think Delaware was trying to do everything she could to protect her people. She cared about the most vulnerable in St. Paul so much that she was willing to die trying to save them. It was more than just revenge. She protected her city, her people. She died a hero, Ivan."

I shook my head. "No, we had them. The plan was working until she raised that gun. They were going to stop, and she put herself right in the middle of the airstrike. Max would have died anyway if she had just waited a couple more seconds."

"Would you have done anything different in her position?"

That question caught me off guard, and I hesitated. *You know she's right.* Three years before, heck, eight months before, I probably would have done exactly what she had. I would have recklessly done anything to end the threat to my friends and the Militia. Something in me had changed since I'd met Julia on that street corner, though. I still had a knack for risking my life, but I feared death now. Before, I knew I was fighting for something, and when I died, someone would take my place. Now, I couldn't imagine leaving Julia behind.

I sighed. "You're right."

She squeezed my hand. "You taught her to be brave like you. She was fighting for what she thought was right. She fought for the people she loved: for Snapback, for you."

I bit my cheek, trying to hold back a second wave of tears. "Why is it that everything we do is for nothing? More people die, no matter what. Delaware is dead, St. Paul is destroyed, Vera is queen. What the hell are we doing?"

Alex called over, "We're living." We both looked up at her, surprised to hear her speak. "We're living so that maybe things don't have to be like shit for our kids and their kids."

My heart twitched as I remembered that she lost someone in

the bombing. "Who'd you know?"

She bit her lip and looked towards the desk, avoiding eye contact. "It doesn't matter anymore. They're gone."

I scooted to the edge of the couch. "Yeah, it does. Even if they're gone, part of them stays with us. Who was it?"

"My friend, Lorelai. She was marching with the Militia." She sniffled.

"How do you know she's dead? The strikes hit mostly the rioters. A lot on our side survived."

She clenched her fist and glared at me. "I know a lot of people in the city. She never came back."

"She could have been taken to Pay..." Julia grabbed my wrist, telling me to stop. I complied. "I'm sorry."

Alex took a deep breath. "It's alright. I get it. She could have been at Payne-Phalen, but someone would have heard from her by now." She paused before continuing, "She was a Yellow and never cared about politics, but she knew she didn't want St. Paul to burn. All she wanted was peace."

Julia looked at me, asking permission to comfort her sister. I nodded, and she joined Alex on the other couch, wrapping her arms around her for support.

My heart still hurt, but I was starting to think Julia might have been right. Delaware was brave. She'd put herself in danger in a desperate attempt to save the city: Revenge or not, it was heroic. That didn't make me want her back any less.

I slumped into the couch and stared at the ceiling. *How do we move forward from this?* I thought about the gift I hadn't had the chance to give her yet. *Happy birthday Julia.* She cared so much about other people. I just wanted her to have one good day.

Faking a smile, I grabbed the tissues from across the room and handed them to Alex. "Well, at least we won't have to go through the disaster of the 'Red King.'"

Alex sniffled and blew her nose before responding, "The what?"

I lay down on the other couch. The conversation wasn't important, but we all needed a lift. "Apparently, that's what the lower colors started calling me ahead of the election."

Julia smiled. "It has a nice ring to it."

"It sounds like I'm going to start impaling people or something," I replied with a chuckle.

Alex took another tissue. "Ivan the Terrible."

"Ouch."

"I think you would have been an amazing king, Ivan," Julia replied.

"Thanks, but we're screwed now, and the woman who wants me dead is now queen. I need to do a better job picking my enemies."

There was silence for a few seconds until Alex took another shaky breath and returned the topic to her friend. "We'll never be able to bury her." She looked up at me. "Or Delaware. How is that fair?"

"It's not, but if you're betting on things ever being fair in this stupid country, you're going to end up broke."

Julia rubbed Alex's back as her sister responded, "When did you get so depressing, Red? I thought you were the positive one."

I shut my eyes and tried to fight the memories that swarmed

my brain. There wasn't enough energy left in my heart or my mind to respond. Jokes couldn't deflect how lost and alone I felt. I had a girl that loved me and friends that cared about me, but all I could think about was Delaware.

After a few moments of silence, my earpiece buzzed, and Snapback's voice cut through the static. "Ivan, you there?"

I groaned and sat up. "Yeah, what's up?"

"Just wanted to check-in. It's been a shitty day, but tell Julia that because of her, almost everybody made it. We did it, Ivan."

I glanced over at Julia. "Snap says the doctors you sent managed to save almost everybody."

"I'm glad I could do something helpful today," she replied with half a smile.

I spoke back into the radio, "You okay, Snap?"

"I don't want to talk about it."

"If anyone understands how you feel, it's me. Just know you're not alone."

He didn't reply for a few moments. "We may have gotten people the help, but the army is searching everything. We'll be dragged back to the Enclave soon, but it'll take days to get everyone moved. How are things at the palace?"

"Vera negotiated a deal for the UPF to give them their businesses and land back."

"What do they get?"

I sighed. "She has to become queen, and the royalty military is going to be reduced to next to nothing."

"Damn."

"I know, we're screwed. Without Julia as queen and the royal military to back us up, I don't know what we're going to do. On the bright side, Julia and Alex convinced her to allow a few of our people to become servants."

He groaned. "This sucks... You know Vera's planning something, right?"

"She's always planning something."

"So, what's our move now?"

I shook my head and glanced at Julia. She looked as lost as me. "We fight back, so this doesn't happen again. Ever."

Chapter 7

By the time Alex left, Julia and I were exhausted, both mentally and physically. Between the massive birthday party, the riots, the airstrike, and everything after, the day had felt like an eternity. We wanted to talk, but she'd put her head on my shoulder and was out in less than a minute. I wasn't far behind.

Sometime in the late morning the next day, Hope's meowing woke us up. The white puffball of a kitten had been my informal gift for Julia a week before her birthday, and in the crazy night, I'd forgotten about her until she was screaming in my ear for attention. I groaned and looked at Julia. She was just waking up and yawned before shock crossed her face. I smiled. "You fell asleep really fast."

She rubbed her eyes and petted the cat, who purred and nuzzled her neck. "You didn't move?"

I shrugged. "It was your birthday. I figured you could sleep how you wanted."

As she started to respond, there was a series of knocks on the door. Sighing, she set Hope to the side and drifted to the door. Vera's pompous butler and right-hand man, Michael, was on the other side. He flicked his eyes to me before bowing to Julia. "M'lady, Queen Vera has requested your presence as the preparations for the coronation are to begin immediately."

I pushed myself off the couch. "What? She doesn't want me to help plan the party, *sir*?"

Michael raised an eyebrow. I always wondered how much he knew about Vera's plans. He had never seemed like an enemy to me, but it was important to remember who he was loyal to. "No. The Queen wishes for you to stand guard outside the room."

"Exciting."

Julia shot me a glare before nodding to the butler. "Please inform her that I will be there soon. Thank you, Michael."

"M'lady." He bowed again before marching down the hall.

The door shut, and Julia rested her forehead on it, her eyes closed. "We were so close."

"I don't think we were."

She turned her head to face me, ruffling her short hair against the door to create a cute little mess instead of her usual perfect look. "What do you mean? The election was only two weeks away."

I poured myself a glass of water and drank it greedily. "I have a bad feeling that none of this was a coincidence. What if we were reaching for a prize that was never really there?"

"What are you saying?"

"I'm saying that I think Vera has been planning this with the UPF for a long time. There was never going to be an election."

She crossed her arms and fiddled with her family ring. "You think my mother conspired with the Front to stop the election?"

I paced towards her and grabbed her hands. "Think about it. Everything that happened cleared the way for her to take the throne: the coup attempt, the Fracture's rise, the riots, the bombing, the treaty, all of it. We've been fighting and fighting, but the whole time we've been trapped in her web."

She shuddered and pushed my hands away. "Ivan, if you're right..."

I stepped back. My temper flared. "If I'm right, Vera is willing to do anything it takes to become queen, and she is responsible for the deaths of thousands of innocent people... and Delaware."

She pulled me into a hug. I couldn't force myself to return it. I didn't need a hug; I needed vengeance. "I do not know if your theory is correct," she said, "but I promise you, we will make things right. Right now, though, you need time to grieve. We both do. Maybe, we should take the time to recover while we can, for just a little while? Together, we can help rebuild St. Paul, and we might have time to be a real couple for once. When the time is right, we will confront my mother."

I took a deep breath, trying to calm down, but my whole body burned with anger and sorrow. "I don't know how to stop after the things I've seen. How can I recover here while the Militia is imprisoned in the Enclave?"

She pulled back and met my eyes as she placed a hand softly on my cheek, wiping away a tear. "I am so sorry for everything that has happened to you, for everything you've experienced. I love how passionate you are about fighting for the poor and suffering, and I know you miss Delaware, but if you try to go on alone, searching for revenge, you will end up lost. We are not done, but right now, your people need you here. I need you here."

Staring at my feet, I tried to regain focus, but my mind flashed with the horrors of recent days. *Get out of my head!* Softly, Julia raised my chin. Her face, full of worry, said it all. *You're not the only one suffering. She's lost her dad and sister too.* I cleared the tears from my eyes. "I'm sorry. I'm complaining about my life and acting like you've never lost someone."

She wrapped her arms around me again, holding me close as I felt her heart beating as rapidly as mine. "We've both lost so much. I know how much Delaware meant to you, and I understand how it feels to lose a sister. Perhaps we should hold a funeral for her?"

"I would love that."

Stepping back, she held my hands. "Then we will make it happen. She deserves at least that much."

I took a deep breath and tried to smile in a futile attempt. "Thank you, and sorry your birthday sucked."

"No need to worry. My birthday is the least of our concerns, and it is nothing more than another festival to stroke royal egos." She gave me a peck on the lips. "Now, I need to shower and meet with Mother. You should change into your bodyguard attire. I probably won't see you until we're finished. Are you going to be alright standing guard?"

I shrugged. "It's my job, and it's better than being in there with Vera."

She huffed. "This is going to be torture."

"I think that's what she wants."

She grabbed my hand again. "Are you sure you're going to be okay? I promise we'll have more time to talk soon, just the two of us."

I smiled softly and kissed her. "Go. They need Princess Julia. We'll have our time."

Biting her lip, she stepped back and opened the door for me. I kissed her forehead as I passed and entered the hall. *Not everything has fallen apart.*

The palace felt different as I made my way to my room. There was no longer a feeling of hope that Julia could become queen and fix things. Instead, a sense of dread hung over me with each step. Everything had collapsed in one quick turn of events, and I still didn't know how to handle it. A piece of me was missing. Julia could make me feel at home again, but now, away from her, I felt isolated.

I grabbed one of my bodyguard outfits and headed to the bathroom to prepare. The ice-blue lion pin of the Hughes family haunted me as I looked in the mirror. That pin now represented Vera, the woman that stood in my way at every turn; I didn't want to think about what I'd have to do now. Our options were running thin, and so was my patience.

One of Vera's guards was posted outside the conference room when I arrived. The bulky Blue glared at me as I approached and reached out my hand to him, matching his look. "Ivan. I don't believe we've met."

He blinked before returning his eyes to straight in front of him. "I know who you are."

I dropped my arm and took my position on the other side of the door. *Of course he does.* "How long you been one of the Queen's guards?"

He didn't speak or move a muscle. *Jeez. New guys.* Ever since the coup, there'd been too many new guards to keep track of, so it wasn't a surprise I didn't recognize him. Something about him made my hair stand on end, though. I just couldn't tell what it was.

Time passed slowly as we stood in the empty hall. Nobody but the occasional patrolling guard passed, and none of them were ever interested in talking. They would either shoot me a glare or avoid eye contact and then continue on, contributing nothing but the echo of their boots on the stone floors. I would have taken anything that could occupy my mind. Instead, as time droned on, I could only think about Delaware, the situation in St. Paul, Vera's plots, and my hatred for the UPF. *Once we deal with Vera, I'm coming for you Bachton.*

I was struggling to keep my eyes open when Jonah showed up. He greeted the other guard, "Good morning, Demetri," before giving me a look of concern. Demetri rolled his eyes, probably upset his name had been revealed. Jonah continued, to me this time, "How are you?" He glanced at my injured arm before leaning in closer. "I heard about our friend..." He flashed another look at Demetri before meeting my eyes again.

Taking a deep breath, I delayed my response. All anyone wanted to know was how I was after the attack, but I didn't want to talk about it anymore. Just thinking about it depressed me. "I'm alive."

He nodded, understanding. "I get it. We can talk more later. Just know you're not alone." He gave Demetri one last glance before heading off to the rest of his duties. I was glad he stopped by, even if it was a short visit.

From the beginning, Jonah had been one of my few allies in the palace, and we'd been through both the Preus family's coup and the Militia raid on the work camp together. I respected him more than almost anyone else. Helping the Militia was a risky move for him, but he did it anyway and was willing to sacrifice his life to save people along the way. Real bravery like that was rare. I didn't know if Vera would allow him to keep his position, but I hoped for his sake and mine that she would.

After another hour, a few butlers arrived with food for those inside the room. Before Demetri could react, I sprung the door open for them and stepped inside, holding it as they passed through. The move gave me enough time to make eye contact with Julia to check if she was okay. We traded smirks while she put her hand to her temple to signal her frustration. I mimicked falling asleep as the butlers served the food, and she bit her lip to avoid laughing. When the butlers finished, I bowed before following them out of the room. *Give me ten more seconds with her, please.*

Demetri huffed when I returned to my position. I glanced over at him. "What?"

"Flirting with a princess is not professional, especially on duty."

"I thought you knew who I was?"

"That doesn't mean you are special."

"You're right." I flicked my tag. "I'm just like you."

With a scoff, he responded, "I would not go that far. One of us has murdered dozens of people."

"Didn't realize you were that dangerous," I quipped, sliding further away from him.

"How has the Queen tolerated you this long?"

I shrugged. "She hasn't."

Silence returned as Demetri refocused on whatever he was staring at on the marble wall across from us. *If this is what a real guard is supposed to be like, then I'm awful at my job.*

It was another couple of hours before Julia emerged with her handmaidens. Anne smiled at me while Rachel wrapped me in a hug that caught me off guard. I'd talked with her more than Anne, but we'd never been that close. When she released me, she spoke, "I'm so relieved to see you are alright. We were all worried when we saw the video."

I bowed my head. "I appreciate the concern, m'lady, and I am glad to be alive. Too many others weren't so lucky."

Sadness crept over her face, and she curtsied in response. "They will not be forgotten."

I dropped my gaze to the floor. "No, they won't."

Julia nodded her head down the hall, and I smiled before turning to Demetri and bowing. He grunted as I walked off with the girls. Julia wrapped her pinky around mine as we walked. "How was guard duty?"

"With charming Demetri? Awful."

"I doubt it was worse than listening to my mother gloat of her victory."

I slid my hand into hers instead as we headed towards the back staircase. "How are we going to beat her?"

Julia quickly stepped away, letting go as a couple minor royals passed by and exchanged a quick greeting with her. When they were gone, she whispered to me sharply, "You need to be careful what you say around the palace. Mother is the monarch now, even if her coronation isn't for a few weeks, and the walls have ears. Now, you should grab your coat. We're going out tonight."

"What's the occasion?"

"Mother is signing the St. Paul Accords with General Secretary Bachton at a fancy villa outside the city. Sorry I didn't get the chance to tell you. She dropped it on us during preparations." She groaned. "That was horrible."

I shook my head. "Don't worry about it. I'll meet you outside your room when you're ready."

She smiled and checked the hall quickly before kissing my cheek. "See you in a bit."

The handmaidens grinned at me as I passed and headed back towards my room. *Why does everyone give me that same look when I'm with her?*

Before I grabbed my jacket, I stopped by to see how my new friends' first days went. Kaja and Lillian were out, but the guys were in their room. I knocked on the open door, and their heads popped up. Manny beamed. "Ivan!"

"How was day one with the horses?"

He shrugged and rocked his head back and forth. "They crap a lot, and I couldn't do much with the whole getting shot thing."

I laughed. "That they do. Getting settled in okay?"

"Yeah. My boss said my first riding lessons will start when I'm recovered, and that'll be awesome. This place is so big. It's hard to figure out where everything is."

"Don't worry. You'll get used to it. Took me a while too. How about you, Tyler? I see Alex already got you a nice blazer.”

He sprang to his feet to model his new jacket. I remembered how I felt wearing the clothes of a royal servant for the first time. It was still alien, but it was hard not to like wearing something better than ripped jeans and shirts full of holes. “He hasn’t stopped talking about his nice stuff,” Manny said, huffing. “I just get riding pants and muck boots.”

“At least they gave you boots,” I said with a shrug.

Tyler signed something and laughed.

Manny stuck out his tongue at him. “At least I don’t have googly eyes for a princess.”

Tyler blushed as I leaned against the door frame. “You have a crush on Alex? That was quick.”

He pointed at his eyes before signing something to Manny.

I chuckled. “You don’t need to translate. There’s more to that girl than what you see, Tyler. Get to know her. Not enough people do that with her, and she’s been through a lot. Pro tip: She likes metal music.”

Manny groaned. “Don’t encourage him.”

I smirked. “The only thing that could possibly piss off Vera even more would be another daughter dating a Red. Maybe she’d try to kill him instead.” Tyler gave me a confused look as I contin-ued, “Long story short, she hired some thugs to kill me in Chicago. I’m still here. They’re not. That’s all you need to know.”

Manny gasped. “Damn.”

“This is a dangerous place to be. You won’t starve, but your food could kill you.” Wrapping my hands around my throat, I pre-tended to choke as I slid down the door frame.

A distressed look crossed Manny's face. "I hadn't eaten yet. Thanks for ruining that."

I struggled to my feet and groaned as my bullet wound reminded me of its presence. "You'll be fine as long as you don't give anyone a reason to hate you. I gotta go get ready for Vera's stupid treaty signing. Wish me luck." Tyler mimed a gunshot, and I chuckled in response. "I wish it was that easy."

The door creaked open as I entered my room and grabbed my coat, the replacement earpiece that Jonah must have had sent for me, and the gift I still hadn't given Julia. I checked my pistol had a full magazine and returned it to its holster before sliding a couple knives up my sleeves. The last thing I wanted was to have to use them that night, but with everything that had happened, it was better to be prepared.

Rachel opened the door when I arrived at Julia's room. I stepped inside, and my heart skipped a beat as I caught a glimpse of Julia in a long and simple black dress that hugged her waist but left the rest to the imagination. Knowing her, the color was a signal of mourning for those who died in the airstrike. Against the black dress, her light skin and golden hair seemed to glow. My jaw dropped. "You look beautiful."

Anne didn't look up from her intricate work on Julia's makeup but responded before Julia could, "Thank you."

Julia smiled at me. "You are handsome yourself."

I looked down at my black suit, shirt, and tie before taking a seat on the couch. "Well, I'm glad you like the clothes you bought me. I'd be concerned if you didn't."

The handmaidens finished, and Julia thanked them before they bowed and made their way out of the room. She returned to the mirror for a moment and patted her hair, still in its asymmetric bob, but there was a new wavy touch to it. *How do girls do that with their hair?* As I stared at her, I reminded myself how out of my league I was in every way: in status, charisma, and definitely attractiveness. It still shocked me every moment that she was mine.

It was only a day after the airstrike, and all my senses overwhelmed my mind every moment. Every sound from the hall threatened to make me jump, and when the brush dropped from Julia's hand and clattered against the floor, my chest felt ready to explode. "How can they celebrate after slaughtering their own people?" I asked.

She glided over to the couch and offered me a hand, which I took. "We can celebrate the end of the Fracture, and we can celebrate that you are alive. Take the time to be happy about something. You have lost so much, but it isn't over. We still have us, and we still have hope." Hope meowed from the other couch, and she laughed before giving the kitten the attention it constantly desired. "I didn't mean you."

I forced a smile. "Glad you and the stray cat are getting along well." It felt wrong to celebrate the day after Delaware's death, especially with the Militia still in danger. My off-hand slid to the gift in my jacket pocket. *We can celebrate what we have left.*

She raised an eyebrow at me, "It seems I get along well with strays," before she made her way towards the door, her dress flowing at her heels. "We need to get going."

I groaned and stood. "Would hate to be late for the black

widow's big treaty signing."

Julia rolled her eyes, and I followed her out of the room. In the Great Hall, we found Alex and her bodyguard before meeting the chauffeur in front of the palace. I climbed into the passenger's seat after helping the girls into the back, and we set off. *Please let this be over quickly.*

Chapter 8

Soft moonlight and scattered purple lanterns illuminated the villa as the SUV came to a stop. I jumped out of the car and opened the door for the princesses. When they were clear of the car, I waved on the chauffeur and tapped my earpiece. "The Dove and Robin are entering the villa. Clear for the Lioness."

Our codenames were way better. Their new royal codenames were stupid to me, but ever since Helena's death, more intense security protocols had been instituted. This one was Jonah's most recent idea, and he was far too proud of it.

Following the girls down the path to the entrance, I admired the wide expanse that was the villa's grounds. The red brick building was incredibly wide, and the snow-covered farmland on either side went on further than I could see. The main path wove through ornately decorated gardens with purple lights sprinkled throughout, creating a hue that hung over the entire front of the property.

As Julia had explained during the ride, the villa was owned by Reginald Patterson, a Purple and the chairman of the UPF's Economic Planning Committee. Famous for its size and difficulty to navigate, the villa had become a popular place for hidden meetings within its numerous courtyards, away from curious eyes and ears. Regardless of Patterson's affiliations, the place was impressive and impossible for me to wrap my mind around. I just hoped not to get lost in it.

I whispered to Julia as we stepped inside, "I wonder if my parents ever schemed in the courtyards."

She responded without turning her head towards me, "As the Secretary of the Prism, Henryk certainly had his share of those."

"You need anything before I take my position?" I asked as we scanned the crowd. A few faces within it had turned our direction.

She pursed her lips and hesitated. *Is she worried about the crown or something else?* Whatever it was, she swallowed it before whispering, "You can go, but be careful. This place gives me an uneasy feeling."

"Tell me about it," I replied before bowing and speaking louder, "Of course, m'lady. Enjoy your evening."

She nodded and gave me a cute, restrained smile with just the corners of her mouth before turning to focus on the task ahead of her. I still didn't know how she maintained her elegance in a situation like that. Vera had betrayed her most of all, yet she stared her mom in the face, never flinching. *She should have been queen.*

It was difficult to find a consistent place to stand because the guests were scattered around the purple hallways. That meant Julia was moving around constantly, keeping me on my toes. Vera would be arriving soon for the treaty signing in the center of the triangular room that was surrounded by the main halls. Until then, everyone was going their own way.

As she flowed through the crowd, Julia seemed to be checking on me more than normal. A quick glance here, a concerned look there. It was disconcerting. *Does she know something I don't?*

My earpiece crackled as Demetri's voice came through. "The Lioness, Goldfinch, and Owl have arrived. Assemble the Pride at the entrance."

Vera, Natasha, and Benjamin. I tapped my earpiece. "Copy." Royals and Purples shot me looks as I maneuvered my way through the crowd to Julia. When I was close, our eyes met, and I mouthed, "Vera."

She nodded, smiled at those she was speaking to, and followed me to the meetup point with the rest of her family. When we arrived, everyone was there, except for Alex.

Vera sighed. "Where is her guard? He should have found Alex by now."

"He hasn't responded via radio," Demetri replied with a shrug.

She rolled her eyes before noticing my arrival. "Ivan, please find my daughter."

"Yes, your highness," I replied with a bow before turning to scan the crowd. Even with Alex's easily identifiable side-shaved hairstyle, I couldn't see her anywhere. *Time to enter the maze.*

The crowd parted for me as I headed down one of the main halls, their dresses and suits tugged away like they'd be ruined if a Red touched them. I smirked at their glares. *At least I'm memorable.*

As I strode down the hall, I observed the variety of offshoots, each stretching off to another section of the villa and each hosting a different style of artwork, not that I was familiar enough with art to identify the pieces or their styles. *How deep did she go?* I tried to think which hall Alex would pick: Some of had various royals and Purples scattered throughout them, and others were bare. *She's hiding.* I chose one of the empty halls, examining the gold-framed classical paintings along the way. Many of the scenes were bloody and grotesque. *Why would anyone want these in their house?*

The maze stretched on as I wound my way through its branches, not knowing where they'd lead. Beyond the sound of my feet against the purple carpets and the variety of art, I'd found nothing after almost fifteen minutes of looking. I decided to turn back and almost did until I heard shuffling from around a corner. When I peeked my head around it, I saw Alex sitting along the wall, her head in her hands and her crimson red dress sprawled around her. For a moment, I put my hand to my earpiece but dropped it quickly. *She doesn't need that right now.*

Her head shot up as I stepped closer and spoke, "The great thing about this maze is it's easy to find a place to be alone."

She clutched her tucked-in legs and sniffled. "They want me to come, don't they?"

"Yeah," I said softly. "Vera sent me."

"Shit. I can't go like this." She rubbed under her eyes, streaking black mascara across her cheeks.

I sat beside her along the wall and analyzed the painting in front of us. A giant pig rested in a bowl of what seemed like bacon strips. "I don't get art."

She laughed through her tears. "It's supposed to represent gluttony, I think. I didn't pay much attention during those lessons."

"Even if I had classes, I probably still wouldn't have figured it out," I said, loosening my tie so I could breathe easier.

A smirk crept over her face as she fidgeted with her hands. It was weird to see her without her confident, rebellious front. "Why are you still here?"

I thought for a moment before looking at her. "Because I know exactly how you feel, and I know the worst thing after losing someone is the feeling that you're alone. We think that we want to be away from the world because it can't understand us, but we really want someone to notice we're not the same."

She stared down the hall. "I haven't been the same for a long time."

I didn't respond. She needed the time to talk and be heard, and in her family, those opportunities were few and far between. So we just sat in silence, gazing at that pig painting. My heart felt at ease away from the crowds and the spotlight. *I get why she hid.*

After a minute or so, Alex broke the silence, "I know what you did for me."

I shook my head. "I don't know what you mean."

"Please don't make me say it."

Dropping my head, I sighed. "Did Julia tell you?"

Of course she did. My chest tightened as I thought about Julia revealing my secret. I didn't know if it was fair or not for me to be mad at her for exposing that I was the one who made Lt. General Gilvan confess to raping Alex back when I'd just become a body-guard. It didn't matter. Alex knew now.

"No, she didn't."

I glanced back up at her. "Then how..."

She raised an eyebrow. "In the ballroom, when you dropped that bandana, it all made sense. Gilvan was ranting about a man in a black bandana when they brought him in. I thought he was full of shit and throwing accusations at anyone he could, but then I figured it out."

My breaths shook. I tried to reply, but the words choked me. That mission was never supposed to be about me, and she was never supposed to know about it. My mind drifted to the memory of Gilvan's wide eyes looking at me in fear and his daughter crying out for her dad. I wanted to forget that night, but it was nothing compared to what Alex had gone through.

She studied my face. "Why didn't you tell me?"

"It was hard enough admitting what I've done in my life to Julia." I bit my cheek to restrain my temper. "The more people that knew about me being Coyote, the bigger the risk. Besides, the mission was about trying to give you a bit of closure, not about me being some hero."

She ran her shaking fingers through her hair, drawing my eyes to the grotesque scar on the side of her head. I hid my scars; she wore hers like a trophy. "You have no idea how much that meant to me, and to Julia. That party was the worst thing that's ever happened to me. Seeing him dragged off, it helped, but..." She sighed. "There are some things revenge cannot fix."

"Too many things," I whispered.

In the few seconds of silence that followed, Demetri's voice crackled through my earpiece. "Ivan, have you retrieved the princess?"

Alex noticed that I was listening to the radio and shook her head. I sighed. "She is currently in some important discussions that she believes will be beneficial for the family and does not want to be disturbed."

He groaned. "Fine. Just get her here when you can."

"Copy."

I glanced back at Alex, and she took a raspy breath before speaking, "Thank you. I don't think I could handle that right now." Her eyes dropped to her family ring, its ice-blue pattern cracking through the platinum shell. "I'm not my sisters."

Leaning my head back against the wall, I responded, "Julia's mourning too, but you knew someone in those strikes. It's different."

"It is, but she is trying to understand. I think it's hard for her to handle both of us."

I chuckled. "We're both a bit of a handful."

She grabbed my hand and squeezed. "You know, I always told Jules that nobody could ever deserve her, but I was wrong. I hope you realize how much happier you've made her. Beyond all the shit that's happened, she's so excited when you're around. Don't blame yourself for all of this. I blamed myself for what Gilvan did for way too long."

The void opened in my chest again, pulling me into its depths. I didn't know how not to blame myself. Over the past eight months, I'd made so many missteps and fallen into traps. Too many people died because of those failures. With a deep breath, I forced away those thoughts. "We'll avenge Lorelai, I promise, but like I told Julia, I have a bad feeling Vera had something to do with all this."

She scoffed. "I wouldn't doubt it. We'll beat her when the time is right, and Jules will be queen."

"We can only hope." I sighed. "I just wish I could do something to make her happy."

She pushed herself to her feet. "Well, if you want my advice, this has been a pretty damn awful couple of weeks. She could use something to cheer her up." She nodded down the hall. "I hear there are some beautiful courtyards here."

Groaning in pain, I forced myself to stand as well. "I don't think taking her away from the reception is a good idea."

Pointing down the hall, she replied, "Take a left, right, and then another left down that hall with her. Remember how much she loved my advice at the nomination ball?"

My heart fluttered as I remembered our waltz in front of the royals, and I felt my cheeks flush. I'd never forget that moment. "Fine, I'll trust you on this one."

Alex stepped down the hall I came from. "You should take a separate route back. I would hate for people to wonder what we were doing back here." I raised my eyebrow at her, and she held up her arms defensively. "It was just a joke."

As she walked off, I smiled. Even if she'd been the one who had come to escape, I needed that time too. For a few minutes, I felt whole again, but I had a job to do. I took a deep breath and headed down the other hall. *How the hell do I get back?*

Chapter 9

The treaty signing had already begun by the time I meandered my way back to the main room. Alex had joined her sisters behind Vera's side of the signing table. Behind Bachton stood both the Directors of the Army and the Air Force—a million shiny gold and silver medals pinned to their uniforms—as well as the UPF's Secretary of Royal Affairs. All four of them wore smug grins, while the Hughes family, outside of Vera, did not seem particularly happy to be there.

Julia looked stunning as always in the spotlight, but I could see the exhaustion in her eyes. I couldn't blame her for being tired. The long days since the raid on the camp and lack of sleep last night had caught up to both of us. I wasn't the one everyone was looking at, though. It was hard enough for me to stand there and watch Bachton effectively hand Vera the crown, but Julia was the one who had been stabbed in the back.

As I took my position off to the side of the meeting, along one of the walls, the Purples finished preparing for the ceremony. I wanted to be able to see the action without anyone noticing my glare. Besides, from there, I could just stare at Julia instead of the depressing signing ceremony.

Bachton scooted his table mic closer to him and cleared his throat. "I would like to take the time to thank you all for being here this evening. In the aftermath of the defeat of the terrorist threat, we must ensure that order is restored to the people of this country and must refocus on the great tasks that we have in front of us. It is with great honor that I sign the St. Paul Accords along with Queen Vera Hughes so that the Treaty of Minneapolis may continue to ensure peace between the collective and the royalty."

Applause filled the room as he removed a white and purple accented ceremonial pen from the tray at the center of the table. One of Patterson's Blue servants then handed him the excessively large parchment. Bachton signed his name and passed it to Vera, who smiled before speaking herself, "I am grateful that Mr. Patterson invited us here this evening, and I am honored to have the opportunity to sign this agreement. It is vital that we continue the peace that has existed between the royalty and the People's Front for a century. Together, we will work to repair the damage done by the Fracture and the Militia, and together, we will ensure peace and stability for all of our families."

Another round of applause followed her statement as she signed the agreement. With wide smiles, the pair shook hands and posed for the cameramen. The cameras flashed, and fire burned my veins as I imagined the praise that would be heaped on Bachton the next day in the state-controlled media. They would call him a champion of peace when he was nothing more than a liar and a murderer.

As I watched their celebrations, one thing stuck out in my mind: *This has been planned for a long time.* The special treaty, the decorations, the pens—all of it must have taken time to plan. There was no way that the agreement would have been reached in the aftermath of the bombing or even the camp raid. Vera had planned this the whole time, whether Julia was willing to accept that or not.

In front of me stood my two greatest enemies, and I could only watch with my fists clenched. Killing them wouldn't help the situation anyway. Vera's death would send the monarchy into chaos once again, and Julia would have no chance at the crown after her boyfriend assassinated her mom. Bachton's death would mean nothing. The hydra that was the UPF would replace him with someone potentially even more brutal, and the Prism would live on.

When the photoshoot was complete, the servants brought out the alcohol, and the real party began as Julia worked her way through the crowd once again. The scene made my stomach churn. *The UPF's solution to everything is parties and alcohol. Disagreements in the Fifth International: party. Dealing with the aftermath of their mass murder: party. I hope my parents weren't like them.*

Before Vera had a chance to disappear into the crowd, Duke Richard Bilgram swooped in and pulled her down one of the halls. The vulture had been circling, hoping to become king himself, so it was not a surprise to see him confronting Vera. I didn't know which of them would have been the worse monarch, but it was obvious that the Accords would deepen the rift among the royals. Many of them would appreciate regaining their businesses and land, but it would be difficult for Vera to regain the trust of Bilgram's coalition after canceling the election.

After a while, Alex slid over to me with a smirk on her face and a glass of wine in her hand. "Mom is in trouble."

"Bilgram?"

She shook her head. "His old farts aren't going to abandon their loyalty to the crown to get him on the throne. The younger royals, though, are not so tame." She held an open hand towards a group of younger Whites, around my age, chatting in one of the halls.

I recognized a couple of them as supporters of Julia, but I still wasn't familiar with all their names. "What can they do? Only the heads of their families have the money and power."

Alex took a sip of her wine. "What good has money and power been for the country? If we want to beat her, they're the way."

Before I could respond, Julia glided over to us and raised an eyebrow. "I feel like I shouldn't leave you two alone for too long. Things might start burning down."

"The only thing burning down is the Duke's self-confidence," Alex quipped back.

I chuckled. "Alex was just telling me that many of your younger supporters are not so keen on giving up."

Julia followed my glance towards the group. "I am touched to hear that they want to remain loyal to me, but for now, let us keep these discussions in private."

Faking a curtsy, Alex smirked. "Of course, my queen." Julia rolled her eyes as her sister continued, "I mentioned to Ivan that I discovered some courtyards while I was hiding from Mom."

Julia smiled, and for a second, I forgot everything but the color of her lips. "I've heard a lot about them. Though, this is my first time here."

"Want to explore?" I asked, nodding towards the hall.

She looked around at the mingling elites. "I would love to, but

I probably shouldn't. Mother is watching me like a hawk."

Taking the last sip of her wine, Alex grinned. "I'll distract Mom. She will be so busy being surprised that I bothered to talk to her that she won't notice."

Julia narrowed her eyes again. "Really? You're willing to suffer through that?"

Alex flicked her eyes to me before shrugging. "You should accept the offer before I reconsider."

Julia glanced at me with curiosity in her eyes. "Fine, but this is exactly why I can't leave you two alone. You scheme against me."

I chuckled. "No, we scheme *for* you."

Alex did a mocking bow to her sister before heading off to find Vera. When she was gone, Julia studied me, probably trying to figure out why Alex was being so nice. "What did you and her talk about while you stalled for her?"

We turned and began towards the hall I'd gone down before. "She's struggling with losing Lorelai on top of her dad and Helena, and she still feels lost after Gilvan's attack."

"It was kind of you to comfort her. I try, but I think talking to someone outside the family is good for her. She respects you, and it means a lot that you're here for us."

We reached the hall, which was empty as most of the guests had remained in the central area. I sighed. "She's important to you, and she's your sister, so I care about her too. She did tell me, though, that she knows about what I did to Gilvan."

Her eyes widened. "I didn't know that. Are you okay with her knowing the truth?"

"I wish it was still a secret, but she said she was glad to see him arrested. I guess that's what matters." I paused. "I should talk to Snap and see if he knows anything about Lorelai. It's worth the effort to see if she's alive, or at least if we can give Alex some closure."

Stepping towards me and holding my hands, she replied, "That's sweet of you. I'm sure Snapback has enough on his plate, though."

I nodded. "He does, but it's worth a shot." I rubbed the back of her hands with my thumbs. "How are you? Everything has been about the airstrike lately. How are you handling all this?"

She pursed her lips and gazed at the paintings as we began walking again. "I never wanted to be queen until Mother took it from me. It's wrong for me to act like it was mine, but it hurts... a lot. Everything we had worked for, your plan, all of it disappeared in an instant. I'm so sorry, Ivan. I feel like I failed you."

As we turned the corner past the pig painting, I wrapped my arms around her waist to stop her. Her eyes watered as I pulled her close, and I smiled to try and cheer her up. "You have sacrificed so much to try and change things. We are more than just you becoming queen, Julia. I love you, no matter what, and there's nothing Vera can do to change that."

Biting her lip and looking down, she responded, "Thank you, Ivan. It's hard to lose it after getting my hopes up."

This close to her, I was hyper-aware of her movements. Her quick breaths. The pull of her lips on my heart. And the adorable strand of hair she could never get under control. I ran my fingers down her cheek. "Don't worry. I'm not giving up on my princess yet." For a second, I considered kissing her, but she would hate me for doing it where a wandering Purple could see. "C'mon, let's find the courtyard."

She gripped my hand as we began to run down the hall. "If someone finds us, my mother…"

"If there was no chance of discovery, this would be way less fun."

She beamed. "True."

We laughed as we ran through the halls and followed Alex's directions. I felt free with her, and seeing her smile and enjoy herself made me forget all the pain for a moment. It was just us, and that felt right.

Soon, we reached a set of wooden doors decorated with an engraving of a river. "This must be it," I said as we held our intertwined hands to the engraving. Curiosity pulled me forward as we pushed together, and as the doors flung open, I realized why Alex directed me to this one. Oak trees and a narrow creek encircled a white wooden gazebo. A thin white blanket covered everything as the open air allowed the snow to drift across the courtyard.

Julia gasped at the sight. With her eyes alight, she raced towards the wooden bridge over the creek. "This is amazing!"

I smiled as she danced through the snow, her hips swaying to some inaudible beat as her hair became one with the sky. *How the hell did I get her?* When I caught up with her at the bridge, we leaned along the railing, looking down at the water below. "Why does he show those stupid paintings and then hide something like this?" I asked.

Her eyes reflected the water as she replied, "Maybe it's showing that the most beautiful things must be found."

I wrapped my arms around her waist and pulled her closer to me as her nose and ears turned red from the cold. "Or stumbled into by accident and saved from thugs."

She kissed me, and for a minute or two, nothing else mattered but the taste of her lips and the feeling of her body pressed against mine. My heart felt full with her. We rarely had time to be alone together, especially outside of the palace. That kiss in the courtyard felt like a great adventure, even if it was only for a passing moment.

When we pulled back, I took the thin ice-blue box from my jacket pocket. "I never got the chance to give you your birthday gift."

Her hands drifted along the edges of the box. "You didn't have to."

"I wanted to. Open it."

She slid off the top of the box to reveal a silver bangle bracelet and a mini-earpiece. Reaching in to grab the bracelet, she let out a gasp and examined the ice-blue spiral that wrapped around its entirety. "It's beautiful. How did you afford this?"

I shrugged, too embarrassed to admit how hard I'd looked to find the perfect one. "It's probably not as expensive as you think, and you guys give me a stipend. It's not much, but between that and the little money I had from the Enclave…"

Before I could finish, her lips met mine again. *Guess she likes it.* I laughed and spun her around, her black dress sweeping through the white night.

The bracelet glimmered in the moonlight as she slipped it on her wrist, beaming. "That means so much to me. Thank you, Ivan. I love it." After admiring the jewelry for a few more seconds, her eyes drifted to the box again. "Is that an earpiece?"

I grabbed the mini-earpiece and held it in the light for her to see. "I figured that you're as much of a Militia member as any of us, so you should be hooked up to our radio. That, and there have been quite a few times where a direct line between the two of us would have helped a lot. It works really long ranges, so we should be able to contact each other no matter where we are, and this one is small enough to not be seen, unlike mine. Jonah got his hands on this one for me. Consider it part of the security budget."

She grinned and pulled me closer. "So I can talk to you whenever?"

Chuckling, I placed it in her ear. "Yeah. As long as we're both in situations where we can talk."

"It feels weird," she said, wiggling her head. "How does it work?"

"To connect to me, hit the top button. For the Militia radio, hit the center. The bottom button turns on your mic."

She played with the buttons for a minute. "I don't hear anything."

"The Militia leadership line is pretty quiet unless one of us needs to contact one another. Here..." I activated my mic. "Hear me now?"

She giggled. "That's so weird!"

"It works better when I'm not right next to you." I wrapped her in my arms again, pulling her against me. Her warmth cut through the cold, and our hearts raced together. "Though, that's where I always want to be." We kissed again, and I wished we could stay there forever, not worrying about the sorrows of the world for once.

When we separated, it was only far enough that the tips of our noses touched. Her eyes shone against the night sky as she spoke, "Thank you for trusting me with this. It's another part of your world I get to be a part of."

"I get to see every part of your life, so it's only fair you get to see all of mine. Besides, you helped plan the camp raid and supply smuggling as much as any of us."

She blushed as she turned around and gazed up at the stars. "You can't spy on me with this, right?"

I chuckled and hugged her. "No, only you can turn the mic on. And besides, I wouldn't do that to you. Trust me?"

"I do," she replied, leaning back into me.

After a few minutes of staring up at the falling snow, Julia shivered from the cold against her exposed arms. I flung off my suit jacket and wrapped it over her shoulders before kissing the back of her head.

She flipped around and smiled cheekily at me before nodding towards the gazebo. We walked to it with my arm around her waist. "I can't tell if I am selfish or determined," she said, "but this whole day... I thought I could stand waiting, that letting the crown go would be the best choice, but I don't know what to do. Part of me wishes I never pursued it; another wants it more than anything."

I lifted my head and opened my mouth to catch a falling snow-flake on my tongue. She laughed as I responded, "I never thought I'd hear you admit you wanted it."

We stepped into the gazebo and leaned over the railing, watching the snow fall over the courtyard. She sighed, creating a puff of fog in front of us. "The crown is not my goal. I see now, though, that it is the only way to put an end to the Front's tyranny and give those little hopeless kids a chance to be happy." Running her hands through her hair, she paced across the gazebo. It was only for a moment, but every second she was away from me, my heart ached for her to come back. When she turned around, her eyes were full of passion. "We have to stop her."

I gripped the wooden railing behind me. The snow along its ridges sent a shiver down my spine and froze my fingers. "I thought we needed time to recover?"

She flowed back to me and gripped my lapels, pulling me closer and trapping me in her gaze. "We will defeat her in time, but now, the Red King needs to rest."

"And what about the White Queen?" I asked as I moved my lips to her neck, the familiar smell of her wintergreen perfume filling my lungs.

Her breaths were quick as she replied, "She will build a coalition stronger than her mother has ever seen. Then, together, they will take the throne, shatter the Prism, fix their broken country, and live happily ever after."

"Ambitious. I like it."

She pecked me on the lips. "And I love y..."

A gunshot echoed across the courtyard. "Get down!" I yelled

and shielded her with my body as she threw herself to the ground. *What the hell is going on?*

Chapter 10

Demetri's voice roared through my earpiece, "All guardsmen, secure the royal family and execute escape plan Omega. There are hostiles in the building. I repeat, there are armed hostiles in the building."

Julia shouted over the gunfire, "What is happening?"

My heartbeat deafened me as I scanned the courtyard. *Empty.* But the shots came from within the villa, and Omega meant escape at all costs. "All I know is there's armed intruders. We need to go, now."

She grabbed my arm, and I pulled her to her feet before we ran to the doors. The shots rang from every direction as I put my ear to the door to check the hall was clear. It was silent on the other side beyond the distant gunfire. For now, we were clear. I pulled my gun, nodded to Julia, and crept my way into the empty hallway.

Demetri's voice returned, "What's the status of the family? I have the Lioness."

Another voice came over the earpiece as we continued creeping down the hall, "Goldfinch and Owl are with me."

That's Vera, Natasha, and Benjamin. Where's Alex? I activated my mic. "Dove is with me. Anyone have Robin?" There was no response. *Of course not.* I broke the silence, "I'll find her."

Julia clutched my arm. "Where is Alex?"

"None of the guards know where she is. Can you text her?"

Nodding, she pulled out her phone as I crept to the corner. She joined me after a few seconds, grabbing my free hand and whispering, "Who are they, the Fracture?"

"No, the Fracture couldn't pull off something like this. Besides, I saw the bodies. They're long gone." I peeked around the corner with my gun raised. My finger gripped the trigger, but it was clear. "We're safe for now. Let's wait a minute to see if Alex texts back."

My mind raced as we huddled back inside the courtyard. *Is this an invasion?* I tried to think of what group could have known about the location of the signing and had enough trained soldiers to eliminate the large number of guards both inside and outside the villa. There wasn't one in Northern Mississippi that I could think of, unless the attackers were from the UPF or royal military, both of which were unlikely, given the circumstances.

For a few minutes, I guarded the door while Julia stared at her phone, hoping for a response. Soon, she let out a sigh of relief before raising an eyebrow when the text came in. "She says she'll meet us at the pig painting. What does that mean?"

I started to open the door. "That's where I found her before. C'mon, it's this way."

We wove our way back through the halls. As we went, the gunshots escalated, rattling my brain. My breaths were short and quick. It took everything I had not to panic. But Julia was relying on me. I didn't have a choice.

When we reached the last turn, I took a deep breath. *Please be alive.* I peeked around the corner, and on the other side was Alex, plastered against the wall with a look of sheer terror on her face. She gasped when she saw me before putting a finger to her lips and nodding her head towards the next hall.

Mouthing back, I asked, "How many?"

She held up two fingers. I nodded and traded spots with her. She crept over to her sister, and they shared a hug before taking cover down the hall.

My injured arm throbbed as I took a sharp breath. *Now or never.* Pistol raised, I turned the corner and smacked into some-one. The soldier stumbled, falling to the ground as I slid into the wall, barely holding my footing. With a shout, he reached for his gun, I aimed and fired, sending a bullet through his head. His body went limp.

That had to draw some attention. I readied my pistol as another black-clad soldier turned the corner. Her eyes widened as she no-ticed me and raised a rifle. *Shit!* I scrambled back behind the wall as a spray of bullets peppered the pig painting full of holes. *Too close.*

My mind spun as I leaned against the wall, my senses flooding my mind. *You've done this before. C'mon!* I focused on the soldier's advancing footsteps, waiting for her to enter my line of sight. Her boots squeaked with each step forward, but as she approached, I realized she probably had her gun trained on my corner. I sprinted back to where Julia and Alex were hiding just as the sol-dier reached the corner. The girls fled down the hall as I took my position.

The soldier checked my previous hiding spot. But before she could swing her rifle to my new position, I slid out from my cover and fired twice. She cried out as the bullets smacked into her torso and arm. The gun slipped from her hands, and she fell to the floor.

Slowly, I moved forward to the corner, checking that no other soldiers showed up. *Clear.* Before going back, I examined the downed soldiers' uniforms. On their shoulders was stitched three letters: *PRH. What does that mean?*

I jogged back towards the sisters and called out, "It's me. We're clear."

Julia scrambled from her hiding spot and gripped my arm with her trembling hands. "Are you alright?"

"I'm fine, but I saw a PRH badge on their shoulder. What does that mean?"

Her eyes searched for an answer as she pursed her lips. After a couple seconds, she whispered, "Huron." I raised my eyebrow before she clarified, "The People's Republic of Huron. Remember, I was telling you about their aggression before the Chicago conference."

"Why would they attack now? Unless, the weapons..."

"What weapons?" Alex asked.

I squinted, trying to focus over the sound of the distant gunshots. "The Fracture's. They had way too much firepower to be getting their guns off the black market. We'd wondered if someone was supplying them with heavy weapons."

"You think Huron was giving the Fracture guns?"

"Maybe."

Julia groaned and ran her hands through her hair. *Why does she have to be so attractive when we're under attack.* "That doesn't make any sense," she said.

I opened my mouth to respond, but a blast of static hit my ear as another guard's voice came through the radio, "Stay clear of the entrance, they're every..." Machine gun fire replaced the sound of his voice. The radio went dead silent.

Damn it. "They have the front locked down. Do either of you know another route out of here?"

Julia pondered for a moment. "We should be fairly close to the southern edge of the villa. If we reach that, there's bound to be an exit to the farm."

"You're a genius! Which way is south?"

She pulled out her phone and opened a compass app before pointing down one of the halls. "That way."

I nodded. "I'll take lead. Stay close."

The gunshots continued, fading farther away as we winded through the halls. With less than a day to recover from the blast, my body ached with each step. I was not physically or mentally ready for another fight, but this was about more than my survival: Julia and Alex were relying on me now. My recovery could wait.

We studied the artwork along the way. The deeper we went into the villa, the weirder and more grotesque they became. Instead of obese pigs, they showed human sacrifices, massacres, naked people strapped down, and endless amounts of bloodshed; it was unnerving.

From behind me, Alex spoke as she gawked at the art, "Hiding his kinks in plain sight I see."

I shuddered. "And he's running the economy... great."

Halfway down what I hoped was one of the final halls, Julia grabbed my shoulder. "We should contact Jonah. If they found a way into the villa, then the palace is not safe. He may have an idea where we can hideout."

If the palace isn't safe, where is? I nodded and tapped my earpiece. "Jonah, this is Ivan."

Static crackled in my ear before Jonah's voice broke through in bits, "Iva… D… Ver…"

"Jonah?" There was nothing but static. *Are they jamming the radios?* I tried reaching the other guardsmen. "This is Ivan. Does anyone come in?" Nothing. *Shit.*

I turned off my mic. "They must have cut off radio signals. I can't hear anybody. We're on our own." I sighed. "I've got some ideas where we can hide, but first, let's get out of here."

The next hall was clear as I swept through it, checking the side passages for any soldiers. As we'd gone deeper into the villa, the gunshots had become barely audible. Sounds echoed well with the marble walls, but the place was massive. It was impossible to know far we'd gone.

A shuffling noise came from around the next corner. I glanced around it only to jerk my head back as a voice came from the other side. "Command, what's the status on the targets?"

I signaled for the princesses to hang back as I peeked around the corner again. There were three soldiers stationed by the door at the end of the fifty-foot hallway. Two stood on either side of the door while the third, who was talking over the radio, paced back and forth in front of them.

Their command center must have responded since the patrolling soldier nodded to his comrades, and the three of them started closing in. *Last-minute sweep.*

Nerves gripped me. It was one thing when my life was on the line. It was another when Julia was in danger. *Stay focused, and she'll be fine.* The soldiers quickly halved the distance between us. I grabbed one of my knives, turned the corner, and threw it at the nearest guard, hitting her in the head and sending her body to the floor.

They raised their rifles as I pulled my second knife and closed the distance between us. The second soldier shouted and fired over my head as I slid. My foot crashed into his shin with a *snap*. He cried out and fell while I lunged at the last soldier, who spun towards me.

Before he could fire, I knocked the gun from his hand and drove my knife into his neck. His body dropped to the floor, bringing me with it. Crimson spewed over my shirt and neck.

Julia shrieked, sending a jolt down my spine. I rolled as the second soldier rushed towards me, my thrown knife in his grasp. He was on top of me within seconds. I pulled my pistol and shot as their blade cut through the air. Inches from my face, it stopped.

He gasped and shook as he stared down at the blood seeping from the hole in his chest. The knife dropped from his hand, and his eyes rolled back into his head. I pushed him off me, but as I did, something caught my attention. There were piercings in his ears. *A soldier with earrings?*

Covered in blood but alive, I let out a sigh of relief and struggled to my feet as Julia and Alex ran over to me. Julia reached towards me but avoided making contact. Her eyes showed her fear as she opened her mouth, searching for words and finding none.

My heart and head pounded when I broke the silence, "Do the other ones have pierced ears?"

Julia furrowed her brow. "What?"

Before I could check, Alex bent down and examined the other soldiers. "They do. Why?"

"Something is wrong, but right now, we need to go," I replied, pointing to the door.

I started towards the door, but Julia grabbed my hand, coating her palm in red. "Are you okay?"

"I'm fine, but we need to go, *now*." Her face told me she was unconvinced, but I pulled her along, grabbing my knives on the way. I wished she didn't need to see me kill three people in such a vicious way, but there was no choice. I needed to get her to safety. They were in the way.

I cursed my injured arm as I struggled to push open the steel door. *I can take out soldiers but not open a damn door?* My cheeks burned as Julia and Alex rushed to my side to help in the effort. With their help, it slid open, and we stepped into the frigid night. I waved the girls to follow, and we crept behind a row of bushes lining the pathway towards the farmland.

Shouting and more gunfire came from in front of the villa as flashlights spewed light across the now otherwise dark gardens. It didn't seem like they heard us, but we were sitting ducks. Still crouching behind the bushes, I led the princesses down the path as sirens and the whirring of helicopter blades became audible in the distance. *The military is coming, but it's too late.*

The breeze whipped across my hair and neck, sending goosebumps racing across my skin as I gazed at the lights flashing in the darkness. I didn't care about the chill. We were finally free from the villa's maze, and that's what mattered.

Julia knelt beside me, her ice-blue eyes sharp in the moonlight. "Where are we going to go?"

It was impossible to know what was going on in the main section of the villa with the radios dead. All I knew was that the soldiers were here. If this was the beginning of an invasion, Huron's troops could be anywhere. We needed to disappear, and I knew exactly where to do it. "Aaron's house. The *Free Press* is basically a bunker, and we can hide out there 'til it's safe."

Alex peeked around the bushes. "Shit. This is so messed up. Do you think they got Mom and Bachton?"

I sighed. "I don't know, but we need to find a car, and preferably one not surrounded by Huron soldiers."

"This is a farm," Julia replied, her eyes surveying the darkness that stretched beyond the villa. "There must be trucks around here somewhere. We should try to find the maintenance building."

With nothing but the moon to provide light, we scanned the field, slowly making our way closer to the farmland. I couldn't see anything but black, but after a couple minutes, Julia tapped me on the shoulder and pointed to our left. I tried to follow her gaze. At first, I didn't see anything. But as my eyes adjusted, the soft outline of a building crept into sight. I smiled. "Good catch."

We crossed the path and headed down the hill on the other

side as we entered the unplanted farmland. As we ran, the semi-frozen dirt crunched under our feet. I winced with each step, half-expecting a soldier to hear us. No shots came, though, and with the hill as an extra barrier between us and them, we sprinted to-wards the building.

Julia ran beside me, the wind whipping through her bobbed hair as my suit jacket flapped behind her like a cape. Everything from my head to my toes was screaming, but as we ran together, I felt alive, free. I'd been through so much shit; she made all of the pain worth it.

Faint tire tracks appeared as we approached the building. Just like the villa, it was made of red brick, and a small garden formed a loop around it. Julia spoke as I peeked through the windows, "We made it because of you."

There was no light inside beyond the moonlight creeping in, but I could see a pickup truck. "We're not safe yet, but because of *you,* we found a truck."

She tugged on the door. "Just one problem."

"Crap, I don't have my lockpicks." I moved next to her and in-spected the lock. It was nothing special. With the right tools, I could have broken it easily.

Alex pushed her way between us with a smirk. "Good thing we don't need them." She pulled the bobby pins from her hair and knelt in front of the lock. "Some of us came prepared."

I crossed my arms and chuckled. "Why do you know how to pick a lock?"

Julia replied before her sister could, "I'm sure it has nothing to do with Eric, or was that Sam?"

"Well excuse me that some of us don't get saved by heroic boys on street corners," Alex said moments before the lock broke open with a loud *crack*. She stood and curtsied. "Maybe, if you hadn't wasted time with Ethan, you would have learned badass skills like I did." Sticking out her tongue at her sister, she held open the door. "Ladies first."

Julia rolled her eyes before entering the building. I loved watching the two of them joke with each other, but my chest tightened with jealousy as I thought about the name Alex had mentioned. *Who is Ethan? Did she have an ex that she hasn't told me about?*

I flicked on the light, and the *buzz* of electricity filled the room. Julia turned towards me, blushing as I raised my eyebrow at her. She mouthed, "Later," and nodded towards the truck.

The grin on Alex's face told me that she knew exactly what she'd done with her comeback. I probably shouldn't have been surprised that Julia had dated another guy, but it had caught me off guard. *Does it matter? You haven't told her about...* My thoughts were interrupted by the keys flying at my face. Alex cackled as I snatched them just in time, and I shot her a sarcastic glare before jogging towards the truck. "Let's get the hell out of here."

The door creaked open as I climbed into the driver's seat and swiped rust from the handle off my hand. Julia and Alex joined me on the truck's one row of seats. I put the key in the ignition without turning it. "Someone have the GPS up? Once we get out of here, I'm going, whether there's a road or not."

The light from Julia's phone burned my eyes as she held it up.

"One step ahead of you."

I shook my head to get rid of the dots in my vision. "Great, now I'm blind."

"Just drive already before they see the light on," Alex replied.

"Just drive already...." I said mockingly as I hit the garage door opener and turned the key. The engine sputtered for a moment, and my heart dropped before it caught and roared to life. *Thank God.* I slid the gear lever into drive and slammed on the gas, spinning the tires before we plowed into the darkness.

My back ached as we bounced through the field. "Worst suspension ever," I yelled over the clanking of the engine. Neither of the girls seemed interested in responding, though, as they watched the mirrors, hoping that no one was following us. Part of me wanted to follow their gaze, but I was too busy gripping the steering wheel and dealing with the limited visibility. "Are they coming?"

Julia replied as she squeezed my leg, probably trying to comfort herself as much as me, "Nothing yet." It was a small touch, but her presence was the only thing preventing me from panicking as I imagined every possible scenario from a small raid to World War III.

I took a deep breath. "Good, but I still have no idea where I'm going, and this truck doesn't seem to understand what a straight line is."

"Is it the truck or the driver?" Alex said with her eyes ablaze. *At least someone is enjoying our life or death experience.*

"Next time we're invaded, I'm leaving you behind," I spat back.

Julia shot me a look. Normally, she would have laughed. "Play nice." Looking down at her phone, she continued, "Veer a little bit to the right. If we keep going south, we should hit a farm road in about a mile."

I smiled at her. "Thanks, 'Dove.'"

"Stop. I despise that codename," she replied sharply.

"Really? I think it suits you," I said, chuckling. "What do you think, 'Robin'?"

Alex scowled. "I swear to god, Red. I will throw you out of this truck."

Another bump sent the whole cabin rattling, and I groaned. The banter was a welcome distraction, and based on how tight Julia was gripping my leg, she needed one too. "Okay, guess those nicknames aren't flying. Julia, I was thinking, though, I don't have a cute nickname for you."

"Really? You're thinking about that *now*? You just killed three people!"

I wiped away the dread that crept into my mind as we hit yet another rough patch of the field. My voice bounced along with the truck when I replied, "Is 'princess' a cute nickname or just a title? I feel like it's kinda both and could be confusing for you."

Her cheeks flushed. "Not now Ivan! I know you're just trying to make me laugh, but I would appreciate you focusing on our survival right now."

We reached a wooden fence-line, and I stopped the truck. "What about 'sweetheart.'"

She blushed again but nodded towards the fence. *I forget some of us aren't used to running for our lives.*

Alex threw her arms forward. "How about 'drive the damn

truck'?"

I put my foot down, sending us ploughing through the fence and onto the road. Wooden pieces flew everywhere, but we landed on pavement, free at last. I turned to Alex. "There, happy?"

She rolled her eyes as we started down the road. "I don't have to know *everything* about your relationship. You know that, right?"

Julia raised her eyebrow at me before flicking her eyes to her sister. "So, how are things with Tyler?"

I love her. I laughed as Alex cleared her throat. "Tyler is an excellent footman, thanks for asking."

"Oh come on," I replied, "We're not blind."

"I don't know, okay?" she said, biting her lip. "I just met the guy yesterday. Don't tell me you two fell in love instantly."

As I turned the next corner, a blast of static hit my ear. I held my hand up to silence the girls as Jonah's voice came through. "Do any guardsmen read me? Anyone?"

I tapped my mic. "This is Ivan. What the hell is going on?"

"I was going to ask you the same thing. Reports started coming in of an attack at the villa, but then everything when silent."

Taking a deep breath, I stomped on the gas, and we sped down the road. "It was Huron soldiers from the look of it." Julia pointed to her ear, and I nodded before adding, "Can you patch Julia into this channel?"

"Oh, she's got the earpiece now? Awesome! Patching her in... Julia, can you hear me now?"

"I can!" A wide smile crossed her face as I turned the truck onto the next road, heading south towards the heart of St. Paul. The truck was still an uncomfortable ride, but at least on pavement it didn't feel like someone was swinging a hammer at my back anymore.

Jonah continued, "Huron? There's been no chatter about them."

Julia replied, "The more I think about it, the more I feel like something doesn't add up. The Front reached a deal with Huron to sell them back the contested old Upper Peninsula of Michigan. Was that not enough?"

I tried to remember what she'd described to me about the deal. Northern Mississippi had loosely held onto Michigan's Upper Peninsula since the Third Civil War, but it made sense that Huron, which controlled what used to be Illinois, Indiana, and Michigan's Lower Peninsula, held their own claim on it. With the border dispute resolved, there didn't seem to be a reason for them to go to war.

"I don't know what's going on," I said, "but something seems wrong. We checked the soldiers: They all had pierced ears. That can't just be a coincidence."

"Interesting," Jonah said, "I agree that something doesn't quite add up."

Julia cut back in, "Do you know if Mother, Natasha, and Benjamin escaped?"

"Sorry, I should have mentioned that. Yes, they managed to get out before comms dropped and are en route to a secure location that even I can't know until this all blows over. From the information I've received from the military, Bachton made it out too."

Something itched in the back of my mind, like my brain was

trying to tell me something that I couldn't quite comprehend. It was the same feeling that I got during Operation Blackout, which was not reassuring. "Huron failed pretty bad if they missed the two highest priority targets."

Julia shrugged. "I'm glad they are safe, though, regardless of the circumstances."

Alex knocked a knuckle against the window, and we both turned our heads to look at her. "Don't mind me. I'm not cool enough to have an earpiece anyway."

Jonah chuckled. "That's definitely Alex. Whatever is going on, though, there's been no invasion from Huron. We'll see how things develop, but for now, I need to help organize the response efforts. Keep in touch, and I'll let you know if I learn anything else."

"Thanks Jonah," I replied before turning off my mic with a sigh. "Well, this sucks."

Alex huffed. "Tell me about it."

We entered Roseville, just north of St. Paul. Something caught my eye on the side of the road. I looked through the side window, trying to figure out what it was as we passed by. "Is that a tent?"

More of them appeared the further into the city we got, illuminated by flashlights, lanterns, and the moonlight. Yellows and Oranges shivered as they huddled around make-shift fires: some in trash cans, others in holes in the ground. Winter was coming to an end, but in Minnesota, it was still freezing. My heart sunk as I watched. *A whole city displaced because of Max's violent delusions and the Front's brutal response.*

Alex gasped. "They're everywhere."

Julia replied, aghast, "This must be where people fled to when the military called for the evacuation. There is a whole city out there, homeless until the conflict is over. We must help them."

"When this crap is over, we will," I said. "But if we do our job, they won't be here much longer."

Her eyes were cold as ice. "We'll fix this."

The tent city was soon a speck in the rearview mirror, and I relaxed as much as I could in the driver's seat, placing a hand on Julia's leg. "We're going to be alright, I promise."

Wrapping my suit jacket tighter around herself, she stared forward, into the darkness. "I can only hope."

Soon, we passed the rusty, bullet hole-ridden sign: *Welcome to St. Paul, Population: 0.* Someone had spray-painted over the number with a zero. I sighed. "Charming as always, but it's mine."

Julia smirked. "Hey, I'm the Duchess of St. Paul, so technically it's *mine.*"

"Oh, really? Tell me, where and when is the underground city market held?"

Holding her chin high, she replied as we neared the heart of the city and Aaron's house, "Between May and August on Saturdays, usually starting around nine in the morning and closing around eleven in the evening. It was formerly held on University Avenue in Frogtown before the Front forced them to suspend operations. They relocated into the rougher parts of town."

My jaw dropped. I was at a loss for words. There were obviously parts of the city, like the Enclave, she knew nothing about, but I didn't realize how much she did know.

She continued, "I have always cared about St. Paul, even if I may have been blind to the worst parts of the city. You opened my eyes to the real suffering beyond the safer parts of town, and I'm incredibly thankful for that. Many royals may not care about the territories they hold, but I do." Alex chuckled, and Julia raised an eyebrow at her. "What?"

Alex grinned. "Oh, you just got lucky. As Duchess of East Minneapolis, I can say St. Paul is way cooler. 'My' area may not be as rich as the west side of the river, but all I've got is a bunch of snobby U of M kids. They do throw great parties, though."

"I beg your pardon? I was one of those students last year." Julia jabbed her sister as I turned onto a dark and dead University Avenue. Seeing the city so empty made my skin crawl. Half the buildings we saw were at least partially burned down, and in my mind, I pictured the flames as I stood on the statue of Law. *Nothing will be the same.*

Grinning, Alex replied, "And you only had fun because I dragged you to those parties… and the city market."

Julia smiled. "And I'm glad you did. I remember when…"

The windows shattered. Glass sliced through the air as the truck flipped. For a second, we hovered upside down. My heart stopped as the truck rolled before resting on its side. I cried out as my head smashed into the pavement through the shattered window. Pain rushed through my skull. My mind wavered. With effort, I looked up, trying to see if Julia was okay. Blood trickled from her temple. Rage burned inside me. *Who did this?*

She clung to the seatbelt, staring at me with fear in her eyes. "Ivan!"

Her voice was distant. I tried to reach for her. But I couldn't move. My arms were numb, unresponsive. There was nothing I could do to protect her. Panic ruled my mind as the door at the other end of the truck opened. The soldiers shouted something, but a ringing in my head deafened me. They pulled the girls out of the truck as I screamed for Julia. With the girls out, one of them looked down at me. "What are we going to do with him?"

Another replied, "Leave him. They want him alive."

The door slammed shut, and my mind failed as I slipped into the abyss.

Chapter 11

Light flooded the truck's cabin when I woke up. My head spun. My muscles ached. I squinted and moaned as I examined my surroundings. *How long have I been out?* The green lights on the truck's clock flashed *12:00* over and over again. *That's useful.*

My head was still firmly planted on the pavement in a pool of crimson. *Is that mine?* I still couldn't move. The seatbelt had tightened in the crash and never released, leaving the rest of my body planted in the seat as I hung sideways. My stomach flipped, but it was hard to tell if I needed to vomit because of that or the pounding that hammered my skull.

I tried lifting my head off the pavement. "Ahhh!" My skull felt like it'd been shattered. A piercing pain flooded my brain, paralyzing me. For the first time in my life, I felt afraid to even move. My breaths were quick but weak. *Am I dying?*

Slowly, the events from the night before came back to me. *Where did they take Julia?* My arm shook as I tapped to my earpiece. "Julia," I croaked. *Shit, even my voice sounds like death.* There was no response. "Julia, are you there?" Nothing. I took a raspy breath. Every word took something out of me, and I felt drained already. "If you can hear me, hold the bottom button down for three seconds."

My heart stopped as I waited for what seemed like forever.

Then, three small beeps came through the radio. *She's alive.* I spoke again, "Are you in danger?" The three beeps repeated, and I took a shaky breath, trying to remain calm. "Is it Huron?" Nothing. *Who is it?*

A voice came through the radio. "Princess Julia, come with me. Your presence is requested."

Demetri. My mind was wild. I wanted to scream, but a void filled my lungs. *Why is she with Demetri? What is happening?* I gasped, struggling for air. "Are you at the palace? Did Vera do this?" The beeps returned. Rage rushed through my body like a wildfire through a dry forest. *I'm going to kill her.* I didn't know how, but I had no choice now. Whatever had happened the night before, she was somehow responsible. My voice wavered as I said, "I'm going to save you, sweetheart, I promise. I'll save you."

Finally, her whisper came from the other end of the radio, "Run."

"What does that mean?" There was no reply. "Julia? I can't just leave." I wanted nothing more in the world than to hear her speak again, but the radio was silent beyond shuffling and the sound of footsteps. *You need to live if you want to save her.*

Adjusting my radio, I called Aaron, "Aaron. Are you there?"

There was static for a few moments before he replied, "Ivan, is that you? What happened? Jonah said you were supposed to hide out here last night. I never heard from you, and he's gone silent."

"I need help. University Ave... gah. Find the overturned truck. Please." Every inch of me shook out of shock or fear or both. The world felt far away. *I don't want to die.*

"Holy shit. I'm on my way. Ivan, are you okay? Where's Julia?"

I coughed. "Gone."

A door slammed on his side of the radio as I shut my eyes. It took every ounce of my strength to remain conscious. I felt my mind slipping into sleep's tempting embrace as Aaron called out, "Hold on man. I'll be there soon."

I opened my mouth to respond, but there was no voice left. Even if there was, I didn't have the energy to create the words. Every inch of me was screaming. My brain was overwhelmed. In a second, my mind slipped, and I lost consciousness again.

Chapter 12

"Ivan! Wake up, kid. C'mon!"

Squinting, I turned my head to see Aaron staring at me through the broken windshield. He stretched his arm towards me.

With everything I had, I tried to unbuckle, but my hands refused to cooperate. I yelled in frustration at myself and the world. *Julia's gone. Vera has her. I failed.*

Aaron spoke again, "You can do it. Focus!"

I groaned again and swung my hands at the buckle. It released, and I flopped into the door and pavement. Pain shot through my head, and my body spasmed as I fought to stay conscious.

Blurry in front of me, I could see Aaron's hand. I shouted in rage and reached out for it. *Not close enough.* My arms acted on their own, pushing me up as I lunged forward. His hand grabbed my forearm, and I forced mine to close around his as he began to pull me out. Slowly, I slid through the shattered glass and into the open air.

The world spun as I tried to stand. My legs failed, and Aaron had to catch me before I fell. His eyes analyzed my face with worry. "Let's get you out of here."

With an agonizing amount of effort, Aaron helped me into the passenger seat of his little grey sedan before climbing in himself. His yellow tag flapped as he worked, silently doing everything he needed to do without complaint. *How is he so calm?* He shifted the car into drive, and we began the couple block journey to his house. *We were so close.*

He glanced at me as I groaned, resting my head on the head-rest. "Are you planning on telling me what just happened?"

The sun burned my eyes, and I winced as my headache pounded harder. "Sorry. My head…"

"You're lucky to be alive. I'll try to patch you up, but I'm no medic."

"Thanks. I owe you."

He glanced at the rearview mirror, checking if we were being followed. "Yes you do. So what the hell is going on? I heard some serious shit went down last night."

I stared out the window. "I don't know where to start. Every-thing fell apart."

"It definitely looks like you did," he huffed.

"It's not funny, Aaron. Somebody shot up the signing ceremony last night. I don't know who survived, but I managed to get Julia and Alex out. We were on our way to you when something smashed into the truck. They took them. They took Julia." My breaths became short and quick. I couldn't control them.

"Who did?"

I yelled and punched the dash. "Vera!" I growled. "The soldiers had Huron patches on their shoulders, but they all had pierced ears. I gave Julia a hidden earpiece, and I heard the voice of one of Vera's guards after they captured her." I shook my head and stared out the window at my destroyed city. "I lost her."

Putting a hand on my shoulder, he replied, "Don't worry. We'll figure it out."

"How? The Militia surrendered, I'm a wreck, Delaware is dead. We have nothing."

We pulled into his driveway, and the garage door slid open. Aaron tried to help me out, but I waved off his support and stubbornly limped my way behind him into the house. He pointed to the brown fiber couch. "Sit. Let's patch you up."

Doing as he said, I groaned before plopping down on the couch. Aaron knelt in front of me with a roll of gauze, studying the wound on my head. He touched it, and I snatched his arm as my body jerked in pain. "Don't do that."

"This is going to hurt no matter what, but some alcohol and gauze are all I can do for now. At the very least, it'll clean the wounds."

Clenching the armrest, I took a deep breath. "Just do it," I muttered through clenched teeth.

The smell of alcohol burned my nostrils as he opened it and poured a few drops on my head. I grimaced as the sting raced through my body. *It's for the best.* I knew he had to disinfect the wound, but my body screamed for it to stop.

He finished with the alcohol and wrapped my head. "I swear, every time I see you, you look worse. I don't want to see what happens to you next time."

I chuckled and then groaned again as laughing hurt my chest. *I'm falling apart.*

After a few more minutes of cleaning up my wounds, Aaron finished. "There, good as new, if new is heavily damaged."

"I feel like a mummy."

He paced over and picked up a smoldering cigar off the ashtray on the coffee table. Smoke filled the room as he pulled a lighter and lit it again. Taking a quick puff, he sat in the armchair next to the couch. "Look like one too. Hey, at least if you die, you're already wrapped up for the sarcophagus."

I raised my eyebrow. "A what?"

"You know, the gold coffin they put mummies in? My god, did Poseidon teach you nothing?"

Shaking my head, I replied. "As much as I'd love to learn about sarcopha-whatevers, I'd rather try to figure out how the hell I'm going to save Julia. She said she was in danger."

"How much did Chuck tell you about the Minutemen after Chicago?" he asked, spinning the cigar in his hand.

The Minutemen? I remembered back to Chuck saving me from Vera's hired assassins. If he hadn't been there, I would have died and my body would have never been found. "Not much, just that it was an organization founded by James Madison and Benjamin Franklin after Jefferson was executed. He said they fight for 'what America was supposed to be' or some bullshit like that."

The grey smoke hovered in front of him, obscuring his dark skin. "Do you think it's actually 'bullshit'? We've talked a lot over the years, and you always said that you wished things could have been different in history."

I slumped deeper into the couch. "What if none of it matters? The people in power are going to fight and kill and steal, and there's nothing we can do about it. I've almost died so many times, and for what? Nothing has changed. I thought I believed in something, in change, but maybe it's impossible. Maybe, I should have just settled into palace life with the woman I loved instead of losing her...”

Aaron shook his head. “We’ve all fought for what we believe in: to end the Prism, to end the UPF’s spying, to bring back rights. Change isn’t easy when our enemies are as big as they are, but Ivan, I’ve seen you and Julia work together. If anyone can beat them, it’s you two.”

“Thanks, but right now it’s just me, and I’m not exactly in my prime.”

“You’re not alone. You never have been. I know at times it feels like you’ve lost everything, but a lot of people are fighting alongside you, because of you. The Militia isn’t done, but you’re right, they’re not going to be able to help. The Minutemen can.”

I shot a glare at him. “Are you telling me that you’re part of the Minutemen?”

He waved away the smoke that hovered between us. “Yes.”

“And you hid that from me for years?” I clenched my fists, trying to hold back my rage.

With another puff on his cigar, he sighed. “It is not that simple.”

I scoffed. “And you’ve been spying on me and reporting back to them?”

“Yes,” he said, waving his cigar to hush me, “but let me explain.”

Groaning, I protested, “How could you sit back and watch our city burn, acting like there could be no outside help when you’re part of the Minutemen?”

He stood, sticking his cigar between his teeth as he frowned. Lines cut deep into his forehead, showing his age. I always forgot that he was more than twice as old as me. “The Minutemen are

126

not an army. We couldn't stop the Fracture or the bombing, as much as we would have liked to. What we are, though, is a network, and together, we should be able to get to the bottom of what is going on. Obviously Vera had something to do with this, but what about the Huron soldiers?"

Dumbfounded, I just sat there, trying to process everything with my woozy mind. *Aaron's part of the Minutemen. Julia is gone. He thinks they can help. How?* I gripped the edge of the couch, steaming. "Fine, maybe you couldn't stop them, but you still lied to me for years." Taking a deep breath to calm myself, I paused before continuing, "I don't know any army that would send a spec ops unit to assassinate the leaders of another country with a flag on their shoulder."

Pacing in front of me, Aaron thought for a minute, then stopped and narrowed his eyes. "What if they didn't?" I shrugged as he continued, "We haven't heard any chatter in our network about Huron wanting a war. Nothing."

"You think the whole attack was an inside job?"

He sat next to me, fired up. "Doesn't it makes sense? The pierced ears, the badges, the lack of an invasion..."

"And both Vera and Bachton escaped. That's either a complete failure by the attackers or something else." A thought popped into my head. *Purge.* I flung myself backwards, looking up at the ceiling as panic overwhelmed me again. "It's a leadership purge. Holy shit, I was right."

"About what?"

"I told Julia that I thought Vera was working with the UPF. Everything that has happened seemed to clear the way for her to take the throne. What if she's been working with the Front to destroy the Militia and any rebels while consolidating power within both the government and the monarchy? They used the Preus coup to eliminate the King. They gave weapons to the Fracture to paint the Reds as violent extremists, giving the military an excuse to occupy St. Paul and mass slaughter their enemies. With the rising tensions, Vera signing that deal with the UPF would publicly look like a return to some stability. What if last night was the culmination of their plan?" The salty taste of blood filled my mouth. I was talking too much.

Aaron groaned as he stood. "Purge their enemies within the elite and pin it on Huron. I have to admit, it's an impressive plan."

"A normal person would say it's horrible."

He huffed. "Since when are we normal? Now, if this was a purge, why would they be so aggressive about ensuring Julia and Alex didn't escape? I assume Queen Vera wouldn't want her daughters to be harmed. A car crash that brutal seems risky."

I narrowed my eyes, staring at the TV across from me. "What if them getting beat up was part of the point? Turn on the TV. I want to see what they're saying."

Aaron grabbed the remote, and the TV flickered on. I squinted as my concussed brain adjusted to the light. On the screen was a video of the aftermath at the villa. From the look of it, they weren't allowing the cameras inside, but they made sure the Huron flag was plenty visible on a few of the fallen soldiers in the garden. The bottom-line read: *Massacre at Chairman Patterson's villa. Huron kills dozens.*

The reporter speaking was outside the police cordon. "The

People's Front police have informed us that General Secretary Bachton is safe and at an undisclosed location until the situation can be accessed. Queen Vera Hughes and her family have also been declared safe after the assault, but others have not been so lucky." He listed off the confirmed deaths: Secretary of Health Patricia Sterling, Secretary of Information Donna Goebel, and Chairman Reginald Patterson among the UPF elites. *They killed him in his own house. Brutal.* Among the royals, they'd killed Lord Franklin McGill, a slew of Bilgram's other coalition members, and a few of the younger royals that had supported Julia.

Flicking back to the studio, the show host replied, "Thank you, Luke. This is truly a tragic day for our nation, and speculation is rampant on how our glorious leaders will react to Huron's aggression. We will keep you updated as we hear more, but until then, we are hearing that Queen Vera has prepared a response to the attack, and we will be bringing that to you live right now."

The camera switched to an image of Vera on the throne. To her right sat Natasha and Benjamin, and to her left sat Alex and Julia. The entire family wore black, but Vera wore a large gold necklace, too large for the day after a tragedy. My eyes were fixed on Julia, though. Dark blue and purple bruises were scattered across her face, and a thin line of crimson ran across the side of her neck. I clenched my fists as rage swelled in my chest.

Before Vera began, I tapped my earpiece, hoping they hadn't spotted Julia's hidden one. "I'm watching with Aaron. We'll make her pay."

She swallowed, and I saw the unmistakable hint of fear in her eyes. *Is she afraid for herself or me?*

I opened my mouth to speak again, but Vera began, and I felt a twinge of regret for being so slow. "As you may have heard, last evening there was an attack by the People's Republic of Huron against my family, members of the royalty, and members of the People's Front government during the signing of the St. Paul Accords. In this disgusting assault, at least twenty highly respected and loved royals were murdered in front of our eyes." She paused as fake sorrow crossed her face before she continued, "I have personally contacted the families of those who have passed, and they all tell me the same thing: We cannot allow this cowardly act by Huron to go unpunished. I have informed the General Secretary that he will have the full and complete support of the monarchy in any actions the government chooses to undertake against Huron."

Of course you did. I could tell Alex was struggling to hide her scowl as she avoided looking at both her mom and the camera. Julia held her chin high, the fear in her eyes replaced by cold daggers that sent a chill down my spine.

Vera continued, "This attack was more than just one country attacking another. It was a disregard for human life, and it was a betrayal of trust from both within our borders and without."

Where is she going with this?

"Multiple members of the royal guard participated in the assault and have been apprehended. One, though, has escaped our grasp. The Red known as Ivan 181375 used his position to abduct both Princess Alexandria and Princess Julia, attempting to take them both hostage on behalf of Huron."

I shot to my feet, yelling at the TV, "Lying piece of shit! I'm going to kill her!"

Aaron shushed me and pointed to the TV. I turned back as Vera continued, "We recently discovered that Ivan is the son of the former Secretary of the Prism, Henryk Matelski, who betrayed his people by partnering with Huron in an attempt to overthrow the People's Front. We believe that Ivan intends to follow through on his father's work. He is currently considered a fugitive from justice, and any information regarding his capture will be rewarded."

She's twisting the truth, and it's going to work. On the edge of the screen, Julia gripped her chair's armrests as she fought to remain silent. As much as I wanted the truth to be told, I needed her safe more than anything.

Vera's grin widened as her eyes focused on the camera. The edge of her mouth twitched for a moment. She looked like a cat ready to catch its prey. "I can assure you that I will do everything in my power as queen to protect the people of Northern Mississippi. In times of trial, we must unite behind the truth and protect those we love."

With that, the screen flipped back over to the newscaster, and Aaron muted the TV as images of my face appeared. *Wanted.* He paced around the room, running his hands along his balding head. "This is not good."

I scowled. "No shit! The whole damn country is going to be out for me now. They think I betrayed Julia."

"And your family history isn't going to help. We knew you were a Matelski, but Vera pulled that card in a way we did not expect."

"Why did everyone know about my parents before me?" I spat. Aaron shot me an uneasy glance before continuing his pacing. I wanted to be mad at him, but considering the mountain of things facing us, that seemed small now. In my heart, I knew I had to rescue Julia, but part of me felt paralyzed by the fear of what could happen if I failed. "How are we going to get her out of there?"

Aaron scoffed. "Your face is plastered all over the news. Everyone is going to be aiming a gun at your head the second you show your face. How the hell do you think you're going to get into the palace?"

Forcing myself to my feet, I walked closer to the TV, which showed an aerial view of the palace. "Do you guys have a boat? Small and quiet."

"I don't like where you're going with this," Aaron said, picking up his cigar again.

"Answer the question."

He huffed. "Why do you always know how to get me into trouble?"

"Because life's no fun without a bit of trouble." I took out my gun and checked the remaining bullets before returning its holster. "Now, do I need to hang two lanterns to get a boat from the Minutemen or what?"

With a puff of smoke and a sigh, he replied, "Poseidon taught you history at least. Fine. You'll get your dang boat. But for now, follow me. We're not done here."

Chapter 13

Aaron led me down the hidden staircase to his print shop, where the familiar old smell of ink and thousands of newspapers filled the air. I looked around when he stopped by the back wall. "I've seen your print shop before. This isn't anything new."

Rolling his eyes, he put his hand on the wall. A green light appeared and ran down his hand as he smirked at me. After a couple seconds, the wall slid open in front of him. "Patience is key." He chuckled as I raised my eyebrow at the scanner. "Biometric. Everyone's handprint is unique. Come." He waved me along and stepped into the room.

All I could do was gawk as I entered the room behind him and analyzed the tech inside. A TV that had to be at least eight feet wide hung on the wall, a computer with five monitors filled the middle of the room, and scattered everywhere were gadgets and blueprints. The little kid inside me wanted to touch everything. It was a boy's playhouse. "Alright, James Bond, now I'm mad. You hid *this* from me?"

He ignored me and sat down at the computer, typing rapidly. While he focused on that, I examined the sheets on the desks. There were files on every major mission we'd run in the Militia and more. Inside each file were pictures and profiles on everyone involved. All the Militia's plans, smuggling operations, and intel were in the files. *They were helping us the whole time.*

The files were sorted by date, and when I reached the past year, my face was in nearly every one. *Operation Blackout, Operation Phoenix, Operation Pridefall...* "What's 'Operation Pridefall'?"

Without looking up from the computer, he replied, "Classified."

"Screw you." I grabbed the file and flipped it open. *Operation Pridefall. Lead Operative: Ivan Matelski. Target: Vera Hughes.* "I'm an 'operative' now?"

His eyes flicked from the screen to me and then back to the screen. "Operation Pridefall was always meant to be our response if Vera were to become queen. Given the circumstances, much of it will have to change, but the concept remains the same."

"How? The rescue is one thing, but how do we beat her?"

"Are you willing to put your hatred of her aside for a moment? For the plan to work, you can't kill her."

"For my relationship to work, I can't kill her," I replied with a chuckle.

He smirked. "Ah. Young love. Now, the plan has always been to discredit her, and this conspiracy can be taken advantage of if we play our cards right. The first step after saving Julia will be the two of you fleeing to Huron. I hear Detroit is only slightly less frozen than we are."

"Detroit? How do we expose her from there?"

He shook his head. "Bachton and Vera are prepping for a war with them, and only you two can stop it. You need to tell Huron what's going on and find evidence that Vera and the UPF are lying. Huron won't believe just anyone, but they'll believe Julia, I hope."

"You hope?"

"Negotiation is an art, not a science, but luckily, your princess is good at both."

I crossed my arms. "We've got a lot of work to do if we're going to pull this off. How did you guys know all of this, and how am I a lead on something I don't know about?"

Aaron sighed. "There are some things in this world that are bigger than us, Ivan. I told you we had a network."

I scoffed. "And who is in this 'network' that you keep referring to? Why do I seem to be left out of all of this?"

"Until now, you didn't need to know. It was better to have you acting independently. The Minutemen have a chain of command, and it's safe to say the people I report to wouldn't approve of everything you did. We didn't want them controlling you. We needed you fighting for what you believed in."

"Who is 'we'?" Rage boiled in my chest again. *There's too many secrets...*

He stood and pressed one last button on his keyboard. The TV lit up, and a group of familiar faces met me. Pacing over to the it, Aaron glanced back at me and continued, "Every single person you see here is a Minuteman, ready to act at a moment's notice."

I held my hand to my head and found myself struggling to stand as I tried to comprehend what was happening. On the screen were at least twenty-five faces. I recognized four: Poseidon, Zeus, El Capitan, and "Is that Alanna Lorenz?"

He nodded. "Countess Alanna has been a key ally for us. She believed, along with our superiors, that we should have brought you and Julia into the loop sooner. Poseidon and I agreed, though, that our job was to support the two of you behind the scenes."

I crossed my arms. "What does that mean?"

"My job, *our* job, for the last couple of years has been to ensure Julia became queen and that you formed the alliance between the Militia and her." He walked over to the stack of files, pulled one out, and handed it to me. Emblazoned on its front were two words: *White Crown.*

My heart began to race as I took the file in my hands. *Have they been manipulating me this whole time?* I scowled. "Are you telling me that this has all been a charade?"

"No. None of this has been a charade. We knew you and Julia combined could be the force that would change things, but we didn't realize how close the two of you would get."

I stepped closer to him, so close that I could smell the cigar smoke on his breath. "So, that street corner..."

He chuckled. "I can't call that anything but fate. We had a plan for you two to meet, but that was perfect. You saved her life that night, Ivan."

"How did you know I would convince her to run for queen, that I'd save her from the Preus coup, that..."

Aaron grabbed my shoulders, interrupting me as he stared directly into my eyes. "We didn't know anything, but we'd studied both of you. We knew that you would never give up your fight, even in the comfort of palace life, and we knew that Julia had the ideas, the heart, and the popularity to make change happen. Chuck lied to you when he said that we didn't have many people in Northern Mississippi, but one thing he told the truth about was that everything relies on Julia becoming queen. You two can unite the two beating hearts of Northern Mississippi: the people and the royalty. No one knows the shadows of St. Paul better than you, and no one can shine in the light better than Julia. The two of you are the plan, you were always the plan, but that doesn't mean it's all on you."

My hands shook as I stared at the file. "Why'd you choose me? Was my dad part of the Minutemen?"

He huffed. "No. Henryk was a power-hungry asshole who used the Prism to gain more power." I winced. "Sorry, but it's the truth. And no, we didn't pick you. You did. We needed an independent mind, and the entire reason we didn't tell you sooner was *so* you could think for yourself. We were trying to figure out who to send to the palace for a long time, and you kept popping up. Every time a problem arose, your comrades in the Militia saw how you stepped up. You had the guts, the passion, and you didn't like taking orders."

"And now they're all dead." I looked up at him. "Tell me that everyone we've lost hasn't been for nothing, that there's still hope."

He walked back to the computer. "As awful as things are right now, there's more hope than we've had since I joined. The bosses back in the Appalachian Confederacy aren't going to be happy with your plan to rescue Julia, though, so the amount of support I can give is minimal."

"I thought the goal was for her to be queen? She can't do that when she's imprisoned by Vera."

Talking as he typed, Aaron replied, "They are more patient

than you, but I believe things like this are exactly why we picked you in the first place. Unlike the bosses, I understand that Operation Pridefall can only be successful before the war starts. When we are at war, the people have a terrible knack of believing whatever the government says." He pressed enter, and a blueprint of the palace appeared on the screen. "You've spent more time at the palace than any Minuteman ever has. What do you think?"

How can I break into the palace when they're expecting me? The blueprint wasn't helping, as its flat map told me nothing new about the palace. What mattered was the guards, the security, the people. Where would they be, and where would Julia be held? Not to mention Alex, Jonah, and my new friends. There was no way Vera would allow them to roam free.

The only weakness I could think of was why I'd asked for a boat. The lake was almost entirely unguarded, and if I could land by the forest, they'd never see me coming. Julia and I had stolen our moments away many times among the trees. Now, they would provide the perfect cover for our escape.

When I cleared the forest, the garden would be no problem. The patrols were always sparse, and with the chill, there wouldn't be many enjoying the air. I would be able to slip through the bushes undetected. The real problem would be the palace itself. With its long marble halls and limited entrances, it would be difficult to sneak around, let alone find Julia.

I quickly explained my plan to Aaron. The whole time, his eyes studied the blueprint, and he made no noise except for the occasional "hmm." When I finished, he remained silent for a few moments, his hand stroking the stubble on his chin. "That might work, although the interior will be tricky. Is there any way you can get in contact with Julia?"

"I've tried with the mini-earpiece I gave her. She hasn't been able to actually say anything." Anger flooded my body again, and I slammed my fist on the table. My hand stung, but it felt good to hit something. I couldn't help it. Just the thought of her trapped made me angry at myself and the world. "Don't you guys have *something* that can help?"

With a sigh, he sat back down at the computer. "We can get you the boat and any other supplies you might need, but you're the deepest person we have in the monarchy. You're a bodyguard. You have to know the lockdown protocols."

"I've got it." I closed my eyes, trying to picture the back of the palace. "If I can knock out the few guards that will be stationed in the gardens, there'll be a clear shot to the balcony outside the living room upstairs. I should be able to make that climb; there's plenty of ledges."

"Still doesn't get you to Julia."

I let out a shout of frustration. My mind was moving too fast to concentrate. All I could do was cradle my pounding head in my hands. *I'm falling apart.*

Aaron stood and walked back over to the corner, where a small bed sat. Compassion filled his normally stern gaze as he looked at me. "We will talk more about the plan later. For now, you need to rest and recover. We aren't going to war tomorrow, and you can't rescue her in the shape you're in. I'll bring down some clothes that aren't covered in blood."

"No!" I stormed across the room and stared at the blueprint, looking for some clue. *I have to find her.* Vera could have changed any of the guards' movements by now, and Julia could be anywhere. "The longer we wait, the longer Vera's grip on power tightens. Julia is in the hands of the woman that tried to kill me twice. I can't just lay down while everything burns around me!"

My head felt ready to blow. Each breath came quicker than the one before it. *Poseidon's gone. Delaware's gone. I can't lose her next.* Everyone had lied to me—hidden a plan that I was the center of. While I scrambled in the darkness for survival, they had planned out my life behind my back. Now, the Minutemen were my only hope to save Julia. The country was collapsing, but all I could think about was saving her.

With a huff, Aaron shuffled over to another stack of papers and pulled out two files. "Ivan, I'm not going to tell you what to do, but it will at least take a day or two to get the boat and supplies for the mission. Take the time to rest. Not every fight is yours to win." He approached and held out the files.

I unclenched my fists with some effort and looked down at the files. "What are they?"

He pushed them into my chest. "Read. I'm going to get the spare clothes for you. Try to contact Julia." With that, he stepped around me and left. His stern voice still hung in the air, reminding me of the fatherly advice Poseidon used to give me.

A sharp pain ran up my spine as I sat on the edge of the bed, threw the files by the pillow, and kicked off my shoes. My feet were wrecked like the rest of my body, but it felt amazing for them to be free. For a minute, I just sat there, alone in the secret room with nothing but the buzz from the monitor to distract me from my thoughts. Inside and out, I was overwhelmed. Everything was crumbling around me. *How can I trust anyone?*

My heart hurt. Every second Julia was in danger felt like another knife in my side. It scared me how much she meant to me. Delaware was my best friend, but Julia was more than that. She was my weakness and the one person that made me feel alive at the same time. I needed her: her eye rolls when I made a stupid joke, her eyes that could switch from alight and alive to daggers of ice at a moment's notice, her warmth when I held her in my arms. Without her, I was broken.

I tapped my earpiece and hesitated for a moment, either afraid she'd respond or afraid she wouldn't. After a few seconds, I took a deep breath and spoke, "Julia, are you there?"

A whisper came in response, "Ivan?"

The sound of her voice unlocked my muscles, and I fell back on the bed, staring at the ceiling. "Hey, I'm alive and with Aaron. Are you okay?"

She spoke in a panic, "I am fine, but I can't talk for long. They have Alex and me locked in our rooms, but they bugged our phones. Jonah and your friends are locked in the basement, and they let our handmaidens go on temporary leave. I could only convince them to allow me to walk in the gardens for a couple of minutes. Mother has lost her mind. You need to get out of the Twin Cities. If they find you..."

With a scoff, I cut her off. "Surviving in St. Paul when people want to kill me is my specialty. Besides, I can't rescue you if I run away."

"Ivan, that crash could have killed you. I can't let you put yourself in danger again. Even if I am trapped, you need to survive."

"We don't have time. Vera and Bachton are going to start a war,
and we need to stop them."

"How do you know that?"

I wanted to tell her everything. "Aaron is part of the Minutemen, and they have a plan for you... for us."

There was no response.

"Julia?"

A few more seconds passed before her voice crackled back
through the radio in a whisper, "The guards are coming. I trust
you, Ivan, but promise me you'll wait until you're ready. I couldn't
forgive myself if you were captured trying to save me."

My heart was heavy as I replied, "I promise, but I miss you."
She was right, but I didn't want to wait. It wasn't in my blood.

Her voice came through one last time, "I miss you too, my love.
Please stay safe." When she stopped, I was left with nothing but
the sound of a guard's shouts and the shuffling of feet on the garden's stone path.

Chapter 14

Subject: Ivan 181375
Birth name: Ivan Matelski
Birth Date: July 19, 1999
Color: Red
Alias: ~~Coyote,~~ Referred to as "The Red King"
Occupation: ~~Steelworker,~~ Militia Lieutenant, ~~Stagehand at the Royal Theater,~~ Bodyguard of Princess Julia Hughes
Affiliations: Twin Cities Branch of the Northern Mississippi Militia, the St. Paul Free Press, the Northern Mississippi Monarchy
Close-Relationships: Henryk Matelski (Father, Deceased: September, 1999), Janica Matelski (Mother, Deceased: November, 1999), Poseidon (Mentor, Birth name classified, Deceased: December, 2020), Penelope 341294 (Alias: Dandelion, ~~Intimate relations~~), Naomi 233942 (Alias: Delaware, Mentee, ~~Possible intimate relations,~~ Deceased: March, 2021), Aaron Jones (Birth name classified, Alias classified, Owner of the St. Paul Free Press, Friend), ~~Otto Preus (Alias: Razorblade, Mentee),~~ Princess Julia Hughes (No known alias, ~~Possible~~ intimate relations), Jonah Clarke (No known alias, Royal guardsman)

The clattering of Aaron's fingers against the keyboard filled the room as I set down my Minutemen file. It was the day after Julia and I had talked, and I couldn't resist looking at the files anymore. When I saw Penelope and Delaware's names, though, my hands shook, forcing me to stop.

I hadn't thought about Penelope in years. Part of me wanted to forget she ever existed, and saying we had "intimate relations" was a bit of an over-exaggeration. We'd kissed once or twice when we were thirteen. Then she decided I was too reckless and told me to pick her or the Militia. I chose the Militia, like any thirteen-year-old boy who was given a choice between a girl and being a badass spy.

Aaron noticed that I'd looked up at him. "Saw the 'possible intimate relations,' didn't you."

"You thought I dated Delaware?"

He held his hands up in surrender. "You two spent a *lot* of time together. Although, that was Poseidon's note, not mine."

I laughed. "If he wasn't dead already, I would kill him for that."

"You're telling me you were never fond of her?"

"Most people don't hit on their sisters. We were best friends, nothing more." Sadness gripped my chest again. "That doesn't make it hurt any less."

Swiveling around, his eyes studied me. "She was a hero to the Militia. I know it doesn't bring her back, but she became who she was because of you. Keep reading. I've got work to do, and you're doing a wonderful job not making your ridiculous number of injuries any worse."

I scowled, only half-jokingly, and returned my eyes to the file, flipping through the pages of reports on my missions. One part caught my eye.

White Crown Recruitment

8/15/2020: As the attached mission reports show, Ivan is a prime candidate for White Crown. He has quickly become one of the most trusted names within the Militia and in St. Paul as a whole. While his style is direct and often reckless, he never abandons his mission, and he never gives up on those he cares about. He will be difficult to control and has a problematic family history, but we believe that he will gain Princess Julia's trust in time. We request authorization to launch White Crown immediately. - Aaron

8/20/2020: Find a different candidate. – (Name Redacted)

8/21/2020: There is no other candidate. – Aaron

8/22/2020: You have approval, but he is your responsibility. - (Name Redacted)

8/25/2020: Ivan has somehow found a way into the palace on his own after saving the princess in St. Paul. White Crown has begun. - Aaron

I set the file to the side again and rubbed my eyes. Between planning for Julia's rescue and reading through the old files, it felt like I'd been trapped in that basement for weeks. My shot arm, damaged head, and sore body felt better than yesterday, but it still hurt to even move.

Who runs the Minutemen, and why didn't they want me? That question ate at me as I watched Aaron at work, radioing other operatives and sending messages through what looked like a chat room. I didn't appreciate the rejection, not that I was a fan of being recruited into a mission behind my back in the first place. Wherever I went, there was always some bigger force behind the scenes. Aaron had said he didn't want them controlling me, and I couldn't help but wonder why.

Aaron spun around and nodded his head towards the other

wall. "There should be a bag over there that you can use. Pick something light since you'll be climbing."

There were a variety of black bags thrown in the corner with no apparent organization to them. I bent down and rummaged through them until settling on a small backpack that had enough compartments in it for knives and the other gear I'd need. My back cracked as I swung it over my shoulders, and I groaned in pain for a moment before tightening the straps.

The computer flipped to a screen saver of Aaron smoking a cigar in front of the Mississippi as he returned to his feet. "That will do, 'Agent Ivan.' I'm going to run some errands and make sure things are ready. I know you said Julia needs until at least tonight, but we need to be ready to pull the trigger the second she gives the go-ahead. Also, I still have a newspaper to run. Please, for now, remain down here in case the black-caps come knocking."

I smirked. "And what am I supposed to do while you're gone?"

Standing in the doorway, he glanced back over his shoulder. "Rest, and feel free to use the computer. Use the screen's biometric scanner to log in. You're one of us now, and anything beyond your classification is password protected anyway. Oh, and don't throw any parties."

I quipped back, "Thanks…"

With a knock on the door frame, he was gone, and the door slid shut behind him. I was alone. In my current state, that was dangerous. A war raged in my mind. Every second of quiet was another to ponder Vera's plot and Delaware's death. All that did was enrage me more.

Julia's file tempted me as I felt the urge to read it in hopes of learning more about her past. There was so much we still didn't know about each other. Our lives since we met had been strangled by missions and merely surviving. I wanted more. *Is that selfish?*

Before I realized what I was doing, the file was already in my hands, and I started to open it before forcing myself to stop. *This isn't fair to her.* As much as my curiosity tried to get the best of me, there was enough secrecy in the world already; we didn't need more of it in our relationship. I needed to trust her to tell me everything, which meant I also needed to open up more.

Why do I miss her so much? When I thought about Delaware, there was just an empty hole, threatening to pull me to its depths. Away from Julia, it was different. There was a longing in my heart that made the world feel wrong away from her. I needed both of them in completely different ways. Without either and stuck in that basement, my hope was fading.

With Aaron gone and no one to talk to, I radioed to Snapback, "Hey Snap, how is the relocation to the Enclave going?"

It was a few seconds before he replied, "Slow. They're still searching Payne-Phalen. It'll be at least a couple weeks before they get us all out of here. No idea why they don't seem to care about time."

"Weird, but thanks for the update. I guess they don't care where the Militia is, as long as we're not armed." I paused and remembered the chaos of the last day. "After the attack at the villa, everything has gone insane for us. Vera and the UPF are responsible, but we have a plan to take them out."

"Glad someone's got a plan, and it's good to know you're okay too. News is hard to come by with the soldiers patrolling here, but we were afraid you didn't make it."

I huffed. "Yeah, I made it out. Barely. That reminds me. Do you know a Yellow girl named Lorelai? She's Alex's friend, and she's worried since she hasn't heard from her since the airstrike."

He paused for a moment. "Nah. Name doesn't ring a bell. Sorry man. I'll ask around and let you know."

"Thanks Snap. Stay safe out there."

"You too, Ivan."

For the next few hours, I researched Huron. Operation Pridefall relied on us getting to and negotiating with a country that I knew almost nothing about. While my job would mainly be to get Julia there safely, the least I could do was have some understanding of the country. After a while, my eyes became tired as I gave in to boredom, and I allowed myself to check social media's reaction to Vera's announcement.

Ever since we'd stolen and published Secretary Heller's journal, the UPF had driven social media into illegal underground networks. Both supporters and opponents of the government were still vocal, though, and everyone had something to say about the last couple days. Depending who you asked, I was now a traitor and a terrorist or a hero trying to save the princesses from Vera's schemes. While no one had uncovered all the information Aaron and I had, many people inside and outside Northern Mississippi didn't seem convinced by her explanation. That being said, stories blasting my history and family were everywhere. It became too much, and a massive headache worked its way into my head. I shut down the computer.

I leaned back and stared at the ceiling. All of a sudden, I felt confined, stuck. My head pounded. *I need fresh air.*

The biometric scanner unlocked the door, and I shuffled through the printers. Their noise hammered at my aching head. The smell of the paper was overwhelming. Everything was spinning. My stomach couldn't handle it. I vomited. I tried to make it to the stairs. My legs collapsed. Curled in a ball on the cold floor, I screamed. *What is happening to me?*

With one hand on the bottom stair, I stared up at the ceiling. *Keep going.* Step by step, I pulled myself up. I had no destination in mind. All I knew was that I needed out. My body was slowly starting to recover, but my mind was shattered. The clash of rage, surprise, and sorrow left me lost and confused. My life wasn't mine. Every step forward confined me more. *Why can't I escape this cage?*

After what could have been minutes or hours, I reached the top of the staircase and stumbled to the kitchen. My hands shook as I filled a glass with water and drank greedily. With everything that had happened, I'd forgotten to eat or drink anything. I didn't want to. Especially after vomiting, my stomach couldn't accept anything more than water right now, even if I needed it.

The carpet scraped my feet as I stumbled to the door. I already felt better after drinking something, but I still felt trapped inside. With a *click*, I unlocked the door and stepped out into the light. The wind whistled through the buildings as I felt the cool cement against the calluses on my feet. I didn't know when Aaron would be back, but that moment finally brought me some calm. *The world hasn't fallen apart yet. Can't someone else fix it this time?*

A course of energy ran through my legs, and I took off in a run, no destination in mind. The splintered pavement jabbed at my feet as I went. It didn't matter. I was just happy to feel something real again. It felt like it'd been an eternity since I could just run. Sure, a war was looming and a couple miles away the Militia was being imprisoned by the military, but right now, I couldn't fix any of it. All I could do was run: from the police, from Vera, from my responsibilities, and from the hole in my chest.

A few blocks down, Julia's orphanage came into sight, along with the royal guardsmen surrounding it. I knew that inside, there were dozens of Black Tags she'd saved from the streets and the work camps. Now, they were encircled by Vera's men.

As I stood in the middle of the street, watching them from a distance, I remembered why all of this mattered. It wasn't about freeing me from the Prism or Julia from Vera's grasp. It was about them being able to grow up in a country where they didn't have to worry if their next day would be their last or if they'd get another meal. Even if I wasn't in control of my life, I would fight so that one day, they could be. Whether I lived or died, I would do it so they had a chance.

Chapter 15

"What part of 'don't go outside' didn't you get?" Aaron said, his nails digging into his scalp as he paced around the living room.

My hunger had returned after my adventures outside, so I ripped a piece of bread off the loaf in the kitchen. He may have been only a Yellow, but with the side money he had from the *Free Press* and the Minutemen, he had more food than I'd seen anywhere in St. Paul. Shoving the piece of bread in my mouth, I replied, "The 'you telling me what to do' bit."

A chuckle forced its way passed his stern demeanor. "Well, I can tell you're feeling better, because you're full of shit again."

"I needed to get out. All of this..." I waved my arm around. "I felt trapped. Other people have controlled my whole life, and now, reading those files...." I sighed. "I needed a reminder why I'm doing this."

"Did you get it?"

I raised my eyebrow as I hopped up on the kitchen counter, hoping he'd be as annoyed with that as he was with the printers. "Get what?"

The side of his mouth twitched in agitation, just like I hoped, as he slowly walked towards the trap door. "The reminder." I nodded, and he continued, "Good. Glad that standing within range of

Vera's guards was worth it." Bending down, he picked up the duffle bag he'd dragged in. "C'mon. I've brought toys."

We walked back down to the hidden spy room, and he heaved the bag onto one of the tables. His face was scrunched as he turned around. I chuckled. "You're getting old."

He cracked his back. "Dang. In a couple of years I'll be yelling at kids to get off my lawn."

I smirked. "You don't have a lawn."

"Shit! I need to get a lawn!" he exclaimed with a smile.

I peeked at the bag, trying to see what he brought. "I've missed you. I hope you know that."

He slapped my back. "The feeling isn't mutual. Now, let me show you the toys." Aaron beamed as he shuffled through the bag, something he only did when he had a surprise. "Got your boat, some protective gear, and you'll like this last one…"

"You got a boat in that bag? You're a spy and a magician? What's next: professional wrestler?"

Ignoring my comment, he tossed me a metal container. I bobbled it for a second, and his eyes went wide until I had it firmly in my grasp.

"From the look on your face, it's dangerous," I said with a smirk.

"Knockout gas. Don't play with that stuff. It's expensive, and you'll be out for a couple of hours at least."

A flash of excitement shot through my body as I studied the metal ball, imagining the shenanigans I could cause with it. "This is real spy shit. What about Julia and the others? Won't they need masks?"

152

"You're trying to save seven people. There's no way to fit that many masks in your bag. You'll get one. Just tell the rest to hold their breath for a couple of seconds."

I scoffed. "Tell two princesses to hold their breath, great idea. I'm sure my beautiful girlfriend will love to hear that."

He turned back towards the bag. "You can give her the mask for all I care. Now, put that thing down before you put us both to sleep." I did as he said as he pulled the bag wide open and stepped aside. "For the rest of it, you have your pick. I got everything I could on such a short notice. In addition," he paused as he paced over to the computer and typed something in before a map of what used to be midwestern America popped up on the screen, "I have arranged transportation for all eight of you to Detroit."

"Why all of them?"

He shrugged. "Their safety would be at risk here, and having more people who have seen what has happened, and been injured by the schemes, will back up your argument. Besides, you need allies that aren't trapped in the Enclave. Anything could happen over there, and the more help you have, the better. There will be a van just outside the southern edge of the royal territory walls. I've got food, water, a change of clothes, money, and a pistol for each of them in it."

Pacing, I thought for a moment. I hadn't considered bringing the others along after the rescue, and to me, it seemed like a risk. "Hopefully Lillian can walk by then, but I don't want Kaja anywhere near a gun."

He stood and approached the map. "You can choose who you want to have the guns, but they are there just in case. Lillian may be an issue, but by the time we're ready, she'll have had a week to recover."

"Fine. We'll make it work." I was happy that my new friends were coming along, but there was already enough to worry about. With so many moving parts to the plan, anything could go wrong before we even made it out of Minneapolis.

"Good." He pointed to the bag. "Pick out your gear. I'll explain the rest of the plan once you're done."

An array of gadgets and guns met me as I opened the bag. It was unsettling to have a pick of gear in a secret spy base. In the Militia, I'd always worked with what little I had. Things were different now. I needed to remember, though, that the Minutemen's tech and weapons came at the cost of control. Even if their help was necessary for now, I wasn't ready to accept their orders. It didn't matter if the directive was coming from the UPF, Vera, or the Minutemen bosses in Appalachia. I'd fought every day to be the master of my own life for once, and in that war, there would never be a white flag.

Reaching into the bag, I grabbed a sleek black knife with a smile. "These look familiar."

Aaron glanced over. "Some of the stuff is from the same black market sellers you worked with in the Militia. I remembered you liked those knives."

"Cute, you remembered my favorite knives," I quipped before shuffling through the bag again, pulling out four of them.

"I got you all types of useful gear, and you grab knives?"

I spun one of them around my finger, feeling the familiar weight in my hand. With everything that was new, it felt good to have my old friends. "What can I say? I'm a creature of habit." When I turned back to the bag, something caught my eye. I reached inside and grabbed a set of small darts. "What are these?'

Aaron smirked and snatched them from my hand, holding them up in the light. "Tranq darts. There should be a pistol for them in there too. They won't last forever, but they'll knock out the target for an hour or so if you hit 'em good enough."

I found the pistol and weighed it in my hand. It felt no different than a normal gun, but mentally, it felt lighter. Having a ranged weapon that wouldn't kill them would be nice, especially since these guys were my coworkers. Well, former coworkers.

I replied, "Man, I could've used this on so many missions."

He handed back the darts. "Like the gas, they're expensive. We have a large budget, but I can't spend all of it funding unapproved missions for you."

"You won't have to. I'm done with the Minutemen after this."

He recoiled, his mouth open in shock. "What? Why? We're here to help you, Ivan."

Ignoring him, I threw the darts and pistol in my bag, along with the knives and knockout gas. His hand snatched my forearm. Instinctively, I lashed out, knocking him back into the table in the center of the room. I instantly regretted it.

"Talk to me," Aaron said, his eyes cold as he rubbed the spot on his chest where I'd elbowed him.

The last thing I wanted to do was talk. Aaron had fought for me to be recruited, but he was loyal to the bosses, who still chose to hide their identities from me. The number of people I trusted was dwindling rapidly. "Your bosses can't trust me with their identities, and you wanted to protect me from them. Why should I be part of a group that wants to control me? Isn't that what we're fighting against?"

"Nobody is making you do anything. You can walk away at any moment, but these people, they're on our side. This is bigger than just the Prism. We're fighting for something bigger, to make America what it was supposed to be, and we need you to do that."

Crossing my arms, I ran my foot along the cement floor. "What are you saying?"

"I'm saying that Northern Mississippi and the Prism will be only the first dominos to fall. Julia isn't just the key to freeing our country; she's the key that will unlock the rest of this continent." He stepped towards me. "You two combined have more influence than we ever predicted, and if we succeed here, everything changes. You can help lead the revolution to end the suffering. Isn't that what we're fighting for?"

I raised my hand to my ear and spun the tag, contemplating where I fit in all of this. Poseidon made me a rebel, Delaware made me a teacher, Julia made me a hero, and now, Aaron wanted to make me a revolutionary leader. "Right now, I just want to save my girlfriend and get revenge on the people that killed Delaware. That's it. I'm not some international revolutionary, and I'm not a king. I'm just a guy who's in way over his head."

Aaron put his hands on my shoulders as I began to shake. For years, I'd fought to end the Prism and change everything. Before all of this, I would have jumped on Aaron's offer to end the Fifth International within the old Kingdom of America. Now, though, I felt old, cynical. Everyone seemed to be either working for me or against me behind my back; I had no control.

He replied, "I know that it seems like everything is spiraling out of control, but you do have a choice. When there is time, I will set up a meeting for you with the bosses, and then, you can decide what path you want to take. You deserve that much."

"I appreciate it, Aaron." I took a deep breath and mustered up some courage. "Let's get back to the plan. The sooner we get this done, the sooner I can figure out my insane life."

Chapter 16

There wasn't a cloud in the night sky as I stepped out of the car a couple blocks from the wall surrounding the royal territory. Coyote may have been dead, but I still loved the night. Especially after days of being trapped in Aaron's basement, the fresh air brought a sense of freedom back into my veins.

We wanted to get as close as possible to the walls for the drop-off but couldn't risk getting closer than half a mile away. Vera would have guards watching for me. It had only been a few days since Julia had been captured, but my body had recovered enough, and my heart was desperate. With my all black spy suit and gear, it felt good to be running a mission again. This wasn't the Militia, but it brought back a sense of familiarity back to me. I had my objective, and it was up to me to complete it, no matter what the Minutemen said.

The houses of the Blues and Greens living around the royal territory were dark as I wound my way through the streets. Even if they weren't as pompous as the Whites and Purples, the size of their houses made me nauseous. While the Militia was rounded up into pens with the rest of the Reds, the higher colors slept in comfort, knowing the system would protect them. I may have softened to them during my time among the royals, but at heart, I would always be a Red. The last few days had reminded me of that. The country's elites spat at me while they schemed against everyone, even the rich few, but the people slept, ignorant to the disaster that loomed.

I focused on my breathing the whole walk, trying to remain calm. There was something more than fear of the royal guardsmen, something deeper. What it was, I couldn't figure out, so I swallowed it and focused on the mission. There were enough obstacles in front of me without me tripping over my anxieties.

Soon, the royal territory's looming marble walls came into sight, just barely more than shadows in the moonlight from this distance. From what I could tell, there were no guards posted at the top, nearly twenty feet high. Regardless, I kept watch. I always had a habit of failing to check twice, and that had kicked me in the butt more than once.

A week ago, I lived in there. My skin crawled when I thought about that—how I'd enjoyed the comforts of life among the royals for months—even if I was only a servant. Those walls were built to keep people like me out; I broke them down. I could only hope they would actually fall in time.

Climbing the walls wasn't tricky. I'd always wanted to. Going through the gates was an honor, but going over, that felt like flying. I tossed the grappling hook well on the first throw. With a *clank*, it latched onto the top of the wall, and I began my ascent. Even with the recovery time, my arms and shoulders were sore. It didn't matter. Each heave up the rope brought me closer to my princess.

Jumping from the wall was a bigger issue. It was twenty feet down, directly into a patch of grass. No bushes to break the fall or trees to leap to. *My ankles are going to hate me for this.* I leapt off the top, and the wind whipped through my hair as I fell. When I hit the bottom, I tucked and rolled. I was of practice, though, and my knee smacked into the turf, sending a jolt up my leg. When I pushed myself to my feet, I tried it out. It throbbed. But I told myself I'd be fine.

The lake was just on the other side of the houses in front of me, where I was sure the minor royals were tucked in, just as cozy as their Blue counterparts. There was no way to know how many of them were in on Vera's plans. I didn't care. In my eyes, they were all hypocrites and traitors. So many of them had pledged their support to Julia, but now, when she was in chains, none of them said a word. They all changed loyalties the second someone waved a useless title in their faces.

The houses were tucked in a bundle of trees, allowing me to wind my way through them, undetected. There were no guards here. Nobody outside the walls cared about these families or even knew their names, and inside them, they'd do anything to avoid making enemies.

I admired the few authentic royals remaining, but the fake smiles of the rest pissed me off. Vera's scheme had unearthed the resentment I'd hidden beneath the surface ever since I'd passed through the royal gates. She didn't realize that her announcement on TV ensured that I was no longer a slave for the first time in my life. Not to the River Falls Orphanage, not the UPF's steel mill, not to the Royal Theater, and not to her. I was free. That made me dangerous.

When I reached Cedar Lake, there was a rowboat waiting for me. Aaron had refused to tell me how he did it, but I didn't care at that moment. He got what I needed.

The water protested as I pushed the boat in and swung myself over the edge. When I landed, the boat rocked and splashed against the water. *Crap....* I scanned the shore, waiting for the shouts to come, but there were only crickets. *In the clear.*

I grabbed the wooden oars and cursed Aaron when a splinter jabbed into my finger. It wasn't the best boat in the Twin Cities, that was for sure. It did its job anyway, and I cruised through the lake with nothing but my breathing and the sound of the oars pushing through the water to keep me company.

The wind whipped across the water, colder than the air on land, and a shiver ran down my spine as the palace came into view. I was grateful this mission didn't happen a month before. The freezing temperatures were one thing, but I was not looking forward to ever ice-walking again. When I wasn't having nightmares about Delaware's death or Julia's capture, I sometimes dreamt of the drowning Militia fighter slowly drifting away from me as my air ran out. That had been less than two weeks ago; it could have been years.

As I approached the shoreline by the palace's woods, I radioed to Aaron, "All clear so far, landing now."

"Roger that, Ivan. Stay safe."

I dragged the boat far enough onto shore to be somewhat hidden by the trees and double checked my gear. The tranq pistol would be my first option, but there were only six darts. If I ran out, I'd have to go back to my old methods. *Knives are more fun anyway.*

The melted snow had turned the ground into a puddle of mud.

I cringed as each of my steps made an unfriendly noise, but I kept moving. Time was not on my side. Sooner or later, someone could notice the boat or stumble onto my tracks. An owl's *hoot* shocked me, and I swung my gun around, almost pulling the trigger before I realized what it was. It cocked its head to the side, studying me before repeating its warning, *hoot.* I chuckled to myself. *Even the owls don't like Reds here.*

I reached the path through the woods and kicked off the mud that had been caked on my shoes. I could picture Aaron's face when he saw that they were ruined. *"Those are expensive. Be careful."* The Minutemen cared too much about how much their gear cost to replace. In the Militia, we didn't bother. We couldn't afford anything, so we reused everything, no matter the condition.

A wooden bench appeared to the right after a minute. I bit my cheek before letting a smile force its way across my face. As much as the mission controlled my mind, that spot pulled me out of it. Julia and I had confessed our feelings for each other on that bench: a nervous wreck and a perfect princess. We were an unnatural couple, but that didn't matter when we'd kissed. All that mattered was her. *We had no idea what was coming.*

I'd radioed to Julia earlier to let her know the plan, but she couldn't respond. Now, as I sat on that bench for a moment, I tried again. "Julia, are you there?"

Beep, beep, beep.

"I'm in the forest. I just found the bench where we had our first kiss. The moon is hanging over the lake like it did that night. Stay strong. It won't be long until we can be together again."

It sounded like she tried to hold back a response.

"I'll be there soon. Love you."

Beep, beep, beep.

With a deep breath, I stood. *Now for the fun part.* The path shot straight through the forest and into the palace gardens. There were five guards in sight, more than I expected. To reach the balcony undetected, I would need to take out any of the guards close enough to see me climb.

The first guard patrolled along the bush-lined edge of the gardens. *Back and forth, back and forth. Easy and predictable.* The second and third smoked in the outer circle, just beyond the patches of flowers near King Timothy III's statue. Guards were technically banned from drinking and smoking. They did a lot of both. Jonah hated it, but he knew how little power over them he actually had, so he let it slide. The fourth and fifth guards were stationed along the back staircase leading to the Great Hall, right below the balcony and in perfect position to see the entire gardens.

My breaths were quick as I snuck to the bushes at the edge of the garden. The first guard marched towards me. *Keep low.* My body ached, but I ignored it as the guard approached. *Wait for the turn.* He about-faced. I pounced, wrapping my arms around his neck and pushing all the force I had into his throat. He sputtered. His face turned red. Blue-clad arms flailed at me, but I held him. After half a minute, he stopped.

None of the others had seen anything. Of course they hadn't. Quick and quiet was what I did best. Plus, with the wind, they were either too far or too distracted to tell what the bush rustling meant.

The guards in the center were in direct view of the ones by the back entrance. They'd have to wait. Creeping behind the bushes, I made my way towards the stairs. Options were thin. I scanned the garden, looking for a way to divert the guards' attention. *Nothing.* The lanterns lighting the gardens would illuminate anything I tried to throw.

Dart gun it is. The guard on the near side of the staircase was in spitting distance. I wished I could grab him like the first, but his partner would notice and alert the others. *I forgot to ask Aaron how long these take... Please be quick.*

The dart flew into the guard's neck. All he could get out was a "huh?" before he slumped backwards onto the pavement. His half-alert partner had just turned his head when I aimed and hit him between his eyes. *Still got my aim.*

Smokers one and two were too busy chatting to notice they were the only ones left as I strode down the main path towards them. The tranq darts would have worked on them too, but I was itching to punch someone in the face. They seemed like good candidates. These guys had made fun of me for months, but they didn't even notice me until I was a couple feet away.

Smoker one's cigarette hadn't even hit the ground by the time I'd knocked him out with two straights and a jab to his face. I snuffed it out on the pavement. With a smirk, I lunged at smoker two as he scrambled for his gun. *Never a good idea in close-quarters.* Not a second after he had it out of the holster, it clattered away from him. Shock filled his eyes as he saw my second kick flying towards his face.

I surveyed my work with a grin. Vera may have been expecting me, but her guards were sloppy. They didn't even put up a fight. That was either a great or suspicious. I couldn't tell which.

Before climbing up to the balcony, I checked the rest of the gardens for guards. The last thing I needed was a surprise. There were none from what I could see, so I jogged back to the stairs, purposely running through a few bushes instead of jumping over them. Vera loved that garden. Even if I couldn't kill her, I could mess up her treasures.

"Aaron, I'm climbing to the balcony now," I whispered into my earpiece as the grappling hook gripped onto the railing. With a deep breath and crack of my back, I started to climb.

"Well done, Coy… I mean Ivan. Sorry, don't go changing names on me again."

I groaned, yanking myself over the edge of the railing. "You knew both names before most people. It's not new to you."

"True. Though, it was easier when I could call you either."

The balcony curtains were shut, so it was impossible to know what was inside. I snuck to the corner, where the railing intersected with the door. With my ear to the glass, I listened for guards on the other side. But there was only silence. *Here we go.*

The door clicked open a crack as I slid inside, and warmth returned to my skin as the living room's lights greeted me. Julia and I had spent a lot of time in that room during the winter. She hated being trapped inside, but the light through the glass comforted her during Minnesota's months of freezing temperatures. Even now, it felt good being in the room. *Focus.*

I slipped on the gas mask and adjusted the straps. It felt weird, but with the family's bedrooms on the tight upper floor, the halls were always flooded with guards. I had to be ready to use the knockout gas if needed. According to Julia's radio call, she and Alex were locked and guarded in their rooms while the others were in cells in the basement. There was no easy way to rescue everyone. Convenient or not, Julia and Alex were the highest priorities. They came first, even if it would be difficult to navigate the halls with them.

My heart raced as I crossed the room and peeked down the hall. *Clear.* Even if the ice-blue carpets muffled most of the noise, I had to be quiet with each step to avoid echoes among the marble floors and walls. A few steps down the hall, those echoes alerted me to at least two guards approaching quickly.

I leapt to the next corner and readied my tranq gun. When the footsteps were a few feet away, I turned to shoot. My gun smacked into a guard's large frame and clattered across the floor. Before I could react, he grabbed my jacket and threw me into the wall. A scowl crossed his face as he spoke, "The Queen said you might be coming, Red."

In the last few days since the bombing, my back had barely recovered enough to be stable again. And as I slumped back against the wall, I realized it might not make it the whole mission. One knock and I could barely move. I just focused on why I was there, why I needed to succeed.

Putting my hands against the wall, I pushed and jumped, kicking the guard's face. He collapsed from the force as the *crack* filled the hall. I hit the floor with him and swept the leg of the second guard as he pulled his gun, sending him toppling. *I hate ground fights.*

The jump kick landing had sent another jolt up my spine, and I struggled to stand. It hurt, but the kick did its job. The first guard still wailed on the ground. From the look of it, I'd broken his jaw.

The second guard scrambled for his gun. I dove towards him, driving my knee into his side as his hand closed around the pistol. He tried to aim at my head. With everything I had, I pushed back.

Bang! My ears rang as he fired a bullet into the ceiling. *So much for stealth.* He was stronger than me, and the gun neared my head again. I spun off him and pulled a knife from my sleeve. He swung his pistol towards me, but I sliced at his arm. Crimson spewed over the white marble floors as he dropped the gun. I crawled back on top of him and rained blow after blow on him until he was unconscious. Releasing my breath, I forced my achy body to its feet.

Guards shouted from down the hall. "Shit," I muttered. They'd catch me before I rescued anyone. I holstered the tranq pistol before pulling the real one. The voices closed in faster than I could think. Julia's room was just down the hall, Alex's a little further, but there was no way to them. My only option was to stand and fight. The stealth knockout game had been fun, but this was about survival.

As I stared down the hall, voices echoed behind me. I was surrounded. *Nowhere to hide.* I pulled out the knockout gas instead. My rattled breaths sounded alien through the mask as I stared down at the canister. Each second felt like an eternity.

A wave of blue turned the corner as the guards raised their guns. "Get on the ground, now!"

I dropped to my knees. They encircled me, and my thumb

tapped the button on the side of the canister before it dropped from my hand.

Chapter 17

The gas canister clanked against the floor as the guards continued shouting. I lay face-first on the ground with my eyes shut. A hissing sound filled the air, followed by the first *thud.* Then another. Then another. I raised my head to watch the guards cough and collapse as a cloud of fog engulfed them. *Holy shit, it worked.*

With a groan, I pushed myself to my feet and tapped my earpiece. "Aaron, you're a genius. That stuff works."

"Happy to be of service."

Julia's room was a stone's throw away. I sprinted to her door and knocked. "Julia! It's me."

After a few seconds, she knocked back. "It's locked!"

Of course it is. I pulled out my lock picks and went to work, my hands shaking like a jackhammer. All that stood between me and the girl I loved was a shitty lock and my fingers were failing me. *C'mon!* Finally, the lock turned, and the door opened to reveal Julia's beaming face. The bruises on her face had yet to fade, and my rage burned seeing what Vera's men had down to her.

Before she could do anything, I pushed my way in and slammed the door. She jolted back in shock. "Ivan, what are you..."

"There's no time. Take the mask."

"Wha..."

"Trust me, just do it. We need to go."

Her eyes were full of fear as she looked at me. Her fingers ran along my cheek while I tightened the mask over her face. "I missed you," she whispered.

No reply came. My lungs refused to cooperate. I'd waited for this moment for what felt like months, but with more guards likely on their way, I was in survival mode. My mind hadn't raced like that since I lost Coyote. She grabbed my hands as I trembled. *What is wrong with me?* I nodded towards the door and pulled her with me. The hall was clear.

I held my breath as we sprinted towards Alex's room. The gas had flooded the hallway up to her door but not beyond it. My already aggravated lungs ached as I knelt to pick the lock. I never got the chance as the door flung into my face, sending me to the floor. Standing over me was Alex, a bobby pin in her hand and a smirk on her face.

I pushed myself to my feet and covered her nose and mouth. "Don't breathe." I nodded down the hall, towards the haze.

She nodded and followed me clear of the gas. "Oh, so only Jules gets a gas mask," she said with a grin.

"Aaron only gave me one," I replied.

How is she so calm right now? I glanced back down towards the unconscious guards. There would be more. We didn't have time. "Back staircase to the basement. We're not leaving without Jonah and our new friends."

"Are you okay?" Julia asked, her hand stroking my arm. I jerked it back instinctively and bit my cheek when I did, instantly regretting my defensiveness.

Her voice through the mask made Alex chuckle, bringing some life back to my mind as she ripped it off and handed it back to me. I shoved it in my bag as I replied, "No, but I got you back, and that's what matters."

The worry didn't leave her face, but now wasn't the time to talk. I shot my eyes down the hall, towards the staircase in the back. We were close, but the guards knew I was there now. They'd be waiting.

My eyes locked with Julia's frozen stare as I handed her the tranq gun. "Just in case. The darts will knock out the guards. There's only four left. Hopefully, you don't have to use them."

Her hands closed around the pistol and felt its weight. She may have been worried, but I'd never seen her face that hard. Whatever her mom had done to her in the last few days, it had pissed her off. "Thank you."

"What about me?" Alex asked, her arms crossed.

Rolling my eyes, I flipped one of the knives from my pack and into the air. My fingers caught the flat sides of the blade instinctively. Alex only allowed the shock to appear on her face for a moment before she grabbed the handle. "Thanks."

"If everyone's happy with their weapons, now, let's go before your mom's goons kill me." I led the way down the hall, ready for anything: one hand wrapped around my pistol, the other clutching a black knife. All of my senses were alert. We were too close to fail now.

At the last intersection of halls before the stairs, I glanced to my right. *Vera's down there.* My trigger finger twitched. *So close.* She would be heavily guarded, and even though part of me wanted to kill her, I had made Julia a promise. Vera had ruined everything. She'd helped the UPF slaughter my best friend. Every inch of me hated her, but I wouldn't drop to her level. The royals and Purples saw me as nothing more than a violent animal; I'd prove them wrong.

Julia gave me a little push from behind. "Don't worry. We have her plans and will expose her later. I promise."

A voice in my head told me to storm in there and kill everyone who got in the way. It was hard to know what scared me more: the risk of death ahead of us or the thoughts that ruled my mind. Something had changed in me.

I swallowed my hatred and crept to the staircase. More than once, Julia and I had taken this back route to avoid the crowds in the Great Hall. Like every inch of this place, it was full of memories with her, memories from a life that at the moment seemed like someone else's.

The stairs were clear through the first landing. I signaled for the girls to wait as I peeked my head around the corner. *Shit.*

Three guards stood on the next landing. Two chatted while the other held his finger to his earpiece and spoke, "North wing stairwell is secure." He waited, seemingly listening to a response before continuing, "We'll check it out."

I scrambled back to the girls and whispered to Julia, "Give me the gun." Her eyes asked me what the situation was as she handed it to me. In response, I held up three fingers and mouthed, "I got this."

The guards climbed the stairs, their steps echoing through the close quarters. I had to be quick. They reached the landing. I fired.

One down. Another swung at me, but I ducked and kneed him in the gut. His arms wrapped me from the top and forced my head towards the floor. As my feet slipped, I threw my weight forward, knocking him into the wall and sending him down the stairs.

Gun raised, I spun towards the last guard. His muzzle was at my head. "Put it down," he ordered.

Based on the rustling from the bottom of the stairs, the guard who'd fallen was struggling to his feet. *No time.* Even if I had the guts to shoot, the dart wouldn't kick in by the time he'd fired back. Without lowering my hand, I dropped the gun. His eyes watched it fall. *Never lose your target.* I jabbed my palm into his elbow. The gun flew from his hand as the joint popped. With all the rage I felt towards Vera, I launched my fist at his face. But I was too slow. He blocked it before connecting with a jab to my cheek. Stunned, I staggered back. My foot met air.

The feeling of falling backwards is one of the weirdest. My brain yelled at me to catch myself. There was nothing to catch with. Before I knew it, I was tumbling down the stairs, crashing into the other guard along the way. Limbs sore and tangled, we both yelled. I yanked my arm free and threw an elbow back into his face. Again. And again. After the third blow, he was out.

Everything hurt as I pulled a knife and stood. The last guard had found his gun. He pointed it at me with his uninjured arm. *How good of a shot are you with your off-hand?* Halfway down the flight of stairs, he spoke, "Drop the knife."

I cocked my head to the side. "Do you have orders to keep me alive?"

"I said drop it!"

Julia appeared behind him. My heart stopped, and it took everything I had not to look at her. "Okay, fine." I dropped the knife, hoping its clattering would obscure her footsteps.

The guard took a step down the stairs. "On the ground."

I didn't budge.

"Now!" He fired into the wall next to my head, sending a ringing through my ears.

Any second now. I dropped to my knees. My knees ached. *C'mon…*

He shouted again, "All the w…"

Before he finished, he fell forward, face-first into the stairs before sliding to the bottom. A dart stuck out of his neck. Above him stood Julia. I beamed up at her, impressed. "Look who's the hero now."

She gawked at his body. "Is he alive?"

"He'll wake up in a few hours, but we have to move. They definitely heard those shots." I picked up my knife and slid it back up the holster on my forearm. "Impressing presidents and prime ministers, negotiating with royals for votes, and now shooting guards during a mission. Anything you can't do?"

Flashing a not-so-confident smile, she replied with a shrug, "I can't pick a lock?"

Alex wrapped her arm around her sister, and they made their way down the stairs behind me. "We'll fix that, won't we Red?"

With a chuckle, I flipped around, walking backwards down the steps. "I teach my lovely girlfriend how to pick locks. She teaches me how to not kill people. We're the perfect couple."

Shouts came from further down the steps. I waved the princesses back up the stairs and crept to the corner. *At least five. Smoke gas it is.* "Don't breathe," I whispered up to the girls as I pulled the second canister and slipped the mask over my face.

The guards reached the flight around the bend as I tossed the canister. Shots echoed through the stairwell before a series of thuds. *Coast is clear.* I waved back to the girls, and we sprinted down the stairs, jumping over the bodies on the landing. As we turned the corner onto the second floor of the basement, the haze grew, forcing us to run far enough down the hall to avoid the gas.

I'd only been to the deeper parts of the basement once before. When I was made a bodyguard, they showed me the bunker deeper underground, where the royal family would be escorted if the palace were attacked. The small prison on this level was off-limits, though, even for bodyguards.

Cement and steel replaced marble down there. A chill filled the place, and the rattling of the palace's air ducts battered my ears. The prison was in the eastern section of the floor. It was nothing but a few cells meant for holding high-priority prisoners before they were executed or transferred to an actual prison. Just a month ago, Cockroach had been down there before Vera got her revenge for Helena's death. A couple months earlier, Wilhelm Preus had spent time there, under the throne he tried to take, before being transferred to the actual royal prison. Neither of them mattered now. I was there for my friends.

Beyond the noise from the machines, there was an eerie silence as we approached the prison area. *Why aren't there more guards?* My feet shuffled along the cement, and I kept my head on a swivel as we reached the last hall. Just around the corner was the door to the prison. No one was guarding it. I searched for Julia's hand and gripped it. "I don't like this."

"How many of the guardsmen were upstairs when you used the gas?"

I shook my head. "I don't know, ten, fifteen?"

Her eyebrows furrowed, the cute way they did when she was focused. "So, you have eliminated approximately thirty guards?"

"Twenty-nine. You had one."

"Regardless," she replied, rolling her eyes, "It is possible that they have not been able to relay your positions, considering how quick the confrontations have been. Perhaps those that heard the gunshots have responded: the guards that were posted here."

I took a deep breath, relaxing a bit. "They have no idea where we are."

"Precisely."

Pulling her around the corner, I quipped, "Then let's move fast. I've had enough guns pointed at my head tonight."

Alex cut in from behind us, "Psst. Leave me with the tranquilizers. I'll guard the entrance, just in case."

"Call for me if there's an issue," I said as Julia handed her the gun.

She nodded, and Julia and I walked towards the door. It was locked, protected by a key code. I knelt to examine it. "Any ideas what the code could be?"

"Sadly, no." She pondered for a minute as I examined it closer. It was a series of eight numbers.

I replied, "Is it a date?"

A smirk crossed her face, followed by a scowl. "Try Natasha's birthday. The third of August, 1994."

The lock turned green. "Holy sh… I mean, it worked!" I rose and gave her a peck on the lips. My mind was at ease when we were working together, and the panic had begun to fade. *How does she do that?*

Alex called from down the hall. "Make out later. I don't want to die in this shithole."

Julia blushed and pushed open the door to reveal a short hall, lined with steel doors. She peeked in the windows on top of each and smiled. "They're all here!" she exclaimed before unlatching the door in front of her. Kaja jumped into her arms, refusing to let go.

We both laughed nervously and opened the other doors, letting all our friends out. Manny and Tyler greeted me with a Red handshake, and Jonah just bear-hugged me with a smile. I missed all of them more than I realized. With Julia, Alex, and all of them free now, I felt a little like myself again, out of the cold shell I'd built over the last few days. Alone, I may have been away from Vera's grasp, but I hadn't been free. Together, with my friends and the girl I loved, I finally was, even if we were in the cold, annoyingly loud basement of the palace.

That moment was pure and amazing, but we needed to go. Guards would be closing in eventually. I tossed my pistol to Jonah and gave Manny and Kaja two of my last three knives. "Don't make me regret giving you a sharp object," I said to Kaja as Tyler just looked at me longingly, jealous he didn't get a weapon. I pointed to Lillian, who was limping. "Help her."

He groaned as I led the group out of the cellblock and back to Alex. As we walked, Julia slipped her hand into mine again. Something inside me was still wrong, cold, but with her by my side, my mind at least wasn't about to explode. From the worried glances she gave me, I knew she could tell something was off. Once we got out of there, then we could talk.

We circled up as I explained the plan, "The southside maintenance staircase will put us just down the hall from the servants' entrance. We bolt out there and run like hell towards the forest. I've got a boat just big enough for all of us. Jonah, any idea where the guards will be?"

He crossed his arms and stared up at the ceiling. "We both know there's only ever one or two guards in the south wing. With any luck, Demetri will have ordered them to coalesce around Queen Vera in a lockdown of the upper floor."

Julia cut in, "Or, Mother will have anticipated our route and have blocked the stairs."

Impatient, I snapped back, "We don't have another choice."

The sisters swapped glances before she replied, "There is another way out of the palace: the bunker. In the rear, there is an escape tunnel for emergencies that leads into a safehouse just beyond the walls."

"You waited until now to say that?" I asked.

Jonah stepped forward. "If I may. That tunnel is secured from the outside. Even if you had known about it, there would have been no way in. We intentionally kept it hidden from all but a few royal guardsmen as it could have been a way for people to sneak out of the palace." His eyes drifted to Alex. "I'm surprised you two know about it."

Alex flipped her hair over her shoulder. "What can I say? I know all of the palace's secrets."

Scoffing, Jonah replied, "You can believe that. Doesn't make it true."

I interrupted their chat, "Okay. I'll admit, that sounds like a good plan, but we need to get moving. How do we open the tunnel?"

Julia held up our still intertwined hands. "Biometric scanner."

"Good. Let's go."

We jogged through the maze of maintenance tunnels and back to the staircase, our steps sounding like a stampede echoing through the halls. I worried that the guards would hear us, but we soon reached the stairs, undetected. As Julia and I began to lead the way down, Jonah whispered from behind us, "Let me go first. I have the pistol, and they will be less inclined to fire at me than Ivan."

Julia replied before I could, "You're right."

I was reluctant, but her eyes cut into my heart as she looked up at me. "Fine. Go," I said.

His steps echoed through the stairwell as he ran ahead. Slowly, we followed behind, Julia holding me back as we went. I hated Jonah taking lead on my mission, even if he was right. It was hard to remember that my job was to protect Julia and save my friends, not put myself in the line of fire every second.

After a few seconds, Jonah stuck his head back around the corner. "Clear!"

There was no reason for a guard to be in the bunker, but it was still a relief to know we were almost home free. Julia's thumb ran against mine as we raced down the stairs, prisoners running for the open air. At the bottom, Jonah was waiting for us by the steel vault door. There was no handle or security code, just a scanner like the one in Aaron's Minutemen base.

Julia ran her hands along her jeans before placing her hand on the scanner. It burst to life with color, and a robotic voice came from around us, "Welcome, Princess Julia Hughes." With a *hiss*, the door crept open. Jonah held it and bowed. "M'ladies."

Smiling, Julia nodded her head and exaggerated her royal accent. "Oh, thank you, *sir*."

The girls led the way into the bunker while I took the rear with Jonah. Instead of the marble of the palace, the bunker was metal. There were couches, TVs, and rugs, but the whole place had the annoying sheen of polished steel. *They'll never step foot in here, and it's still way nicer than even a Green's house.*

"Will things ever change?" I asked Jonah as the others opened the door to the tunnel.

He stood like a soldier, probably out of habit, with his hands behind his back. "We can change the system, but we can't change the people. There will always be more Wilhelms, Veras, and Bachtons."

I kicked at nothing on the floor and huffed. "I was hoping you would be more optimistic than me."

"I didn't finish. There will always be people who seek to take advantage of others by any means necessary, but that's why we need people like Julia, and like you. People that believe in something bigger than themselves and who are willing to sacrifice a part of themselves to make it happen."

My heart twinged at his compliment. I didn't like it. When I looked up, his face was dead serious. I replied, "When does that sacrifice stop? Because it hurts like hell."

"You're fighting against the world as it is. I think there are only two possible ends to that: you break it or it breaks you." He glanced over at Julia waving for us to follow them into the tunnel before returning his gaze to me. "How I see it, this world can't break you, Ivan, because that happened a long time ago. You can't shatter something that's already in pieces, but those shards sure as hell can cut you deep."

He nodded towards the door, and we began walking. I could only stare at my shuffling feet as he continued, "You've seen more terrible things in your lifetime than I ever will, and after everything that has happened, I know you want to go into a shell. Hell, I wanted to after what we saw in New Ulm. That pain you're trying to block out, it makes you human. It's the reason you're fighting. Let yourself bleed. It'll remind you that you have a heart."

We'd reached the entrance to the tunnel. I forced my eyes from my feet. They met Julia's, and I took a shaky breath. That pain Jonah talked about was a river caught behind a dam. I didn't know how to let it out without the whole thing crumbling. Seeing her concern, though, forced my heart to soften. *You can trust her.*

Together, Julia and I followed the rest of the group through the cement tunnel, lit by nothing more than a few flickering overhead lights. It was a stark contrast from the bunker, but I assumed fanciness didn't matter if the fleeing royals got to this point. Survival meant more than decorations.

With Julia's hand back in mine, I couldn't get Jonah's words out of my head. We faced a giant mountain if we wanted to beat Vera and the UPF, but we also needed to talk about everything. I didn't know where I would start when we got the chance.

A screeching noise came from ahead of us as Manny pushed open a trapdoor in the ceiling. He looked back, beaming like a kid who found a stash of candy. "We're free!"

"Thank God!" Kaja pushed him out of the way and jumped up the ladder. "I thought we were going to be trapped in that shithole forever."

Julia and I both laughed and smiled at one another. Meanwhile, Manny brushed himself off and followed Kaja, muttering under his breath. When we caught up, Tyler was letting Lillian down. Julia touched her arm. "Will you be alright?"

"I think so," Lillian said as she tested her weight on her recovering leg. "Besides, Tyler deserves a break." She smiled at him.

He bowed, exuberantly waving his arm to the side. *Pretty good copy of Michael.*

With Julia's help, Lillian climbed the ladder, and the rest of us followed her into a dark room. Jonah and Manny flipped on the lights to reveal a dusty living room, obviously untouched for years. "Even your abandoned houses are better than the Enclave," I said with a chuckle.

Tyler signed something to Alex, who translated, "Tyler believes there's not much worse than the Enclave."

I huffed and crossed my arms. "You guys didn't see that camp. It gets worse."

We shuffled our way to the front of the house. Jonah went ahead to scout as the only person that was both not recognizable by most Blues and a color that could legally be in the areas surrounding the royal territory. Soon, he returned and waved for us to follow.

The wind had not faded during my time in the palace, and it blew Julia's normally perfect hair into her face as we crept out onto the sidewalk. She noticed me grinning at her and quipped, "You're missing half the hair on your head and you're making fun of *me*?"

I wrapped my arm around her. "I'm just lucky the pavement wrecked my hair, not my brain."

Kaja turned around and said, "Not that you had much to lose there," before sticking out her tongue. *Jeez. Her sarcasm is Delaware on steroids.*

Kissing my cheek, Julia replied, "I don't know. He's pretty smart... for a Red."

"Ouch," I said. "I save all of you from the evil queen and this is what I get?"

With a smile, Lillian said, "And we are all truly thankful. Right, Kaja?"

"Could have been faster," Kaja quipped.

I laughed. "Sorry, you didn't pay for the express rescue package."

We wound our way through the streets just beyond the walls, heading towards the van Aaron had waiting for us. Along the way, I checked in with him.

After listening to my explanation, he replied, "You made a huge deal about the damn boat and then just leave it there?"

"It's not like it was a speedboat."

"Do you know how hard it was to get that boat to the... You know what, never mind. Glad to hear you all made it. Keep me updated."

I chuckled. "Will do."

Soon, we reached the van. I jumped in the front along with Julia and started it with the key Aaron had given me while the rest of the group piled in the back. The mirror showed the chaos behind us as Tyler scrambled to sit by Alex and Manny tried to avoid Kaja. In the middle of it all, Jonah and Lillian sat quietly, waiting for everyone else to figure themselves out.

Shaking my head, I put the van in drive. "Buckle up kids. We're going on a road trip."

Chapter 18

Escaping Minneapolis was easier than I expected. We heard the sirens back around the walls as we pulled away, but they were heading away from us. By the time they figured out how we escaped, we would be too far to find.

Even though I had given Julia a basic rundown of the plan over the radio ahead of the mission, the others were still clueless. I had to explain not only what we had to do, but who the Minutemen were, what Vera's scheme was, and how she'd done it. My mind was fried, and the words came without thought. As I rambled, part of me remembered looking down the hallway to Vera's room, how I was so close to killing her once and for all. I would have had my revenge, at least on her. But that hatred wouldn't have fixed anything. Revenge cost Delaware her life. I promised myself it wouldn't do the same to me.

I drove with one hand clutching Julia's. Every inch of me was exhausted from the crash and now the mission. Bruises covered my body, and I could feel all of them. What I wanted, what I needed, was a hot shower and a bed. It didn't matter if that bed was the grass on the side of the road or the back of the van. Whatever energy I'd regained resting at Aaron's was gone.

When I finished my explanation, Kaja said, "So, when we were rotting in jail, you had a nice comfy bed?"

"Did you get hit by a truck, have a severe concussion, and almost die?" I shot back, my temper unruly. Julia squeezed my hand, telling me to calm down. I couldn't help it. Everything stoked the fire in my chest.

She tried to break the tension. "At least this van is more comfortable than that maintenance truck."

Alex moaned. "Holy shit that thing was awful."

"So, what actually happened to you guys?" Jonah replied. "I tried to get in touch with Aaron, and he had no clue what was going on. Then, Demetri's men came for me."

I scoffed. "Some royal guard assholes t-boned us. We flipped, and I smacked my head on the damn pavement through the window, knocking me out while they dragged off Julia and Alex. I didn't wake up until the next morning." Glancing at Julia, I asked, "What happened after that? Obviously Vera dragged you guys out there for her 'destroy Ivan' speech."

"Both of us were rattled after the crash." Her free hand drifted to her cheek. My heart ached at the dark bruises across her face. It was my job to protect her, but here she was, battered and bruised. Vera had put her in danger, and that alone was enough to piss me off. She continued, "The soldiers that forced us out of the truck bound us and shoved us in the back of their car. I was so scared, but once they turned towards Minneapolis, I knew Mother did this. She bugged our phones and confiscated our computers, locking us away unless called upon. I would have contacted you sooner, but she could hear everything. I didn't want to risk the one line of communication we had left." She released my hand and raised hers to her temple. "I'm so sorry I didn't believe you sooner about her."

I shook my head. "No, even I didn't see this coming. None of us could have. Aaron said the Minutemen had their suspicions, but Vera and Bachton made us all look like idiots. It's funny. I always wanted to be on the top of the 'rankings': Northern Mississippi's most wanted. Guess I got it."

From the back, Lillian replied, "So, how will we convince Premier…"

Julia smiled at her and filled in his name, "Taggart."

"Right, Taggart. How will we convince him that hacking into the Northern Mississippi TV networks to broadcast Julia's statement works in his interest?"

Jonah replied, "Hmm. That is a valid point. Huron's military is comparable to, if not stronger than, ours. They might take the excuse for war as a welcome one, and the broadcast would be a lot easier if we had Vera's emergency access key."

Gazing out the window, Julia said, "We must hope that Nathaniel Taggart is as rational as he is passionate. He has spoken often of bringing Chicago back into Huron, but with the sale of the Upper Peninsula to them, they likely have no further desires for *our* territory at the very least. A war would be a distraction from his prize."

Kaja yelled from the back, "I don't know anything about these people, but couldn't they just attack after we show people Queen Vera and Bachton are assholes?"

Tyler scowled at her for being so loud right next to him and elbowed her in the ribs. The resulting slap was even louder, and Tyler groaned, the first sound I'd ever heard from his mouth.

"Touch me 'gain. I dare you," Kaja said, not a bit of sarcasm in her voice.

From the rearview mirror, I watched the action and laughed as Tyler pled for help from Alex, a bright red handprint gracing his cheek. Alex held up her arms. "Nope. My face is damaged enough as is."

Julia returned her hand to mine. "Do you have a dashing man waiting for you in Det-wa?"

"No, but you never know who you might meet," Alex replied with a flip of her hair on the side that still had some.

Tyler looked like he'd been slapped again and slumped down in his seat, pouting. She noticed and flashed him a smile. It didn't seem to work.

There were a few moments of silence before Manny spoke, his eyebrows furrowed, "Det-what?"

With an understanding smile, Julia glanced back at him. "Detroit used to be a French fort before the British captured it during the Seven Years' War. Det-wa is how it is pronounced in French."

His mouth gaped open. "Whoa! Do you speak French?" She could barely nod before he continued, "How many languages do you speak?"

She pondered that for a moment as she counted to herself. "I believe eight, besides English: Spanish, French, German, Portuguese, Russian, Lombardish, Arabic, and some Cantonese."

Tyler must have signed something from the back because Julia replied in sign language. *Nine...* It was one of those moments where I was proud of how much she knew and could do, but I felt like an idiot next to her.

Manny flipped around to repeat the question to Alex. She mumbled, "Four," before speaking up, "Some of us weren't over-achievers with crushes on the language tutor."

No response came from Julia. She only blushed and giggled before noticing my joking glare. "What? Are you going to make the ridiculous claim you never had a crush before me?"

I grinned before dodging the question and returning my eyes to the road. "No, but it's still funny." The car beeped, and I looked down at the gas meter. We were almost empty. I tapped my earpiece. "Oh, come on Aaron! Who sends someone on a secret mission without a full tank of gas?"

His voice crackled back over the radio, "I was in a rush. Be grateful you have transportation at all."

Jonah checked out the window, looking at the road signs. "Faribault? We're not even through Rochester yet!"

"Not my fault." I pulled into a dinky gas station. It was nothing but two pumps and a small stand for the cashier, who rested his chin on his hands as drool ran down his arms. "Jonah, you need to go pay. Aaron should have some money in the bag in the back."

He nodded and climbed out of the van. We would need to find a place to rest eventually, but with two untagged princesses and my face being well-known in the country, we'd have to wait until we reached Huron. Jonah was both the person likely to draw the least attention and the one least likely to complain about me asking him. When he knocked on the glass, the Orange behind the counter jolted awake in shock and fell off his chair. It was unlikely he saw many Blues, and his eyes were full of fear as he popped back to his feet, understanding that a Blue reporting him for sleeping on duty could mean being knocked down to Red. I knew Jonah would never do that to him; most Blues weren't so forgiving.

As he pumped the gas, Julia looked out at him. "How much has he sacrificed to help us? While his world is falling apart, he is always courteous and brave. After his arrest, his wife must be frantic."

I followed her gaze. From that angle and no longer with his guardsman jacket, he could have been just an average rich guy. Like all Blues, he was clean-shaven with perfect hair and teeth, but there was something more to him, even at the surface. While most people of his color looked down on everyone they met, he carried himself with humility. He'd been right by my side when we rescued the Blacks and Reds from the New Ulm camp. His life was perfect, comfortable, but he risked it all to help free those of us in chains. I replied, "He's the closest thing this crappy country has to a hero, and no one knows his name."

Lillian spoke in almost a whisper, "I think that's the point."

Flipping around again, Julia looked back at Kaja. "I'm so sorry Kaja, we got distracted, and I didn't answer your question earlier. Taggart could choose to invade once the Front and Mother's bases are weakened, but as part of this meeting, I intend to negotiate a larger deal, one that could prevent future conflict."

The door slid open halfway through her statement, and Jonah replied when she was finished, "Don't go talking about foreign policy without me."

She smiled. "Of course not, Ambassador Jonah Clarke. Kaja and I were simply discussing how we planned to prevent a war with

Huron post-Operation Pridefall. Weren't we Kaja?"

"Yeah, and I was about to say that I know how we can do it." A wide smile spread across Kaja's face. That concerned me.

Tyler signed something to Manny, who chuckled. "He thinks you don't know anything about diplomacy."

The second smack sent a shockwave through the car. *He really didn't learn his lesson the first time?* Kaja cleared her throat as Tyler held his head in his hands. "It's simple: we give him what he wants. Who cares about Chicago?"

"While our sentiment towards the city may be different, I must agree," Julia replied. I gawked at her. She noticed. "Those in charge of the Chicago Union are no better than Huron. If we can prevent an unnecessary war that would kill thousands of innocent people over a border dispute, we should do it."

I gave her a small smile. "You sound less like a princess everyday..."

"That's not..."

"...and more like a queen."

She blushed. "Oh. Thank you." Her lips pursed. "If I am to replace my mother, it will be my responsibility to find solutions to the problems she has created. In addition, Chicago assisted in Mother's plan to kill you. Some things I am unable to forgive."

How do I react to that? So far in our relationship, I had mostly been her protector, but it was hot seeing her willing to fight for me. There was a fierce side to her that her time in confinement had revealed. We'd both been through a lot. All I could do was squeeze her hand tighter.

Kaja shouted to Tyler in the back, again acting like he wasn't right next to her, "See! Maybe I do know about diplomacy."

With a chuckle, I started the van up again. "It's gonna be a few hours until we reach the border. You guys should get some sleep. We can rotate drivers later."

Julia studied me. "Are you sure?"

"Yeah. I'll be fine." I forced an unconvincing smile.

Her eyes narrowed, but she slept anyway. For at least another hour, it was just me, the road, and the sound of Manny snoring in the back. My mind was exhausted and my body was numb, but for the first time since Delaware died, my heart felt like it might be okay. The hole was still there, and it still hurt, but I could feel emotions beyond pain and anger again. Opening myself to happiness meant accepting sadness. That hole would never be gone completely; that just meant I would never forget the girl who stood in front of the flames and decided to fight back.

When the time came for our next refueling, my eyes were crusted over. I hadn't slept well since the camp raid, and those weeks with little sleep—on top of getting the crap beat out of me multiple times—had finally caught up with me. Just outside the next town, I pulled over. Julia and I moved to the back next to Alex, while Jonah took over driving. Tyler practically jumped out of his seat to join him in the front, and a groggy Alex groaned as his shoulder was no longer an available pillow for her.

As comfortable in the back as we could get, I rested my head on Julia's shoulder. My eyes shut as she ran her fingers along my cheek and through my hair. We were back together, and I let my muscles relax with some effort. After what must have been only a few seconds, I faded to sleep.

Chapter 19

"We're approaching the border," Jonah said from the front.

Light flooded into my eyes, and I squinted. It was morning. A humming, disrupted by the occasional bump in the road, filled my ears. The empty cornfields on both sides of the road were a blur as my eyes adjusted.

Julia stroked my head as I straightened up and stretched. "My prince awakens."

"How long was I out?"

She tried to fix my disheveled hair. "I was asleep for a part of it myself, so I'm unsure."

"Three and a half hours," Alex said as she watched the landscape out the window. I cocked my head to the side, and she shrugged. "What? I couldn't sleep."

Jonah replied without looking back, "Perhaps if you didn't sign with Tyler the whole ride..."

If Alex had something to throw at him, she would have. Her cheeks were bright red, and she glared at the back of Jonah's head. In the front, Tyler smirked before staring out the window, his fingers drumming on the armrests. It was a rare sarcastic comment from Jonah, but it struck beautifully.

With the border crossing approaching, we would have to be careful. Tensions were escalating between Huron and us, and they would not be enthusiastic about letting people into their territory. That's why we had an alternative route: farm roads. Just west of Beloit, a city on the border of Huron's state of Illinois and Northern Mississippi's state of Wisconsin, there were farms scattered along the border. Aaron's intel had revealed a couple unguarded dirt trails that criss-crossed their way into Huron territory. It was an easy plan, but if we were caught, everything would fall apart.

We bumped along into the city. It was one of the only industrial cities I'd seen outside St. Paul, and things were rough. Factories lined the road, their windows smashed in and their walls crumbling. And those were the ones still in operation. Reds, either barefoot or in tattered shoes, lined up and down the sidewalks to be searched and checked-in for their sixteen-hour shifts. It reminded me of my time in the St. Paul steel mill. Those years had created a hard shell that Julia still tried to break through. She'd freed me from that place. Now, it was my turn to free them.

"It's horrible." Lillian gasped as she watched the Reds. As a Yellow, she probably never had life easy, but even they rarely saw our work conditions.

I replied, "It's our lives."

"You never showed me where you worked. The conditions," Julia said to me, her eyes full of sorrow.

"There are some things better left in the past." My fist clenched just thinking about that place. The heat of that steel mill melted me, molding me into the guy I was. It would always be a part of me; that didn't mean I wanted to talk about it.

She didn't reply but put her hand on my leg. Even though I

194

knew she wanted me to open up more, there was so much shit in my past. I'd told her everything I thought was important; the rest of it didn't matter anymore.

Jonah called back, "Police. Keep your heads down. The windows may be tinted, but it's not worth the risk."

I caught only a glimpse of a cop's black cap as we passed by the patrol. A van with a Blue driver and Red passenger wouldn't draw attention, but if they saw us in the back, they'd ask questions. It was weird to see cops instead of soldiers. A few months ago, before the Fracture, St. Paul felt a lot like this. Things were normal here—not burned to the ground. The Fracture's influence had been based almost entirely in St. Paul, and the Militia was thin beyond the largest cities. Here, the chaos of the Twin Cities didn't matter. Life went on: Reds in chains, Purples and Blues with whips. *Even if we take over the capital, there's the rest of the country. They probably have no idea what's actually happened.*

"It is impossible not to wonder what the people here believe has been happening in St. Paul," Julia said, reading my mind.

"Lies," I said.

Sadness filled Lillian's eyes. "I'd like to think that they hear some of the truth."

Factories gave way to the downtown strip of the city. Greens and Yellows meandered among the storefronts, ignoring the suffering we'd seen only blocks away. *Why would they care? We're just lowlife Reds. They have no reason not to believe that.* I took a deep breath before replying, "It's hard enough in St. Paul, and we have the *Free Press*. Out here, there's nothing to counter the UPF's bull."

Tyler signed from the front. Alex translated, "They need a voice."

All our eyes went to Julia, but she shook her head. "While I may be a voice for change among the royals, I cannot be the voice of the Reds. The last thing they need is another faction of the elite telling them what to do or who to be."

She glanced at me before speaking to the rest of the van, "This plan, and every single thing we have done, is not about me acting as some savior. It is about us all putting aside our differences to realize none of it matters: the Prism, the royalty, or the Front. These things are nothing but mirages to blind us and divide us against ourselves. My duty is to shatter that perception. Once that is accomplished—when Blues and Reds see each other as unique individuals, not colors—we will free ourselves. Every person in this van is a representation of that fact, and that is why, when we send our message to the Front and my mother, we will all speak." Her eyes were solid in resolution. She meant every word.

There was a chorus of agreements as I smiled at her. Effortlessly, she'd managed to unite everyone behind one cause. When Reds rarely could trust even each other, she could make them all trust her.

Kaja grabbed her orange tag. "We should rip out our tags during the message."

Lillian winced. "Maybe cut them off? It would probably be best not to destroy our ears."

Give up my tag? Part of the idea seemed obvious, but it felt like she was telling me to tear out an organ. Being a Red was part of my identity—all that I had left of my life before Julia. Coyote was gone. Poseidon was gone. Delaware was gone. The Militia was all but destroyed. Now, I was being told to give up my tag. I didn't know if I could do it.

When I looked at Julia, her eyes were fixed on her family ring. That ring symbolized her allegiance to the monarchy and her family, her own divide. It was one thing to remove a symbol of oppression; it was another for her to turn her back on her family. When I scanned the van, I saw we weren't the only ones wary of the idea. Jonah and Tyler both clutched their tags, and Lillian's mouth hung open as if she was already regretting her contribution to the plan.

Alex was not so hesitant. She held up her platinum and ice-blue family ring. "Screw you, Mom."

With a smirk, Kaja replied, "You're supposed to wait until the video. Duh."

Julia's eyes hadn't moved from her finger. I whispered in her ear, "You don't have to do this."

Her eyes flicked to me, the frigid composure she had before replaced with sorrow for only a second. "No, but it is the right thing to do."

My hands shook again. "I don't know if I can."

Jonah and Tyler remained silent in the front as the others continued their joking banter. Julia took my hands. "When we find time alone, we can talk more, okay?"

"C'mon, you can still be the Red King," Kaja exclaimed, obviously noticing my discomfort.

"That's not it!" I snapped before reining myself in with a sigh. "I've lost everyone and everything from before all this. Removing my tag... it would be admitting that part of me is dead."

Manny replied, his face curious, "Isn't that what we're doin', letting go of that stuff?"

Jonah's voice came from the front. "The punishment for removing your tag is death, not just for you, but also for your family."

Silence met his comment. We all knew what they would do to his wife if he was seen on TV without his tag. He had everything to lose. It made my objections feel petty, childish. After what felt like an eternity, Julia spoke, "You have already risked everything for us. I cannot ask you to give any more. Christina deserves to be safe and for her husband to return unharmed."

"I'm the only high color in the group." His voice was little more than a whisper.

Julia's voice became stern. "Jonah, as you are still technically my servant, I forbid you to remove your tag."

In the mirror, I could see him holding back tears. "As you wish, m'lady." He waited a moment before continuing, eager to change the topic, "We're almost to the border. Once we're across, I can drive a few more hours, but I think we could all use a proper place to sleep."

I groaned as we hit a bump in the road. Many of my old injuries had finally healed, but the ones from the night before were still raw. "We don't have time to stop."

Manny replied, "How are we going to find a place when we're all obviously not from here?"

"Aaron packed scarves, hats, and hooded jackets in the back," I said, pointing to the trunk. "We can cover our tags."

Julia nodded. "We will need to be selective as to where we

choose to stay. We would likely draw suspicion at any preferable places."

Alex threw her arms around her sister. "Shitty motel it is!"

Kaja laughed. "M'lady, would you like the dealer's room or the hooker's?"

"It doesn't matter where we want to stop," I said, trying to hold back a chuckle. "Bachton and Vera could start a war any day. If we stop, we risk being too late. And I don't think any of us want to fail because we spent a night sleeping in a crack house."

Julia replied, "According to what Alex and I overheard from Mother, no invasion will take place until after the Militia has been relocated back to the Enclave. That will not be complete for at least a week."

Still with her arm around her sister, Alex said, "Mother is devious. She will have planned this for months, if not years. The last thing she would do is rush to war. There's something else she's waiting for." Julia raised her eyebrow, and Alex shrugged. "Hey, I may not want to be queen, but I know information is power."

Tyler signed something to her, and I caught the word "what." I hadn't learned the language yet, but I'd picked up a few signs just watching him.

Alex thought for a moment. This mission had her engaged more than I'd ever seen. She actually seemed to care and was actively helping in planning. I figured she'd finally had enough of Vera trying to control her, but it was hard to know if there was something more to it. "I don't know. Her coronation? Without the crown on her head, it would be difficult for her to bring the royals behind her."

Something seemed off to me, but I couldn't figure out what. "She dissolved the royal military."

She raised an eyebrow. "How is that rel…"

"Listen to me. The royal military was dissolved, right? She had to, based on her agreement with the UPF."

Jonah shifted in the front. "It's impossible to know. A few weeks ago, they further encrypted military correspondence, so even I, as head of the royal guardsmen, did not have access."

"As far as I am aware, Mother did, in fact, dissolve the royal military," Julia replied, her eyes searching. "Why do you ask?"

"Because, if she did dissolve them, it doesn't matter what Vera thinks. But what is the one thing Vera wants more than anything?" I bit my cheek, trying to think through what to say next.

Alex scoffed. "She always said she wants to keep us safe."

My mind was racing again. "Control. 'Keeping you safe' was an excuse to control your lives. She manipulated your dad to do what she wanted. She wanted to do the same thing to Natasha, but when Bilgram and Julia challenged her, she went around the system. When she realized she couldn't control me, she tried to kill me. Everything she's done from the very beginning has been to be in control."

Kaja furrowed her brow. "What's the point?"

"If she wants to be in control, why would she let her army go?"

Julia gasped. "She wouldn't."

"I'm sorry," Lillian said with a confused look. "I'm not one for plots or war. What are you saying?"

Julia answered for me, "Mother didn't dissolve the royal mili-

tary. If the Front invades Huron, the Twin Cities will be left unde-
fended, and she will start the next civil war."

Chapter 20

"What are we going to do?" I laid my forehead against the side of the van, ignoring the shiver the cold metal sent down my spine. "Vera is always two steps ahead of me… ahead of us."

Julia pulled a navy beanie down over her head as she scanned the fields around us. Jonah needed a break, and I'd volunteered to drive the next stretch. During the switch, we decided, or more specifically, Julia decided, that we would stop at a motel soon, meaning we had to wear hats to disguise that we were from Northern Mississippi. "Yet, Mother did not expect you to rescue us."

I scoffed. "Of course she did."

She rolled her eyes and threw another beanie over my head, smirking as she tucked away my tag. "You look cute in purple."

"Just like my parents," I snapped as I ripped it off my head. Regret gripped my chest instantly. The rage in my heart had returned, but Julia didn't deserve to have it fired at her.

Without a word, she pulled me into a hug. Reluctant, I returned it after a few seconds. *Remember, you love her.* As much as I didn't want to calm down, holding her in my arms always cooled my temper. Since the rescue, I could feel her desire for revenge against Vera, but she managed to balance that with the tender side of our relationship. *How does she do that?*

I plopped the hat back on my head. "I'm sorry."

Her smile returned, and her eyes shone in the sunlight as she pulled it over my ears. "I love you."

"I love you too, sweetheart." I kissed her for the first time since we'd been separated. For that moment, I felt whole again. When I opened my eyes, though, I returned to the real world.

"Ew," Kaja said, gawking at us. "Get a room."

I chuckled. "The dealer's or the hooker's?"

She must have liked the joke because she giggled and jumped back into the van. *Glad to make someone laugh.*

Julia grinned at me. "What?" I said.

"You are so good with them, and they love you."

I huffed. "They barely know me."

"When they were without hope, you saved them." She gripped my shirt, pulling me closer. "Lillian told me everything that happened. They see you as their king, and they admire you, just as I do." She gave me a peck on the lips. "I know you are struggling, Ivan, but none of this chaos is your fault. My mother believes that she is protecting me. She does not understand us: our relationship and how you make me feel alive and free. Let her misunderstand us. Let her underestimate you. In the end, that is our advantage over her."

Why does she have to be right? I stared past her, at nothing. My heart still ached, and I couldn't bring myself to look at her. Every time I thought I was okay after Delaware died, I broke again. "I can't do it."

She slid her hands into mine. "Remove your tag? Defeat my mother?"

I felt myself beginning to cry, but I forced back the tears. Now wasn't the time. "Life. I don't know what I'm doing anymore. I don't know who I am. Everything is a trap. I can't trust myself."

Her arms pulled me in again as I began to shake. There was nothing she could say that could fix me. I was broken before all of this, but now, I'd lost too many pieces to count. As stupid as it sounds, I wanted my old life back. It was simple. The fate of the country wasn't resting on my shoulders. Now, I was being crushed.

After a minute of silence, she whispered, "You are the bravest, most honorable, and most loving man I have ever met. You are Ivan Matelski, inspirer of the lost, leader of the broken, and the Red King. You will do anything to protect those that you love, and you have lost everything to free the suffering. I love you, and I promise you that you will *never* be alone." There was fire in her voice.

"Thank you," was all I could mutter as she held me there. I wished I could say more, but the words wouldn't come. My chest was a void. No matter how much love she poured into me, I felt empty.

Manny hopped out of the van, a Russian style fur hat on his head. *It suits him.* His foot caught on something, and he flopped onto the ground before he could say anything but "Ah crap..."

We watched him lie on the pavement, covering his face in em-barrassment. Unlike me, he wasn't used to speaking with prin-cesses. I smirked as I thought about what his recovery might be, and he didn't disappoint.

"Your majesty," he said as he scrambled to his feet. "Long way to go…uh… We should probably get on the road."

Julia smiled and bowed. "Of course, sir Emmanuel. We will make our way into the carriage imminently."

Her light-heartedness brought a smile to his face as he stumbled back into the van, still flustered from his fall. Something made me like the guy, even if he was a little clumsy. We needed his spirit when it felt like the world was falling apart.

With him gone, Julia squeezed my hands. "We can continue this conversation in a room that has not been occupied by drug dealers or prostitutes."

I laughed. "I'm not sure that exists where we're going."

We climbed into the front of the van, and I turned the key. With the stutter of an engine that has lost one of its cylinders, we began the next stretch of our journey into Huron. Less than a hundred miles to the east was the stretch I'd driven within the Chicago Union as I fled their police. Now, months later, things weren't much different. This time, though, I wasn't alone.

I was thankful to have the people I cared for with me on this mission. Pridefall was bigger than anything I'd done yet, and without them, I would have been a wreck. Julia had brought me calm, and together with the friends I had left, she also brought me purpose. As much as I was fighting for my freedom, it had become so much bigger. Delaware had sacrificed herself to free those she loved. The least I could do was continue her fight.

The dirt road rumbled along as I drove. After an hour of Jonah's off-roading and now this, my back was ready to surrender. *Whose idea was it to go through no man's land?* I called back to Jonah, "I get why you gave me the wheel."

He chuckled. "And you fell for it."

"But now I'm in charge."

From the rearview mirror, I could see Tyler sign something. Alex laughed and signed back. He responded one more time before she said, "Alright, Tyler needs to hit the restroom."

"We're in the middle of nowhere," I said.

Tyler replied through her, "Sooner rather than later would do best. Thanks."

"Pee in a bush."

Soon, we hit pavement. It was cracked, but it was better than the hills and bumps of the farm trails. The aches from the car crash had combined with the bruises from last night's rescue, and I was grateful for the relief. We drove in silence, winding through the country roads until signs appeared for the next city: *Rockford.*

Before I could say anything, Tyler fidgeted and tried to get Alex to tell me to stop. I watched him struggle in the mirror for a few seconds before relenting. "We have to stop for gas anyway, but you better go faster than I can fill up the tank. We're leaving without you if you're too slow."

I smirked as he flipped me off. But as we entered the city, the joking stopped. I'd always thought the Enclave was as bad as things could get. I was wrong. Ahead of us, rubble covered every square block on this side of the massive river that split the wasteland from what looked like a regular city. Even we had a few buildings left standing, but here, there was nothing.

Julia covered her mouth as she watched the destruction in horror. "How could this happen?"

"This must have occurred after the Third Civil War," Jonah said,

206

analyzing the sights as we went. "This level of destruction couldn't have been done with the technology either side had at that time."

Manny gawked out the window. "Then who did it?"

Jonah shook his head and returned his eyes to the rubble. "It's impossible to know. Either Huron squashed a revolution, or there is a darker story here."

Tyler's hands shook as he signed to Manny. "He says he can wait to pee…"

How does a city like this just become a wasteland? So far, we hadn't seen any people, and I started to doubt that there was anyone left among the piles of brick and steel. Jonah was right about the damage. In the Enclave, buildings were wrecked, but there was a lot left. Rockford must have been carpet-bombed. There was no other way for a whole city to be reduced to nothing. *If Huron did this, do we really want to work with them?*

Julia's eyes met mine. "Do you think…"

A *bang* filled the air. A tire hissed. I fought against the steering wheel. It wasn't enough. We careened off the road, smashing into what little remained of a brick wall. The car moaned and died. *What the hell?*

I unbuckled and pulled my pistol. "Stay down," I whispered to Julia. She cradled herself in her arms, keeping her head beneath the window. "Ready, Jonah?"

From the back, I heard his safety click off. "Ready as I can get."

We jumped out of the van, and I scanned the area around us. There was nobody in sight. "How did they…" Another bullet whizzed by my head. "Shit!" I jumped over the hood of the van and crouched on the other side.

Jonah slid around the back. "It must be a sniper."

"Vera?"

"There is no way she would know our route."

"Then who?"

Another shot rang through the air, followed by the crunching of rocks beneath boots. Jonah glanced at me. "We're about to find out."

"Drop guns and come," a gravelly voice yelled.

We nodded to each other and stood with our arms raised. "We surrender," I said.

A straggly bearded man stood less than ten yards away, a pistol in his hand. A teenage boy and girl flanked him. "Give guns. Them, out!" His spare hand, or the mangled mess where a hand should have been, pointed at the van.

I followed the order, sliding the gun to him and opening the door for the others. Julia stepped beside me as I spoke, "What do you want?"

The leader scoffed. "Not from?"

"No, we're not." I stepped towards him.

"Stop." He pointed behind him to the solitary building left on this side of the river. "Snipe."

"Who are you?"

The girl replied. Her voice was quiet and barely audible over the wind. "We are the Knights of Auburn."

Jonah replied, "Auburn?"

Shaking, the boy pointed to a street sign nearby: *Auburn Street.*

"What happened here?" Julia asked, sweeping her arm towards

the rubble.

"Them." She nodded towards the river. On the other side was a series of skyscrapers. If I didn't know better, I would have thought I was staring across the Mississippi at downtown St. Paul. The only thing missing was the High Bridge.

Tyler tapped Julia on the shoulder and signed. She replied as the leader shouted again, "Stop. What is?"

Julia held up her hands. "Our friend cannot speak. We were communicating in sign language as he wishes to know who 'they' are."

His pistol swung wildly as his face turned red. "East."

She stepped closer, her voice calm. "Why would they do this?"

The boy held his fists clenched in front of him, smashing his knuckles together before flinging them apart and making a popping noise with his mouth. *He's like Tyler.*

"Was there some sort of war?" Julia asked.

The girl shook her head. "No. Test."

Julia and I glanced at each other before I replied, "What kind of test?"

Pointing down first this time, the boy repeated the same motion. At the end he danced his fingers through the air before lowering them to the ground. *What is he trying to say?*

"Oh no..." Julia looked like she's seen a ghost as she glanced from the leader's grotesque hand to the groups' glazed over eyes and then to the ground. Finally, she grabbed my hand. "If I am interpreting them correctly, Huron conducted an underground nuclear bomb test beneath our feet. These poor people are suffering from complications caused by radioactive fallout. It must have leaked through their containment during the test, poisoning those on the surface."

The leader croaked out, "Ground shook. Mom sick." He spasmed, and the girl had to hold him up. When he regained his balance, he pointed the gun at Julia. "Give van, food."

Rage replaced my sadness as I stepped in front of Julia. My fists clenched as I spoke, "Drop the gun. Then we'll talk."

He grunted. "Now!"

It didn't matter to me that he'd suffered. In that moment, he threatened Julia's life. I could sacrifice the van, but she was all I had left. "Drop the damn gun if you want our help!"

"Diplomacy," Julia whispered in my ear.

"He aimed at you."

"Stay calm." She stepped out from behind me, and it took everything I had not to hold her back. My instincts told me to fight. Hers told her to negotiate. This was her specialty. "We will be more than willing to gift you the keys to our vehicle and our remaining food supplies. All we ask is that you allow us to collect our things and go in peace. We are sympathetic to your plight, and we have no wish to do you further harm."

He coughed and wiped his sleeve across his mouth. "Do."

Julia spun around with a smile. I grimaced. "How are we going to get out of here now?"

"Alive," she said as she rounded the van and grabbed a pair of bags from the back. "We have more than enough money to purchase another van. From how it appears, the 'East' appears to be a place where we can find one."

I took one of the bags from her, and we made our way towards our attackers. "He pointed a gun at you."

"And they were poisoned. It does not grant them an excuse, but these people have nothing through no fault of their own. We can afford it."

When we reached them, the leader snatched the bags. His eyes snapped from me to her and back to me. He didn't trust us. I wouldn't after everything he'd seen. If Huron bombed this side of the river to cover up the effects of the leaked radiation, these "Knights" had been left to die. There was something wrong with them, but I wasn't any different. While I didn't have deformed limbs and fogged eyes, my time in the shadows had done its own damage.

In the distance, I could see the bridges spanning the river—four of them. Three were collapsed in the center. "Can we cross that bridge?" I asked the girl, pointing at the remaining bridge.

She turned to stare at it. "It is guarded."

"To stop you?"

She nodded.

Julia replied, "Would they allow us across?"

"You not broke. Probably," the girl said with a shrug.

We turned back to our group and waved for them to follow. It would be a couple mile walk to the bridge, and even if Julia was right about the time it would take for the UPF to declare war, we needed to hurry. The longer we waited, the stronger Vera's grip on power would become. I didn't know if we would ever be able to make Julia queen, but there was no way I could let Vera rule.

Manny groaned when he caught up. "We have to go all the way over there?"

I chuckled and threw my arm over his shoulder. "Just thought we could use some exercise today. Stretch our legs."

Tyler signed to Alex, who bumped into him with a grin. "He's right. That van sucked anyway."

When I looked back, the Knights were restarting the van and trying to fix the tire. There were so many questions I wanted to ask them. Besides my short stint in Chicago, this was my first time outside of Northern Mississippi. I was already realizing how little I knew about the rest of the world and even the areas not far from St. Paul. I wondered if everywhere was like this—divided and broken—or if there somewhere that things were different. *Are we trying to do the impossible?*

Chapter 21

Julia and I led the way to the bridge as the rest of the group lagged. She slipped her hand into mine. "Talk to me. I can feel your suffering."

My chest was a knot that I couldn't untie. I didn't know where to start. "My entire life has been nothing but loss and violence. Everyone I ever cared about is gone. I was on those missions, and those bullets could have hit me if I was less lucky. I could have been in that work camp if I never ran into you. That airstrike could have killed me if I was in the lines with the rest of the Militia instead of standing above them like some general sending them to die." A shiver ran down my spine. "What if I could have saved them? What if all this crap has been my fault? You always said the world is made of cracked glass. What if I shattered it?"

She wrapped her arm around my waist and pulled me closer. "Everything we are attempting to accomplish is stopping those that shattered our world. You are experiencing survivor's guilt and possibly PTSD, but none of this was your fault. When I was apprehensive of your past, you opened the book for me to see, and I saw a caring and brave boy fighting desperately to protect the little that he had left. The shards had scarred your body and mind, but your heart was gold. None of that has changed. You are still the boy I fell in love with. The world has tried to break you, but every time Bachton or Mother or a snobbish Blue knocked

you down, you stood back up. You told them to hit you again because you believed that if you stayed down, they would take everything you had left."

"They did it anyway," I replied with a scoff. "Whenever you're
in danger, my mind turns off. You're everything I have left, and I
don't know what I would do without you." I shuddered. "When I
saw Delaware's body, something inside of me broke, and I haven't been the same since. I've tried, but it hurts to laugh. It hurts
to feel anything. If you died…"

"Shh." Her other arm wrapped me into a hug as we stopped in
the middle of yet another abandoned street. "I am not going anywhere. Even heroes have their doubts and their worries, but
something they often forget is that they are not alone." She
glanced towards the rest of the group.

I followed her gaze and was met with a smile from Jonah, the
joking between Alex and Tyler, and the faces of friends who had
been complete strangers a week before. It was a rag-tag, mish-
mashed group. If someone had told me a year before that I would
be in Huron with a gang of Reds, an Orange, a Yellow, a Blue, and
two Whites, I would have called them insane. Now, as I watched
them approach us, a rush of emotion hit me. I couldn't tell if it was
sadness, happiness, or something else. It was just a relief to feel
something. I flicked my eyes back to Julia. "How did we do this?"

With a knowing look, she ran her hands down my arms.
"Hope."

"Everything alright?" Jonah asked when the group reached us.

Julia nodded to me before I replied with a chuckle, "No, but
right now, I don't think anybody is."

He patted me on the shoulder. "There's some truth in that. Speaking of being alright, can I borrow the burner phone Aaron gave you? If possible, I would like to warn Christina of what is about to happen."

I handed him the phone. "Sure, but what do you mean?"

"If they have not come for her yet, they will when I remove my tag."

Julia stepped in-between us. "I can't let you do that."

The smile he gave her in response was forced. This wasn't a decision he had made lightly. "Forgive me, m'lady, but you are not the queen yet. I am going to do my duty to prevent this war."

As he turned to make the call, Julia grabbed my arm. "Please, Ivan. Tell him it is not worth the risk."

I swallowed, afraid of what I was about to say. "I can't, because it is." Her glare dug into me as I took a shaky breath and continued, "I'm willing to do it. If he is too, then I respect his decision. We can get Aaron to take her into hiding until we get back."

"If that was me, would you do it?"

"Jonah is a braver man than me."

She groaned and tried to chase after him, but Alex cut her off. "We're all making sacrifices, even Tyler."

We all looked at him as he signed to Julia. Sorrow replaced desperation on her face. "Are you certain you want to do this?"

He nodded.

"What'd he say?" I asked.

Her hand slipped into mine, shaking as she replied, "His two younger sisters are still in the Willmar work city."

My heart sunk. *Why didn't he tell us before?* We had only managed to rescue people from one of the five camps in Northern Mississippi. That ate at me, even though I knew we'd saved everyone we could. "I'm sorry." It was all I could say. I'd seen what happened in the camps. His sisters were suffering if they had survived this long.

Alex translated, her voice cracking as she did, "They're either dead or starving, and the only way they will survive is for us to succeed. He says that we can't ask others to risk their lives and their families if we won't."

Nobody had a response to that. It just deepened our sorrow, and all we could do was continue the journey to the bridge in silence. Just over halfway through the trek to Detroit, we had already lost our van and all our food. *What would Vera say if she could see us now?* We were nothing but a band of misfits trying to change the world as we walked through a sea of destruction.

The buildings on the eastern side became clearer as we approached the riverfront. Three skyscrapers lined with glass reflected the sky, but beyond them, there were no buildings more than a couple levels high. "That's mildly intimidating," Alex said, shielding her eyes as she gazed up at them.

Julia stared with awe. "It's fascinating how different they are from the rest of the skyline."

"Gives me a bad feeling," I said. In the Twin Cities, any building that tall was a symbol of the UPF's elites. It didn't make much sense to me, but I guessed they got some weird pleasure out of staring down at us.

Kaja quipped back, "Because this side of the river is so pretty."

Chuckling, I replied, "You know what I meant."

We reached the only standing bridge after a few more minutes of walking. It was not even close to as tall as the High Bridge in St. Paul, but it was in similar shape. Cracks ran through the entire structure. Whatever metal railing that was left was rusted and frail. As we crossed, I couldn't help but think the bridges had the same purpose. They crossed the rivers, but they couldn't—and weren't meant to—mend the divide.

On the other end stood four soldiers. Their uniforms were the same as those worn by the UPF and royal goons that had ambushed us at the villa, and fear crept into me as we approached. *Maybe I do have... What did she call it? PTSD?* Whatever it was, I swallowed it for now. There was too much on the line.

The soldier closest to us called out as the others raised their rifles, "State your business."

Julia stepped forward before anyone else had a chance to react. It was a smart move as I was not in the mood for diplomacy with an army that had killed so many of their own people. "We are travelers on our way through the city. Our vehicle was taken, and we are in seeking another mode of transportation."

"Where is your destination?"

"Detroit," she answered honestly. *Bold move.*

He raised his eyebrow. "Why?"

Glancing back towards us, she replied, "We have yet to see the glorious capital of our collective. Is it not right for the people to experience it with their own eyes?"

I held back a grin and hoped the socialist language would work. Of course she spoke it well after spending years with her dad around the UPF elites. Her fakes were getting better. Before, she avoided lying as much as possible; the last week had changed something in her. She was more determined, shrewder. We'd both seen the ugly within the elite but understood this was a game to them. It reeked, but we had to play it to win.

The guard waved, "Oh," and straightened his jacket. "Of course. If you are looking for a car, there is a shop to the southeast."

Julia bowed her head. "Thank you, sir. Your service for our people is appreciated."

We advanced before he had a chance to reply, but the other soldiers had already lowered their guns. I doubted they expected us to be allowed in. With Julia's wit, though, they had no choice. If Huron's government was anything like the UPF, failing to respect the collective was a mistake.

A strip of parks wandered their way along the shore of the east side, the only thing separating steel from water. They were empty. When we were out of ear-shot of the soldiers, Julia blocked the sun from her vision and said, "Apparently, 'if you build it, they will come,' does not apply here."

My stomach turned as we stood there. Everything was wrong with the city. Sure, it was the middle of the work day, but *someone* should have been out besides the soldiers. "Let's go. The sooner we get a car, the sooner we can get out of here."

We made our way through the streets. Cops lined the sidewalks every twenty feet or so, each of them staring up at the buildings. Besides them, if we hadn't been able to see people through the windows, there would have been no sign of life. *What are they doing?* With them there, it was easier to walk down the center of the empty street. If they were trying to keep people inside, we must've been somehow exempt, since they all but ignored us.

As we approached the used car dealer, a loud bell rang, stopping my heart for a second as Julia clutched my hand. The ringing echoed through the streets. I spun around and watched as a flood of people exited the buildings all at once. Within a few seconds, they had shuffled into a line, waiting for the cops to pat each of them down. Then, they were on their way.

"Why are the police searching them?" Lillian asked, gawking along with the rest of us.

Before anyone could reply, Manny took off towards the sidewalk yelling, "They're coming!"

"Oops," I said with a chuckle as a chorus of horns hit my ear. There was a line of cars waiting for us to get out of the middle of the road.

We joined him on the sidewalk as the cars passed by, their drivers shooting glares at us as they went. Kaja scoffed. "Assholes."

Julia smiled. "They are most likely saying the same thing about us."

Tyler and Alex signed back and forth, laughing. *Get a room.* With a bump into me, Julia grabbed my hand and led me towards the dealership. I laughed. "Okay then, you're lead."

"You were too busy staring at the flirting couple," she quipped.

"Don't worry. I stare at you too."

Blushing, she pulled me through the rows of cars. I was caught in the moment and watched her more than them. Laughing and joking around with her made me feel free, but those moments were rare when people studied our every move in the palace. *When can we be a normal couple? Can a princess ever have a normal life? What about a queen?*

Eventually, she settled on a SUV with enough seats for all of us. Like all the others, it was depressing and grey. But it would do the job. Jonah popped the hood, and Tyler peeked at the engine before signing to Manny. "He says this thing's a beast." He signed something again and Manny groaned before finishing, "Just like him."

"I get why they ripped his tongue out," Kaja said with a smirk.

"Kaja!" Lillian glared at her friend. "Was that necessary?"

Tyler crossed his arms as Kaja shrugged. "Depends how you describe 'necessary.'"

A man in a sloppy tie stumbled out of the building. "Oh, hello! I wasn't expecting customers so soon."

I leaned over to Julia. "Are used car salesmen the same in every country?"

Ignoring me, she beamed at the man. "Our apologies. We are travelers that encountered some car troubles per se." She held an open hand towards the SUV. "We were particularly interested in this model."

A puzzled look crossed the man's face as he examined us. *Is he surprised by her royal accent or the weird mix of our group?* After a few seconds, he reactivated salesman mode and spat out a dozen useless or false spec numbers. There was no way the car had 700 horsepower.

Nodding through it all, Julia asked the questions she assumed a normal person would ask. Naturally, I derailed that. "Can we pay in cash and skip the paperwork?"

His puzzled look returned as Julia swooped back in. "What my *friend* is trying to say is that we are in quite a hurry. We would be willing to pay extra if we could skip the legal hurdles."

That caught his attention. He grinned. "Four-million-three-hundred-thousand Hurons will do nicely."

Manny wasn't able to hold in his reply. "Four million? That's crazy."

Bending down, Alex whispered in his ear, probably telling him one Northern Mississippi dollar was about a thousand Hurons. In our prep, Aaron had informed me of the massive printing Huron had to do decades ago to pay off their debt. The Huron hadn't been worth much ever since.

Julia took the distraction and held out her hand. "You have yourself a deal, sir."

He chuckled. "Perfect! Though no one has ever called me 'sir' before. Where did you say you were from?"

"We didn't," Alex replied, her voice stern. "Do you want the money or not?"

Flustered, the salesman stepped back. "Of course. It's yours."

Julia nodded to me. I pulled the cash out of my bag and counted it before handing it over to the man. "Now, the keys?"

"Oh, yes. One moment." He scampered inside before returning with the keys. "Pleasure doing..."

I had already taken the keys and jumped into the front seat. Tyler smiled as he passed the salesman and patted him on the shoulder. *Cocky. I like him.*

The SUV was far from new but had plenty of space, and its seats didn't feel like they wanted to kill me. Its transmission groaned as I put it in drive and set off. Within a few minutes, we were on the highway and out of that strange city. So much was wrong with that place; I felt like I needed a shower. There was a bigger story there, but now was not the time. We had enough ahead of us already.

As we passed the *You are now leaving Rockford* sign, Alex said what we were all thinking, "Goodbye and good riddance."

Chapter 22

The rest of the drive was going to be simple. All we had to do was bypass Chicago and it was a straight shot to Detroit. In-between would be nothing but mismanaged government-run farmland. I could smell the dying crops already.

Our time in Rockford ate at me. We were trying to stop a war between the UPF and Huron, both groups that shamelessly killed their own people. It was hard to see the bigger picture when I'd stood hours before in the rubble of what used to be half of a city. The Knights of Auburn had been poisoned by a nuclear weapons test. That meant that Huron both had dangerous weapons and was not afraid to slaughter people to cover that up. *Do we really want to work with them?*

It was tempting to think allowing Vera to take over would be better than this. We were trusting tyrants, allowing Huron to take Chicago. I couldn't help but picture the city I'd seen just a few months ago burned like Rockford's west side. With a shaky breath, I glanced at Julia as she gazed out the window. "Are we doing the right thing?"

"What do you mean by that?" she asked.

"What if letting your mom take over is better than stopping the war? What if we try to take her down after she beats the UPF?"

"That would be after thousands of people gave their lives in yet another war. Huron could take vast parts of our country, and

Mother would have secured her hold on power by then. This is our best chance to save lives and still eliminate the Prism. I truly believe that."

Alex replied from the back, "Mom has no intentions of destroying the Prism. She will continue to use everyone as her puppets."

I stared at the endless highway. "I hate that this is the best option."

Somewhere in Michigan, we found a motel in the middle of nowhere. The manager didn't ask any questions and just seemed excited to have customers. We all needed an actual bed to sleep on, especially since we would soon be meeting the Premier of Huron. It would be mostly Julia's job to convince him of our plan, but the rest of us needed to be on our A-game too in order for our broadcast to have a big impact.

With the motel's desperately cheap prices, we could afford four rooms without worrying about money. Naturally, Tyler and Manny paired up and practically sprinted to their room like it was a kid's sleepover. I laughed as they went but remembered this was probably their first time in any hotel. It was crap, but a year ago, I would have been excited too. Reds didn't get opportunities like that. Across the hall, Kaja and Lillian disappeared into their room as well, leaving the princesses, Jonah, and me. To avoid any awkwardness, I went with Jonah, even though I wanted to spend the night with Julia more than anything.

My body ached as I lay on one of the beds in our room and stared at the off-white and peeling popcorn ceiling. I needed to shower. For now, though, I couldn't find the energy as Jonah talked strategy at me. Most of it went in one ear and out the other.

Eventually, he jumped in the shower, and after a few minutes, I forced myself to go over and knock on Julia's door. Alex answered. Behind her, my girlfriend was curled up with her eyes closed, a pillow in her arms. "She was wondering if you'd want to talk."

"Apparently I waited too long."

"I'm awake," Julia claimed with a yawn.

I chuckled. "Not convinced."

She joined her sister at the door. "What's up?"

"Got a minute to talk in a room that isn't a drug dealer or hooker's?"

"I was going to visit Tyler anyway," Alex said, taking the hint as Julia bit her lip. I grinned at her. Nervous, Alex ran her hand through her hair. "What?"

Retreating into the room, Julia giggled. "I have only seen you like this twice before."

I joined Julia on the edge of her bed as Alex shut the door and held her arm across her body. Seeing her so vulnerable still was a surprise, a welcomed one. She replied, "And both of them ended up being assholes."

Julia smirked. "Most boys are."

"Hey!" I said, wrapping her in a hug.

She kissed me on the cheek. "And I am ecstatic to be in love with an exception."

"Apology accepted." I glanced back towards Alex. "I think Tyler is one too. Though it's hard to tell with the silent types."

With an elbow to my ribs, Julia said, "Just let him know the White Queen and Red King are watching to ensure he treats you right."

"Believe me, if he doesn't, I'll punish him myself," Alex replied before sliding out the door.

Finally, we were alone. The bed creaked as Julia flopped backwards and let out a laugh. I smiled down at her as she stretched, exposing her midriff. "What?" I asked.

"Sometimes, things are so ridiculous and awful that you can't help but laugh."

"You're starting to sound like me," I said, lying down next to her.

Her eyes studied the ceiling. "When did life become so complex? Things were simpler before, but honestly, I struggle to remember what it was like before I met you."

I chuckled. "Is that a good thing or a bad thing?"

She turned her head towards me, causing a few stray strands of hair to drape over her face. My heart skipped a beat, and I fell in love with her again in that moment. Her sharp eyes locking with mine. Her sense of humor that few people got to see. Her bright blonde halo. I loved every part of her, inside and out. Fighting for our lives and country too often distracted me from that. There was nothing I wanted more than to lay there next to her forever.

"I was blind before," she replied, "and you opened my eyes. Once you know the truth, it is difficult to continue living a lie."

Wrapping my arms around her, I pulled her closer. Her chest rose and fell against mine as I said, "And you showed me not every White, Purple, and Blue is a jerk. Most of them, but not all of them."

A cute little smile appeared on her face before she pursed her lips. I could tell she was conspiring. "Speaking of before, I feel like we still don't know that much about each other's pasts beyond the basics. I know much of it is painful, but it helped shape you."

My chest tightened, but I forced myself to breathe. *We really haven't been able to talk like a real couple. Besides, you've told her the worst of it.* After a couple seconds, I replied, "Okay, but let's make it a game. You ask a question, and then I get to ask one."

She popped up and spun to lean her back on the headboard. Her eyes were alight as she thought of what to ask first. "You haven't said before: Have you ever been with someone else?"

The passion in her eyes made my heart race. *Of course she went there first.* I sat up and scooted next to her. "When I was thirteen, there was a girl I had a crush on: Penelope. She was an Orange on the east side that would come to the Enclave occasionally. We kissed like two or three times and then she never wanted to talk to me again. So, no, you're my first real girlfriend."

Her gaze dropped to the silver bangle I'd given her before she glanced back up at me. "Where is she now?"

I shook my head with a smirk. "That's a second question, but I guess I'll allow it." I took a deep breath. "No idea. When you get abandoned like that with no explanation, it's hard to think of a reason to care where they are."

"Well, her loss is my reward." She kissed my cheek slowly. "Though, it is quite a surprise that a dashing young Militia lieutenant like you didn't have girls fawning over him."

Her hand tucked into mine, and I felt the tension in my back loosen. "Aaron and Del claimed they were," I replied with a shrug.

"I wasn't paying attention. I was never looking for a relationship, but with you, it was easy. Now, it's my turn." I thought for a moment, then asked her the same thing, "Who's that Ethan guy Alex mentioned?"

She blushed and glanced towards the door, avoiding eye contact. It took a while for her to respond. That made me nervous. "Growing up in the palace was lonely. There were always dignitaries, ambassadors, and royals bowing to me and calling me 'princess,' but none of them bothered to get to know me. I spent my days in books, wishing I was the princesses in them: exploring and fighting monsters. Though Alex took it harder than I did, it was lonely. To make matters worse, from the moment I turned thirteen, Mother was lining up boys whose families would be helpful allies. One of those boys, Ethan, was different."

My heart twinged with a bit of jealousy. "How?"

"He was *real*. At first, it was uncomfortable since we had been friends for years, but he actually cared about me and for me. More than anything, I needed that."

That hit me. Maybe that was why things felt so easy between us: She felt alone, I felt lost. I'd always had Delaware and Poseidon, but I never had a real home. Whether it was the orphanage or the Enclave, I was fighting to leave. Now, home was wherever she was. It didn't matter whether it was the palace or a crappy motel room. I pulled her into a hug. "I'm sorry you were so alone, but I get it. My whole life was as an outcast, and in a way, so was yours. We watched the 'normal' people live their lives while we were trained to become what we had to be. What happened to him?"

Her hand ran across my forearm as her eyes remained fixed on her lap, the passion replaced with sorrow. "What happens to every royal boy with an eye on the throne. He began to see me as nothing more than a conduit for his political career. We had been together for four years, but my opinion stopped mattering; I stopped mattering. So I broke it off, and Mother was furious. Part of the reason why I went to college was to escape the palace for as much of the day as possible. Ethan was everywhere I looked, but at college, I had real friends."

I didn't ask another question. There was no reason to push her further. The wound he left obviously still hurt. For a few minutes, we just sat in silence as I held her. I could feel her heart racing as she took a deep breath. "It's my turn again."

"Maybe we should stick to more positive topics," I quipped.

She chuckled and nuzzled her head against mine. "What is your dream? After all of this is over and we are free, what do you want to do?"

I sighed and shut my eyes. With her in my arms, I had a rare moment at peace. It was hard to think about what was ahead when I could just cuddle with her. "My life has been fighting the Prism since I was eight. It's hard to imagine what it'd be like without it."

Her eyes locked with mine, challenging me. "There must be something you have always wanted to do."

I groaned but relented. "Fine. My dream is to one day stand on the High Bridge and see my city alive. I want to see people crossing the Mississippi freely and without a color assigned to them. After that, it doesn't matter to me. So, I guess after all of this crap is over, my dream would be to standing there, watching it with you. It doesn't matter if there's a crown on your head. All I want is the peace of knowing people are free and that I'm with you."

"You are adorable," she replied, biting her lip.

I failed to hold back a smile. "What about you?"

"I would be lying if I said I don't want to be queen. After the Front and my mother are gone, someone will have to ensure Northern Mississippi does not shatter into pieces. While I am not arrogant enough to believe it must be me, my heart tells me I must try."

"Do you think we have to be a monarchy?"

"Of course not, but at first, the route to a different system would be difficult."

With a peck on her lips, I replied, "Good thing we have each other. Julia Elizabeth Hughes: Queen of the Whites, Prime Minister of Northern Mississippi, savior of the Reds, and the hottest woman in the country."

She grabbed the pillow from behind her and smacked me with it. "Stop it!"

Returning fire with my own pillow, I replied, "You know it's true."

She laughed and pushed me onto my back. Her ice-blue eyes gazed down at me as she said, "Then you shall be Ivan Matelski: King of the Reds, Mayor of St. Paul, secret agent for the Minutemen, and the most handsome man in my queendom."

A rush of excitement rushed through me as her lips met mine. I held her hips and pulled her down to me. When we parted, I smirked up at her. "My turn."

Her eyes narrowed as the ends of her mouth curled. "You just asked me that last one."

"Doesn't count," I quipped, raising my eyebrows to challenge her.

She kissed me again, forcing me to submit.

"Fine, you can go."

She grinned, and her eyes filled with passion. "When was the moment you fell in love with me?"

My chest tightened. *Why does that question make me nervous?* "I had a crush on you from the start, especially after the night the Duke hit me. You were the first person outside the Militia that bothered to care about me."

"You didn't answer the question."

"Fine," I said with a chuckle. "I don't know... The night in the Enclave, when you were willing to see my world and how awful it was. Then that Timberwolves gangster was trying to run you down. That night, I realized I'd do anything for you." That felt like the most difficult thing to say, but at the same time, it felt like a weight off my chest.

She smiled. "I loved that night too. It meant so much to me, and it was the first time I was sure about you."

"Oh, that's great," I said sarcastically.

"No," she said, rolling her eyes and running her hands under my shirt and up my abs and chest. "I mean, you showed me so much about yourself that night, beyond even what you said. Before that, you seemed like the cute mysterious Red boy who had a dark side, but after that, I understood."

Now I felt myself blushing. "Cute mysterious Red boy?"

She narrowed her eyes. "Learning about you sometimes feels like its pulling teeth, and other times it seems so easy."

My chest felt trapped in a vice as I replied, "When I lost Coyote, I felt like I lost part of myself. There's so much I've done and been through. Now, it feels like a whole 'nother life. Part of Coyote just became me, but the rest... Now Delaware's gone. It's like that whole life went with her, and I'm left holding bits and pieces of who I was, trying to fit them back together."

That hurt to admit. I'd been stuck between two worlds, and instead of choosing, the chasm between them ripped me in half. This new, comfortable life made life in the Enclave feel like a nightmare. It was hard to remember that those nightmares were the reason I was who I was.

We sat in silence for a few moments as they processed what I'd said. Heck, I needed the time to process it, and I'd been living it for the past eight months. Julia ran her fingers through my hair as her lip quivered. "I'm so sorry that life in the palace has torn you away from everything you've known. How can I help mend that gap?"

I sniffled. "You do more than enough, forcing me to be myself, but I don't know if it can be mended. Maybe that's okay." I sighed and gazed into her eyes. Water instead of ice. "Sorry. I didn't mean to ruin the mood."

She slid next to me and wrapped me in her arms. "No, Ivan, I love hearing about you and how you feel, even if it's heavy."

After a few seconds to think, a smile crept to my face again. "You need to answer your own question."

She bit her lip. "After Gilvan, when you wept for that little girl.

I saw your heart so much in that moment. Obviously, I liked you a lot already, but that night confirmed how much I loved your soul."

"And now, you have the orphanage."

She smiled. "Because a cute mysterious Red boy stole the heart of a princess with his tears over a small child." Slowly, she lifted up my shirt, "Since you returned my question, it is my turn again. Tell me the stories of your scars."

"All of them? I don't think we have that long."

"Then, for now, tell me of this one." Her finger traced the one that arced from my abs to my chest, sending a chill down my spine. I watched her beautiful eyes as she did it.

"You picked the one that wasn't because of an attack."

The side of her mouth twitched in curiosity.

I closed my eyes and tried to remember the scene. "I was either ten or eleven, racing through the Enclave like a kid who forgot his place in the world. There was an abandoned warehouse by the Mississippi that was surrounded by barbed wire from years ago. As a kid, I thought it was fun to play around, until one time I tripped and fell into it. The wire scraped straight up my front. Blood was everywhere. I remember hearing the other kids shouting and screaming. The last thing I saw before I passed out was Poseidon scooping me into his arms." I wrapped her hand into mine. "Never went near it again. The other kids respected me for having such a badass scar, though."

She bit her lip. "Why am I not surprised you were a rambunctious child?"

"Because I didn't grow out of it," I said as I pulled her closer, starting a make-out session that lasted longer than I bothered to keep track of. The feeling of her body against mine was all I wanted in that moment. It was more than a relief to just enjoy our time together for a few minutes and ignore the journey still ahead of us.

When we parted, she laid her head on my chest. "You have one question remaining."

"Hmm." I decided on the question that had been eating at me since the rescue mission. "Something changed when your mom took you last week. You're more rebellious and determined. It's hot to see you taking lead and fighting for what you believe in, but I just want to know what happened and if you're okay."

A smirk crossed her face. "Aw. That means so much to me."

I stroked her head, running my fingers through her hair. "It's my job to care about you. Everything has been about me falling apart, and I haven't given you the time you deserve. I'm sorry."

"No, Ivan, I completely understand." She sat up and swung her legs over the edge of the bed, looking at me over her shoulder. "Your best friend died less than two weeks ago, yet you were strong and brave enough to keep going. I know you have changed too, and that is okay. You lost a piece of your heart."

"We weren't..."

"You loved each other like brother and sister," she said as her icy eyes told me to listen. "It is okay to be heartbroken, to feel sorrow and pain. In your world, they told you pain is a weakness, so you calloused yourself. But I promise you that I will not take advantage of your wounds and your sadness. We are here to support each other, and you came here for more than just time with me. I see it in your eyes." She slid her hand into mine and ran her thumb along the back of it. "You never have to hide from me."

I cried. Everything I'd been holding in around the others was released at once. Julia pulled me into a hug as I failed to speak. I wanted Delaware back. I wanted Poseidon back. I wanted a life where I didn't feel like the world was on my shoulders. After a couple minutes, I whimpered, "How do you go on when so much of you is gone? I don't recognize myself anymore."

Cradling me in her arms, Julia chuckled. "That's just because you need a haircut."

I failed to hold in a laugh. "I love you sweetheart."

"I love you too."

"Every day I feel a little better, but things will always be wrong without her," I said, wiping the tears from my eyes.

"Time heals most wounds. She will always be with you, but out there, right now, there is a group that loves you. Kaja and Lillian admire you so much, and I see how Tyler watches your every step. She would be proud of you for fighting on with her people, and she would want you to be happy."

"You're right," I said with a deep breath. "But, you didn't answer my question, because I fell into my own trap."

She brushed a hair from in front of her face. "I love when you open up to me. Life is hard, and that is why we need each other. When it comes to my time in Mother's captivity, perhaps the same occurred to me. Growing up, I wanted to please my parents and do what I had to in order to be the best princess, even if I did feel lonely. Now, I see the flaws in them and our way of life, and it frustrates me that I floundered so much time chasing something that did not matter. What we are doing now feels to me like penance for the easy life I've had. I have been given so much. But when we discovered what Mother did, I had never been so angry. She betrayed everyone she ever claimed to love or care for. I've been manipulated my whole life, and I have had enough. In a way, I finally was able to put myself in your shoes."

I sat up. "It's funny. Anger was the thing that motivated me most for so long. Now, it's fear of losing what I have left. When we met, you were always glancing over your shoulder to see who was watching. Now, I see the most confident woman I've ever met, willing to take on rogues in Rockford, negotiate with dangerous dictators, and confront her scheming mom. We've both been through hell, and it's changed us."

She pulled me to my feet, and I wrapped her in my arms. We rocked back and forth before she pecked me on the lips. "When all of this is over, it will be the two of us forever."

I kissed her back. "It already is."

Chapter 23

The next morning came too fast. Jonah shook me awake as the light began to creep through the blinds. I groaned and rolled over. "Ten more minutes."

"Was it not you who said we couldn't afford to stop in the first place?"

"Maybe."

He picked up my jacket from off the floor and chucked it at me. "Take a quick shower. We leave in fifteen, and I don't think her royal highness would appreciate you being tardy."

"You're supposed to be the nice guard," I said, throwing off the sheets and struggling to my feet.

With a smirk, he brushed off his sleeves and grabbed the door handle. "We may no longer be guards, but it is still our job to protect her. C'mon, the shower will knock you awake. They don't have hot water."

He was right about one thing. The water could have been icicles and I wouldn't have been able to tell the difference. We had escaped winter in recent weeks, but now the cold was inside again and reminding me of why I was grateful for the palace's hot water. After a couple minutes of shivering and slapping soap on my skin, I gave up, changed into the jeans and t-shirt Aaron had packed for me, and met the group in the hall.

We piled back into the SUV for what I hoped would be the final stretch of the journey. Alex insisted on driving, and Kaja insisted on sitting with her. None of us objected. While I'd never seen her drive before, I imagined she would get us there quicker than Jonah, and I was happy to sit in the back. After my drive yesterday, anything sounded better than staring at pavement for the next few hours. Besides, it would give me the time to learn some of Tyler's sign language.

The car lurched into gear as we took off. "Does she know how to drive?" Manny asked himself.

Alex's middle finger shot up for all of us to see. "I heard that."

Manny's eyes were wide in fear, and we all laughed. *He should be scared.* The meeting with Premier Taggart stared us in the face, but those moments made the situation bearable. Even if laughter couldn't cure our anxiety and sorrow, it was still a great distraction.

For the next couple hours, there was nothing but forests and farmland as we sped through Michigan. I was clumsy with learning sign language, and it kept both Tyler and Julia entertained. She translated for him as I tried to copy his motions. It was hard. His hands flowed through the motions. Mine jolted.

I studied another sentence and attempted to decode it. It didn't feel like a language. "Someone is driving... I don't know that last one," I said, recognizing the steering wheel motion of the word "driving" but not much else.

Tyler smacked his palm against his face before shaking his head at Julia. Her hand ran along my back. "You are making progress, my love. It takes time."

He moaned and signed, "He's an idiot."

"Hey! I'm not an idiot," I interjected before realizing I understood him. "Wait. I did it!"

She chuckled. "Of course, you are already familiar with the insults."

"Most important part of any language."

"Sign something to us."

I took a deep breath and cracked my knuckles for effect. Most of the symbols for things were still fuzzy, but I found a phrase I could do. "I am a Red."

Finally, I earned a smile out of Tyler, and he offered me a fist bump. *It's the little things in life.* Beyond my victory, it felt good to finally have some idea of what he was saying. Life was hard enough for Reds that had the ability to talk. He deserved to be heard.

Lillian watched us with interest, her eyes curious as her hands followed our motions. Besides the fact that she was a Yellow, I knew almost nothing about her past, but she held herself like a Green. Delaware called them wannabe Blues because Greens had one foot in the pool with the elites, and they wanted people to know it. Even though Lillian lacked that arrogance, the way she talked told me she had gone to a school in either in Minneapolis or the best schools of St. Paul.

My curiosity got the better of me. "Were your parents Greens?"

"How... How did you know?" A flash of worry crossed her face.

"Yellows are usually pretty content with a simple life, not being Oranges or Reds. You have ambition. Plus, you have a high-color accent."

Her hand covered her mouth. *Shoot.* I was right, and she was ashamed. Julia noticed too and said, "Whatever the color of your tag, I am grateful to have you with us."

"My family rejected me after I failed the Prism," Lillian replied with a sniffle. "I honestly could not have cared less about the test, but I wanted to make them proud."

Julia unbuckled and turned around, her arms under her chin on the back of the seat as she offered Lillian a smile. "I have felt the exact same way my entire life. Approval is, unfortunately, a fickle fiend to grasp, though."

"Fickle fiend... fickle fiend. That's a tongue twister," Manny said, breaking some of the tension.

"It is," Lillian replied. "The amount of pressure placed on us for the Prism is ridiculous. It was six months ago... My life has never been the same. All of my Green and Blue friends turned their backs on me."

"I didn't." Kaja beamed back at us. "Ain't she lucky."

"I am, but I never guessed we would end up here," Lillian said with a smile.

I scoffed. "Tell me about it."

Julia settled back next to me, sitting so our legs touched. "So much has changed in such little time, for all of us, and I can only imagine that pace will only continue if we succeed."

"Or fail," Manny replied.

Tyler shot his friend a glare and gave a sign no one needed to translate.

"What? Just trying to be realistic. We could fail."

With her fist held high, Alex replied, "That's the spirit!"

Julia tried to hold back a laugh. "He does have a point. We

should prepare for the worst."

"Considering Huron has nukes, I'd rather not," I said.

"What would we do?" Tyler replied.

There was only one option. "If we fail, we run."

"Oh, and you said I'm the negative one," Kaja quipped from the front.

I couldn't help but laugh. "I don't think we'll fail, but if we do, that's our only option. There'll be a war, and both the UPF and Vera will try to hunt us down."

Julia sighed. "That is a possibility, but..."

"Guys, we have company!" Alex called back. I looked out the back window to see three black SUVs tailing us. A white lion emblem glared back from the front of each. *How?*

Manny ducked as I pulled my gun. "They already shot me too many times."

"Floor it!" I yelled. The engine roared. I aimed and fired. My ears rang as the bullet ripped through the back window, sending glass flying through the air. The first SUV swerved, its driver slumped in his seat.

"What the hell Red?" Alex screamed while Julia and Lillian covered their ears.

I ignored her. "One down." Every inch of me was on fire. But as I raised my pistol again, my chest tightened. The world shook. I tried to pull the trigger. My finger didn't move. *What is going on?*

It seemed like slow-motion as Jonah fired from the back row. My ears screamed at the sound. In my mind, the shot was distant. Everything blurred. Another *bang* hit my ears. I couldn't tell from where. Someone was yelling. Maybe everyone was yelling. I couldn't tell. I couldn't move.

A force knocked me down to the seat. My face smacked into it, sending the pistol clattering from my hand as it disappeared. Tyler fired rapidly. Each shot was a cannonball destroying my brain. Julia shook me, her eyes wide in fear. Her hands quivered against my cheeks. I wanted to tell her I was alright. I wanted to pick up my gun and fire back. *Where's my gun?*

Our SUV swerved and jolted. Weak, I pushed myself off the seat with Julia's help. Her hands pushed my head beneath the top of the seat as bullets rattled against metal. *She saved my life.* My vision slowly cleared along with my mind. I could thank her later. Right now, I needed to do something.

My hands blindly searched for the pistol as I mumbled, "Where is it?" The floor bounced, making it impossible.

"Are you sure?" she said as she grabbed it from beneath our seats. I could tell she was shaken, but her eyes were cold as ice. "You don't have to do this for me."

A raspy breath escaped from my lungs. "Yes, I do." I peeked over the seat to analyze the situation. We were on a gravel road, slicing through the woods as the two SUVs tailed us. Bullet holes riddle their windshields and grills. To my right, Tyler was crouched beneath the seat, waiting for his next chance. *When did he learn to shoot?*

In the back, Jonah shielded Lillian as he fired. When he ducked back down, he saw me. "You alright?"

I raised my pistol and fired, clipping the hood of the closest SUV. "Good enough," I replied and glanced at Julia. "Where are we going?"

Alex answered for her, "Not a damn clue!"

Julia's hand closed around my wrist. "Let me have one."

"No." I popped up and fired again, missing. "Damn it!"

Her grip tightened. "I wasn't suggesting it, Ivan. Give me a pistol."

"Once you kill someone…"

"I know." Her voice was soft yet confident. She knew exactly what she was asking to do.

I had promised myself I'd never let her do it. My first kill changed me, and every kill after had made it worse. You can only plunge into those unforgiving waters once. There's no going back. I couldn't let her do it. "No, I'm sorry."

She released me. From the look on her face, I knew she felt betrayed. But I had no choice. The shootout risked her life. I couldn't let her risk her heart. *Why does it hurt so much?*

A bullet whizzed over my head and through the windshield. Kaja yelped as the car skidded. *Time to end this.* I gripped the gun and spun, firing in a series and missing wildly on all of them. Before I could complain, Jonah sent a bullet through the driver's head, and his SUV skidded to a stop.

When the final car was in range, I pulled the trigger again. There was nothing but a *click*. "Crap! I'm out."

"We were using the ammo from the back, but that's out too," Jonah replied before popping up and firing. "We just need one good shot."

Tyler signed something to me, but my mind was too scattered to comprehend it as he rose. Four shots echoed through the car as the hot shells flew at me, searing my arms. A looked back just in time to see the SUV fly into a tree. It creaked but held. Their SUV didn't fare so well. It was over.

"Yeah!" Kaja exclaimed, her face alight. "That was so cool, Tyler!"

He brushed off his shoulders with a cocky look on his face. *Is that sign language for "I'm too cool for you"?*

The car slowed as Alex pulled over and laid her head on the steering wheel. I could hear her sobbing.

Julia reached up to rub her back. "Alex, are you alright?"

Her sister screamed and slammed her fist into the horn over and over again, startling the crows nesting nearby. They took off, turning the otherwise grey sky to black. The sound of their wings made her stop and stare up at them through the broken windshield. "How could I be okay after that? Holy shit, Jules, we almost frickin' died! And now, our *second* car is ruined, your boyfriend is falling apart, we're in the middle of nowhere, and Mom is probably sending more people to kill us."

That was harsh. I stared down at my hands. They trembled. *Is she right?* After I got Julia back, I thought I was okay again. Obviously not. Whether it was the PTSD thing she'd mentioned or something else, it could have gotten us killed. Because of my breakdown, Julia was desperate enough to ask for a gun. I trusted her with one. That's what scared me. She could have succeeded.

It was at least a minute before Julia responded. I couldn't tell whether she was mad at me or worried about her sister, but it was taking time for her to process things too. "We will figure this out, all of us. We don't know if Mother or the Front sent those men, but it doesn't matter. All they have done is revealed their

fear. They know what we can accomplish. They know we can succeed."

"Do you actually believe that?" Alex replied.

Jonah hopped through the nonexistent back window and
strode towards the totaled SUVs, cocking his pistol along the way.
Manny called back to him, "Where are you..."

"To figure out who they are."

Julia and I made eye contact. She nodded, and I pulled a knife
before following him. Part of me wanted to be mad he would go
after them himself, but I was no different. If he hadn't gone first,
that would have been me. Except I would have done it with only
a knife.

"Stay with the girls," Jonah said as I ran to catch up. His voice
had a new edge to it. *His wife is in danger. You're the same way.*

Alongside him, I smirked and spun the knife around my finger.
"And miss all the fun? Hell no."

He scoffed and shook his head. "Do you know what I thought
of you at first?"

"No idea."

"I thought you were either incredibly brave or incredibly reckless." He raised his pistol as we approached the first SUV. "Everything you've done since proved me wrong. You're both."

We both laughed and scanned the area. The driver was definitely dead; Tyler had made sure of that. There had been a second
person in the car, but he was nowhere in sight. *This is bad.* Our
feet crunched on the gravel as we moved in from opposing sides.
My heart quickened. I grabbed the door handle and yanked it
open. Nothing.

Jonah lowered his gun. "Dang it. Where did he…"

The shot shook the trees. For a moment, the world stopped. Jonah's eyes filled with fear, and I could only watch as he collapsed.

Chapter 24

While I stood, planted to the ground in shock, the shooter grinned and aimed at me. *Demetri.* Julia screamed, knocking me out of my daze. I flung myself behind the car as a bullet flew past my head. *Damn the royals.*

I whispered under the car to Jonah, "Are you alive?"

He groaned. "Thanks for the positivity."

"I'll take that as a yes."

Demetri spoke with authority, "Hand over the princesses, and then you two can go."

I tried to creep to the other end of the car, but my steps on the gravel made too much noise. *So much for stealth.*

A scuffle came from the other side of the car. "Come out, or he dies."

Jonah muttered, "Don't."

No choice. I raised my arms and stood. Demetri's grin met me. "Perhaps you are not as stupid as you appear to be."

Jonah coughed. Blood seeped from his side, but from the look of it, it wouldn't be fatal. "The one time I tell you to be reckless. Ack!"

Demetri shoved the gun harder into the side of his head and nodded to my knife. "Drop it."

I glanced towards our SUV. Julia and Alex were scrambling

with something between them, but I couldn't tell what it was. Tyler gripped his gun. He could shoot but was out of ammo. The last bullets were in Jonah's pistol, lying somewhere on the other side of the car. There was no help coming. It was up to me. I couldn't lose Julia again, but Jonah would die if I attacked. My hand quivered as the knife slid from its grasp. My breaths were weak, but I asked him, "Why'd you do it? All those people at the villa... You helped kill them."

He chuckled. "No innocents died that night. The blood spilled was tainted with greed and corruption. My job is to serve the Queen. She and the Front wished to purify the elites of the rot. The princesses would have been safe if you had not intervened."

"Safe? They were imprisoned!"

His finger tightened around the trigger. "Stop talking, or you will regret it."

I nodded in compliance, and my face burned as Demetri waved for the girls to follow him. With Jonah at gunpoint, there was nothing I could do but stare at Julia as she followed his instructions. Her shirt was ripped, and a bleeding scrape graced her cheek, but she pressed forward. In that moment, she wasn't a princess. She was a fighter, staring down her fear without wavering. My heart ached. I wanted to lie next to her with my hand around her waist and her body against mine, forgetting the world. *Why do I want her so badly when I'm about to lose her?*

When they arrived, Demetri threw Jonah to the ground and pointed the gun at me as he retreated with them. I rushed to Jonah's side and ripped the sleeve off my shirt to cover the wound.

Blood was everywhere, and my mind scrambled to find a solution. Once I tied the shirt as gauze, Tyler helped me bring Jonah to his feet while he mumbled, "The bullet grazed me. It didn't hit anything important."

"You sure?" I replied.

He groaned and nodded. "I'll be fine. But you let them go."

Demetri heard and huffed. "You made the right...ack..." His eyes rolled back into his head. A second later, he was on the ground, motionless.

I could only stare at the hole in his head as crimson pooled around him. "How..."

Above him stood Alex, her eyes sharp and focused on his body. A black knife coated in blood dangled from her fingers. *Where did she get the knife?*

We all remained still for what felt like hours. Nothing but our breaths filled the air until a flock of crows took flight, the flapping of their wings like a chorus. Seconds later, they were gone. Even the trees seemed quiet as nature mourned a princess's first kill. The knife slid from her fingers and clattered against the gravel. My heart felt like it struck me instead. Alex wasn't Julia, but she had been through enough, suffered enough.

The look on her face was familiar to me. It was the same one I had after my first real kill. I remembered standing over the thug's body, my knife in his chest. He had attacked Delaware a couple months after I rescued her from River Falls. In my mind, I could still hear her scream as it pierced every inch of the Enclave. She'd fought him off, but after her initial escape, the scrawny boy had pulled a knife and was in pursuit.

My chest had caught fire as I watched him prowl after her. In full stride, I tackled him the way Poseidon taught me: wrap their legs and pull them to the ground. In seconds, he wriggled loose and nailed me in the cheek. I growled and broke his nose with my elbow, and when he tried to crawl away again, I grabbed his leg and twisted. He yelled and grabbed at his knife. But before he could stab me, I rolled and pulled my own, its black blade nearly invisible in the night. When we struggled to our feet and lunged, it guided itself between his ribs.

In the present, I stared at my hands, just like I did that night. Delaware's screams still haunted me. If I'd been any later, anything could have happened. In my rage, I sacrificed part of me to protect her. I would have done it again, a hundred times if I had to; that didn't make it feel any better. There is weight in a life, and it was heavy on my chest. For weeks after the kill, nightmares would force me awake in a cold sweat, and I'd spend the rest of the night watching the world from the bridge. In the years since, each kill got easier. That scared me.

Now, watching Alex stand where I once stood, my heart broke for her. The trickery involved in her attack impressed me, though. She must have taken one of the spare knives from Aaron's bags without telling us. The move reminded me of Delaware, and that broke my heart again.

Julia intertwined her fingers with her sister's and whispered to her. Tears streamed down both of their cheeks. I didn't know my place. *Do I comfort them or keep my distance?* My feet refused to move anyway, so I stayed rooted to the spot as Lillian and Kaja joined them.

Jonah's groan knocked me back into reality. "We need to get to safety."

My eyes met Julia's. That fierceness was still there, but it was mixed with shock now. She was as lost as I was. After the lull, the wind had picked up again, and clouds rolled overhead. With the chill in the air, my hairs stood on end. "Let's go back to the car," I said, watching the darkening sky. "We'll figure it out from there,"

Julia pulled at Alex, trying to bring her along. She wouldn't move. The girls all comforted her, and as much as I wanted to help, the best thing I could do was help Jonah limp back.

As we walked, I focused on the sound of the gravel under my shoes and the wind whistling through the trees. My panic from the shootout was gone, but Demetri's attack and death rattled me. Something inside me felt misplaced—not broken but not where it should be.

In front of us, Manny scanned the trees and sky as if he would find a building. Alex was right, we were in the middle of nowhere, and with our crappy car now windowless and riddled with bullet holes, it wouldn't protect us from the storm. For now, though, it was a place for Jonah to rest while we figured out a plan.

I set him down in the passenger seat, and he shut his eyes. "Thank you. Now, please, go check on the girls. They need you," he ordered through raspy breaths.

I shook my head. "You're the one that got shot."

"I'll be fine, Ivan. It just grazed me. We've both had worse. Right now, you're the only person that can bring Alex some peace. And besides, I've got Tyler to keep me company."

Tyler crossed his arms and nodded sharply.

"Fine," I replied. Even if he wasn't my boss anymore, I gave a salute and jogged back towards the girls. I felt like a wimp compared to Jonah. The guy had been shot but didn't scream or complain. He was strong, a soldier at heart. *Princesses sometimes save the soldiers, right?*

Alex's eyes were stuck on the ground as I reached the girls. I tried to give Julia a reassuring smile, but I think it came out more as a grimace based on her worried reaction. "How is our fearless guardsman?" she asked.

"He says the bullet just grazed him." I glanced back at him. "There was a lot of blood but looks like he'll be okay."

Lillian let out a sigh of relief. "Oh, thank God."

I met Julia's gaze. "He won't admit it, but I think he could use your company." At the end of my statement, I flicked my eyes to Alex.

She took the hint and waved for the maids to follow her. We grazed our hands against each other as she passed, and I felt a little sense of pride that we could communicate like that. With Delaware gone, she was my best friend now, and it was comforting to grow with her outside of our romantic relationship.

While they walked away, I stood in silence, waiting for Alex to speak. Her fist clenched and unclenched for a few seconds before she let out a sharp breath. "I don't need to talk."

"I know."

She scoffed. "Then why are you here? I have already received *all* the comfort in the world."

"Because I know you don't need comfort. You need to hear it like it is." Her eyes jumped up to mine as I continued, "You killed

Demetri. That will never leave you. He'll haunt your nightmares the rest of your life. You'll go through phases: regret, denial, hating yourself, hating fate or God or whoever put you in this position, and then you'll accept it's part of you now. You've taken a life."

"Shut the hell up!" She shoved me, sobbing.

I didn't budge, and passion burned through my voice. "You'll accept that you killed the man who shot Jonah. You killed the man that tried to kidnap you and Julia. You killed the man who helped slaughter dozens of people at that villa. You killed him to protect the people you love, the people you'd do anything for. And once you've accepted that, you can accept the fact you're broken and that nothing can change that. Nothing can put that piece of you back, because some of us have to break so this piece of shit world doesn't shatter, so that those we love remain whole. I've stood exactly where you stand, and I wish someone could have told me the truth. Not that 'it'll be okay' or 'time heals all wounds.' Some scars never fade. They make us who we are, who we have to be."

Her arms wrapped around me as she broke down further, her head on my chest. I hugged her back. The sister of the woman I loved. The black sheep of the royalty, a White stained in crimson. She was lost and broken like me.

Alex cleared the tears from her eyes as she stepped back. "Why does that bring me more relief than my sister's support?"

The crows' calls faded as I gave her a solemn smile. "Because it's the truth." Behind me, our wreck of an SUV shuddered to life. It had been in bad shape before, but now its backfire echoed through the forest like a shotgun every couple seconds. "You gonna be okay to go?"

She chuckled and took a shaky breath. "If the shitmobile doesn't fail before we get there."

"Looks like Tyler is waiting for you," I said as we made our way back. He sat on what remained of the back of the SUV, his eyes fixed on his hands in his lap.

A closed-mouth smile forced its way across her face. "Like a sad puppy."

When he noticed us, his head popped up, and he started signing faster than I could translate. "Exactly like a puppy," I said.

They hugged, the tight kind where you never want the other person to let go. Confident I'd done my job, I grabbed the door handle but stopped when Alex called over to me, "Hey Ivan." I glanced back at her still holding Tyler. "Thanks."

Did she just call me Ivan? I nodded and flung myself into the car, next to Julia. Her hand slid into mine, and my heart calmed. "Let's get out of here."

Manny was in the driver's seat. Once the royalty's newest item joined us, he screeched more than shifted the car into gear. "And never come back."

Chapter 25

The thunderstorm struck as we stumbled upon an abandoned gothic church just outside a village. Nestled in the woods, it would be the perfect place to hide and wait for better weather.

With the windows shattered and roof peppered with holes, the car provided little protection from the rain. Manny skidded us into a gravel patch that must have been used as a parking lot ages ago. Now, it was overrun by weeds and even some small trees. It didn't matter. It would hold the shitmobile.

I held my jacket over Julia to protect her from the rain as we scattered from the car. When we reached the entrance, I pulled open the church's massive door and held it for her and the group. She curtsied as she passed. "Oh, why thank you, sir Ivan."

With an eccentric bow, I replied, "Your highness."

Kaja squeezed past Julia. "Am I the only one who *doesn't* love being soaked?"

To keep Julia out of the way, I threw my jacket around her and pulled her close to me, bringing out the smile that I loved so much. When she laughed and smiled at the same time, her own royal walls fell. Her hair was drenched and stuck to her forehead, and the cut on her cheek looked deep enough to scar, but away from the fancy dresses and royal spotlight, she was perfect. And she was mine.

I'm going to marry her. The thought went as quickly as it came, but it was there. For so long, with the talk of me being king and having to be a royal, I had been scared. I'd lost who I was and it had felt like the world was trying to redefine my life without giving me a say. But for some reason, after everything we'd been through, that moment in the rain washed away my doubts. Even in the freezing rain, I felt warm next to her. I loved Julia, my princess, and when the moment came, I would ask her to spend the rest of her life with me.

I must have been smiling too much, because she offered a weak laugh. "What?"

"You're beautiful," I replied, brushing the hairs from her face.

She countered with a kiss before glancing into the church, where Alex, Tyler, and Kaja were laughing about something. "Whatever did you say to her?"

"I told her what I wish Poseidon would have told me. Some scars stick with you for life, but that doesn't mean they're not worth it."

Her eyes flicked to the ground. "That is the opposite of what I told her."

"I know, but that's okay. You did what any good sister would. It'll just take time for her to accept what happened. Some things come with experience."

She gave a half-hearted smile before gripping my hand and pulling me into the church. "Have you ever been to a service?"

"No," I replied, gazing up at the somehow still intact stained-glass windows encircling the sanctuary. Wooden benches lined the aisle up to the altar. The rest of the building was stone, and the group's voices echoed through the room as I continued, "I've never really been in a church before." I ran my fingers along the benches. "Why do the benches have those pads in front of them?"

A cute smirk crossed her face, meaning I'd said something wrong. "These benches are called pews, and those pads are for kneeling in prayer. We used to have services in the Royal Chapel before the General Secretary commanded that it be torn down. It was likely the only remaining church that did not meet underground, but Father did not wish to provoke the Front by resisting."

"Why am I not surprised?"

"My father made mistakes. All of us have."

I followed her as she approached the altar. "You haven't told me much about your faith."

Her voice quieted. "And I'm sorry for that. Even among royalty, the topic has become taboo, and I was afraid of how you would react."

"Why?"

"Because a part of me didn't believe that you would understand it." Her eyes studied the wooden cross, illuminated by the little light that snuck through the stained-glass window behind it. "It was wrong for me not to trust you. My faith is an important part of my life, and if you are willing, I'd like to share it with you."

I wasn't sure what to think. Besides that old English Bible in the Militia headquarters, I'd never been exposed to religion. It was important to her, though, and I wanted to be open-minded. "I'm willing to listen and learn."

A smile crossed her face as she knelt on the stone steps and lowered her head. "Pray with me?"

I followed her lead. "Now what?"

She turned her head to look at me. "It's a conversation with God. You can just listen if you'd like." I nodded, and she shut her eyes. "Dear Lord, thank you for granting us shelter from this storm and for watching over us during this trying time. Even as we find ourselves lost in the wilderness, I know you are with us. I thank you for the new friends you've given us during times of tragedy. Please watch over us as we enter the final phase of our journey to Detroit and grant us your guidance as we seek to find peace. I ask that you be with Mother. She has strayed into a dark place, and I pray that you show her your light once again. Be with our group as we rest and heal, and please help Alex find your grace while her soul mourns. Lastly, I ask that you reach into Ivan's heart, Lord, and show him your love and mercy. Thank you for bringing him into my life to love and protect me, and I ask that you help me do the same for him. In your name we pray, amen."

When I opened my eyes, she was beaming at me. I didn't quite understand it, but the idea of her asking her God to show me mercy felt big. My heart felt weird. I glanced at her but wavered and stared down at the stone floor. "Thank you."

"Thank you for being open." Her eyes returned to the cross in front of us. "That chapel may have been nothing more than a building, but it was my escape. When they tore it down, I lost my place of solitude. It's one thing to pray in my room. It's another to be in a beautiful building such as this, built to honor God. It means so much to me that you were willing to do this."

I wrapped my hands around hers. "I'm sorry I made you feel

like you needed to hide this. Faith is something new to me, but it's important to you, so I'm willing to try, even if we don't have a beautiful building."

"It only takes two to make a church. As long as I have you, it doesn't matter if we're in a chapel in the forest, a great palace, or the ruins of a great city."

Her hands shivered, so I wrapped my jacket tighter around her. Back towards the center of the sanctuary, Kaja seemed to be telling a story to the rest of the group, acting out scenes within it. With the echoes, it was difficult to understand what she was saying. I nodded towards her. "We should check on the group."

"Of course. Leaving Kaja and Alex together for too long sounds like a dangerous proposition."

"You were the one that let her be Alex's maid."

We stood and walked hand-in-hand. "Gaining Lillian's positive spirit was worth the risk of some added shenanigans." She chuckled and glanced at our hands. "We all need a partner in crime."

Alex's head popped up as we approached their circle. "Did someone say 'crime'?" she said, grinning like a maniac. *At least she's feeling better, for now.*

"Is being a fugitive and fleeing from justice in one country not enough for you?" Julia quipped back. There was something about Alex that brought out that edge in her. It was both entertaining to watch and attractive to see her in a battle of wits.

Alex's eyebrows raised, anticipating the verbal combat. "Nah, I want to go for a triple crown, unless her royal highness Queen Julia can find two more before my humble self."

"If I were to have three crowns, I may let you have one. Though,

I would rather you not return that favor," Julia replied with a smile. She sat down next to her sister with her back against one of the pews.

Alex threw her arm over her Julia's shoulders. "Why wouldn't you want to spend time in prison with me? I promise I'm a worthy cellmate."

"After a lifetime trapped in Mother's vice, I would say I have had quite enough of prison."

I scoffed. "Believe me. Jail is a lot worse than that."

Kaja coughed deliberately, and we all turned to look at her. "If you're finished…"

Julia bowed her head and waved for her to continue her story. "Of course, Lady Kaja."

"Good," Kaja replied, straightening her shirt before striking a pose and continuing, "We were sprinting through Dayton's Bluff, a couple loaves of bread in each of our hands. The black-caps were right behind us. Those fat assholes wanted the food more than they wanted us. A cop car swooped in front of us." Using her arm, she mimicked a car drifting, with sound effects and all.

I raised my hand. "What's going on?"

She dropped her arms and groaned. "I'm telling the story of how Lillian and I met. Enough from the peanut gallery."

We all chuckled as she regained her stance. "There was no-where to go—black-caps behind, black-caps in front—but then, a head popped out of a townhouse nearby. The girl waved us in, but before Tommy and Sky could make it, the cappers grabbed 'em. I barely slipped through the crack in the door and slammed it before they reached me."

"You were frantic," Lillian said with a smirk.

"You would have been too if the cappers were on your ass from trying to get some food. And we were both panicking when they tried to knock the door down. I remember you pointing towards a door in the back. We sprinted through it, and the rest is history."

"Unfortunately, the bread was rather stale."

Kaja huffed and crossed her arms. "Some of us struggled more than you."

Julia chuckled under her breath at their squabble. "What convinced you to open that door?" she asked Lillian.

"It had only been a couple of weeks since my parents had kicked me out of the house for my demotion to Yellow. I'd been sleeping in that abandoned house, and when I heard the shouting from outside, I knew I had to do something. It ended up as the best decision I've made." She took Kaja's hand and smiled at her. "I'm glad we found each other."

"And I am glad Ivan found you," Julia replied, grinning at me before speaking to the group, "This would be so much more difficult without all of you here. Despite our struggles, we all make a pretty great team if you ask me."

Jonah moaned and lay down on one of the pews. I paced over to him and knelt as the group scattered across the room to rest. "How you feeling?"

He chuckled to himself. "Like I miss my wife."

"I'm sorry."

"It's not your fault. If anything, you're giving me the chance to get back to her. Vera isn't patient with prisoners."

"No, she isn't." I paused for a moment, thinking about the day.

"How was she when you talked?"

His nose twitched like he was trying to hold back his sorrow. "Christina is strong, but she is in a tough spot because of me, even with Aaron's help. The faster we return, the better."

I nodded. "Agreed, but we need to get back alive. If Demetri found us, Vera's going to send more people. She knows our plan."

"Or she is that desperate to get her daughters back. There's nothing that drives the Queen crazier than them being out of reach." He lifted his head to look over at Julia. "We will need to move soon, but enjoy this time for now. It sounds like the rain stopped. Get some air. I think both of you could use it."

I followed his gaze. He was right about the rain and the fresh air, but I wasn't going to let him off that easy. "You talk about other people relaxing a lot for a guy who got shot."

"Do I have to order you to keep your girlfriend company?" he quipped as he rested his head back onto the pew.

I pushed myself to my feet. "You also give a lot of orders for a guy that got fired."

His eyes were closed, but I swear he was glaring at me. "I may be incapacitated at the moment, but I can still beat you in a fight."

"You wish." I hopped over the next pew and met up with Julia, who was chatting with her sister. "Jonah gets cranky when you shoot him."

"I heard that!" he yelled back, his voice echoing through the room.

Julia gave me the usual look to behave. "I know another body-guard that often becomes moody himself when things get rough."

"Didn't I just break you out of the palace singlehandedly?"

She smirked and raised an eyebrow. "I do believe I saw you use both of your hands, sir."

Someone's in a snarky mood. I reached my hand out to help her up. "Well, take the second one and come with me, your highness."

"Where are we going m'lord?" she replied, taking my hand and hoisting herself to her feet.

"I don't know. That's the fun part." I offered her my arm, and when she took it, we mimicked a royal stroll down the aisle.

From the second I walked over, she hadn't stopped smiling. That alone made me forget about the pain for now. My heart was full with her, and right now, that was all I needed. When we reached the doors, I held it open for her, and hand-in-hand we sprinted into the late afternoon light. "Where to?" she asked, her eyes gazing out into the forest.

"I see only one place to go, but you gotta keep up." Before she could react, I took off towards the forest. Running was one of the most freeing things in the world. It cleared my mind, stretched my legs, and got me outside. I needed it and so did she.

"What are you doing?" she called after me.

My hands clung onto the lowest branch of a tree as I started climbing. "Follow me or you'll never know."

"We shouldn't stray too far from the church," she said with a laugh. I could see the gears turning in her mind. She was always analyzing the situation, trying to choose the best move. I needed her to act. It took her a few seconds to contemplate what to do, but she loved the forest—I knew she'd come.

"Curiosity is amazing, isn't it," I said with a smirk when she reached the tree.

"Curiosity is a cunning beast," she quipped back.

The leaves obscured the sun except for a few splashes scattered across her face. I loved her in this mood, and my heart raced as I gazed down at her. With her, free in the forest, I felt like I could fly.

I laughed and leapt from the tree, landing with a roll. On impact, my shoulder smacked into the ground harder than it should have, and instead of my feet, I ended up on my back. With a groan, I muttered, "Delaware was always better at that."

She laughed and reached down to help me up from the grass, but I pulled her down to me. After a little yelp, she smiled as I wrapped my arms around her. Looking up at her with the sun's retreating light illuminating the trees and her golden hair, I could have been in a dream. She brushed a hair from my face and kissed me. It didn't matter that we were battered, bruised, and in the middle of a forest. I could have spent an eternity there.

After what could have been minutes or hours, she pulled back. "I love you."

I rolled to the top and gazed down at her as she laughed. "I love you too, my princess," I said and kissed her again.

When we parted, the grass had become one with her hair. I smiled down at her as her eyes gazed into mine. Her hands ran along by body, tracing my scars and muscles alike. "Thank you."

"For what?" I asked with a chuckle.

"For making me feel safe and giving me a purpose."

"Says the girl that pulled me from the slums and gave me a home." I slid next to her, and we watched the trees wave in the wind.

She smiled cheek to cheek. "It's nice to know that even if we fail, there is some beauty left in our world."

"There always will be as long as you're in it," I said. She blushed as I jumped to my feet and offered her my hand. "Run away with me?"

"But where will we go?" she asked as I pulled her into my arms.

"Wherever you want. Lead the way."

Her hand slipped into mine, and she glided through the trees at a full sprint, the wind whipping through the ripped fabric of her clothing as she pulled me along. We raced deeper into the forest without direction until a creek blocked our path. Julia stopped as I crouched next to it, letting the frigid water run over my fingers.

She studied me as I traced the creek's stones. "What are you doing?"

"Stick your hand in the water."

"It's going to be freezing. Are you joking?" I flicked some water at her, forcing her to jump back, laughing, as it splattered across her shirt and face. "Well, now I'm soaked."

I stuck my other hand in the water. "Don't make me stick my face in too. It would be awful if I got hypo-whatever-ia."

"Hypothermia," she replied with an eye roll before kneeling next to me and racing her fingertips through the water. Her eyes focused on the ripples dancing among the rocks. "I told you it was freezing."

With a shrug, I replied, "Really? I can't feel anything."

My hands really had gone numb, but the joking was helping me as much as it was her. For the first time since the shootout started, it didn't feel like there was a cloud in my head. The water helped me cling to reality as my anxiety threatened to drown me. In the distance, the thunder rolled, and the trees creaked with the force of the wind.

Julia giggled and stood. "You're adorable, but we need to get back before that next front hits."

"You're right." I pulled my hands from the creek. They burned, but the pain felt good. "But not until you climb that tree."

Her eyes followed my finger, a touch of curiosity filling them. "Mother never let us climb trees."

"There are thousands of trees around the palace, and you haven't climbed *any* of them?"

She shrugged. "I guess I never had a reason."

I flicked the stray water on my fingers at her again as I passed, prompting her to stick her tongue out at me. With a running start, I put my foot on the trunk, jumped, and gripped a branch. My sore arms groaned as I yanked myself up. "Are you coming or not? I promise it'll be fun."

The storm grew closer as she scanned the skies, her brow furrowed. Determination replaced her worry as she copied my motions exactly. She leapt up, grabbing hold of the branch, but her hands slipped. Out of instinct, I dove towards her and gripped her wrist before pulling her to safety. Seated on the branch, her cheeks were flushed red. "For the first time in my life, I understand my mother's command," she said with a sigh of relief.

I sat next to her, my arm around her waist. "See, I told ya it would be fun."

Her eyes dropped to the bracelet I'd given her, and a cheeky smile crossed her face as she nuzzled her head into my shoulder. "Every moment I spend with you is my favorite. As horrible as these past couple days have been, I've loved tackling every challenge together." She sighed and rolled the bracelet around her wrist. "With you, I don't feel like I need to prove that I'm something I'm not. You have given me the confidence I needed to be free, to actually confront the world's problems and mine. I'm so lucky."

"Dang, I need to save you from falling more often," I replied, stroking her head. "I've loved watching you become the leader your dad thought you could be. He can't take any credit for that, and neither can I. You are proving why you should be queen. All I am is friendly support."

"Oh, only friendly?"

"Wait, are we a thing?" I joked back.

She rolled her eyes, sat up, and stared at the dying light as the sun passed below the trees. "Tomorrow is a new day with new adventures and hopefully new solutions."

My chest tightened. I didn't want to think about tomorrow's negotiations and whether we'd prevent the next great war or not. All I wanted was her. So much it hurt. But she couldn't be entirely mine until we figured out this mess.

"Why does it scare me so much?" I asked. "Negotiating with Huron, stopping Vera, ending the Prism... Everything is so uncertain. We're so close to doing what I always dreamed about, and that scares me. I'm paralyzed just thinking about what things would be like afterward. Who am I without the Prism to fight against, without my tag? The only thing that I know for sure will be the same is you."

For a few moments, she was silent, looking at me before spinning her family ring. "I don't quite understand why, but this feels all too natural for me, like it's what I was meant to do. For so long I dragged my feet when you asked me to step up and lead. I was blind, keeping my head down for so long... Change can be difficult. I was afraid of what my family would think and what the future would hold, but when I challenged the Front in those interviews, something in me began to change. You showed me the truth, but it was in that moment that I realized I really could do it. Everything that has happened since has forced me to become the princess I always told myself I wanted to be, and that is because of you."

"I'm glad this is easy for someone."

She took my hands. "Ivan, the only reason I am not a nervous wreck right now is because of you. When you remove your tag, and we defeat the Prism, nothing about you will change. You are the brave, caring boy that saved me on that street corner and gave me hope. You are the boy that showed me how blind I was and how I could change things for the better. I did not fall in love with you because you are a Red or a rebel. I fell in love with you because I saw who you are despite those things, and you saw beyond my titles and status. When this is all over, my ring and your tag won't matter." Thunder clapped overhead, and she shot her eyes up at it before squeezing my hands. "We should head back to the others."

I took a deep breath and hopped down from the branch. I wanted to believe her, but even if my mind was convinced, my heart wasn't. But my heart trusted her, and that was enough. As I stared up at her, I couldn't help but smile. "C'mon sweetheart, let's get out of here."

She yelped and fell into my arms, but my body was not in the shape for catching girls after the beating I'd taken in recent weeks. We flopped to the ground, laughing before she scrambled to her feet. "Race you back!"

Chapter 26

The Sun peeked over the horizon, illuminating the squalor as we reached the suburbs of Detroit. After a rough night of sleep in the church, I'd taken the wheel for our final stretch. My insides were twisted, and driving gave me something to focus on other than my anxiety. But it returned when I saw the conditions the people lived in.

Looks like home. Homeless wandered the streets with torn clothes hanging off their bodies. They glared at us as we passed.

It was hard to accept that we couldn't do anything for these people. Our mission would bring us one step closer to ending the suffering in our own country, but that didn't make it any easier to drive past those men, women, and children. *Maybe one day we can fix this.*

Workers were also filing out of their houses, if you could call them that. Most of the buildings were little more than shacks that appeared from the outside to have no more than one or two rooms. The men and women hopped onto bikes and pedaled towards downtown along with us. Their clothes were better than those of the Enclave, but their faces were grim.

"This tears at my heart," Julia said as we passed a group of kids playing in the street. We could see every rib through their torn shirts.

"Is this what you wanted to see when you said we should

travel?" I replied. I hadn't traveled much, but everywhere I'd gone so far had been no better than the Twin Cities. Part of me doubted anywhere was.

Her eyes dropped. "There are beautiful parts of the world, even on our continent, yet the tragic elements are far too common. I see now that when we traveled as a family, we received a filtered view of the world beyond our borders and within."

Alex huffed. "Mom claimed she was protecting us."

"We realized far too late how much she used that claim to manipulate us," Julia replied, pinching the bridge of her nose. "With us blind, we could be her puppets, but that is over now."

In the distance, the skyscrapers of downtown Detroit came into view. Aaron had said that the tallest buildings formed a semicircle around the government's "Axle" along the bank of the Detroit River. *We're so close.*

The further we went into the city, the better the conditions became as the cyclists split off towards the cloud of factory smoke to the south and were replaced by nicer and nicer cars. Shoppers popped in and out of stores along the main strip. They all wore similar clothes to those that we saw in Rockford, but even without tags on their ears, it was still easy to tell the elites from those they considered lower. Certain women wore elaborate pieces of jewelry while men had an array of hats, the more elaborate seemingly representing status.

Kaja chuckled when she noticed the hats. "They're so stupid."

"They are very silly," Julia replied before glancing towards me. "You would look cute in one."

For a second, I tried to picture myself in an elaborate bowler cap and squirmed. "I'd go bald before wearing one of those."

Alex stuck her head between Julia and me. "We can make that happen."

"One of us has plenty of experience with that," Julia said with a smile, tapping the shaved side of her sister's head.

"Guys, look," I said as the car rolled to a stop. In front of us, a police cordon blocked the path to the river and the Axle.

A chorus of groans came from the back as Julia and I traded looks. "One of us needs to figure out what is happening," she said.

I nodded. "We can go. Jonah, stay back just in case something goes wrong."

"Is that the best strategy?" he asked.

Julia nodded to me, and I turned back to him. "Why wouldn't it be?" Before he could reply, I hopped out of the SUV and jogged towards the cordon with Julia.

The cops were already watching us. Considering we were driving a loud, shot up car missing half its windows, I couldn't blame them. Facing the police was my territory, and I could feel Julia's nerves as her hand gripped mine. I tried to flash her a reassuring smile, but her eyes were focused on the police ahead of us.

"Be careful," she whispered.

We approached a cop in the middle of the street and were greeted by his glare. "This area is off-limits to civilians. Go about your business elsewhere."

Julia batted her eyes at him, making my heart twinge. "May I ask why?"

"Foreign officials are visiting the Premier."

"From which country?"

"That is none of your business. Now leave."

"Do I not have the right to ask who is meeting with our leader?"

He stepped forward, towering over her. "Do I have to ask you again? I'd hate to ruin that pretty face."

Go to hell. I stepped between them, leaving only a couple inches between his face and mine. "Is curiosity illegal?"

Before I knew what happened, I was on the ground. Blood rushed from my nose. My head spun as Julia stepped forward, pleading with the officer. "Excuse my friend, officer. We have urgent business in the Axle."

He scoffed. "Ha! You?"

As I stumbled to my feet, she straightened her posture. "My name is Princess Julia Elizabeth Hughes, and I am here to request an audience with the Premier."

The cop lost it. Julia's fists clenched as he laughed hysterically. When he finally collected himself, he said, "That is the stupidest thing I've ever heard in my life. If you were a Northern Mississippi princess, why are you here when your mother is inside with the Premier?"

"My mother?" Julia's eyes were wide as we looked at each other in shock. *How did Vera know our plan?*

"Get out of here, kid."

I could only stand there like a wounded puppy as Julia stared him down. "No. You will allow us in. Look at my ring. Would a random civilian wear the ring of the royal family?"

The cop stepped back, mumbling to himself. "I, uh... Give me a sec."

While he scampered off, the fear from what he said started to set in. Julia paced, obviously agitated by the arrival of her mom.

"This is bad," I said with a groan. "If Vera is meeting with Taggart…"

"Then we are in extremely hot water. Why is she always so far ahead of us?" She groaned and tried to fix her matted hair. The other cops watched us while she pondered what to do. "We thought Mother wanted to use Huron to distract the Front, but she must be here to form an alliance. If she can blame the Front for the villa massacre, then Huron would have a weapon against them in the war. They will expose the Front's involvement while making Mother appear as a hero, not another perpetrator."

My mind was scattered. For days we'd traveled to get to this spot just to find it was all for nothing. We had only two options: run or face Vera. The choice was obvious. "Julia, you need to take her down. Expose her for the liar she is, and our plan stays the same."

She shook her head and stared back at our friends. In her eyes, I could see the determination of recent days fading, replaced by the fear of facing her mom. It was one thing to defy her support for Natasha, but now, we were standing in the way of her controlling Northern Mississippi. Vera killed hundreds and would slaughter more to achieve that goal. Julia was the only one who could beat her.

Her eyes flicked back to me. "I don't know if I can. Just look at me, I'm a disaster."

"I am looking at you, and all I can think is you're perfect. Forget the fancy distractions of the palace. This is life or death for thousands of people. They believe in you, the hundreds of Whites that supported you believe in you, and every single person in that shot up SUV back there believe in you. You told me last night that you finally felt like you were doing what you were meant to do. So do it. Show your mom she was wrong to control you, and show her how much she underestimated how strong you are."

A raspy breath escaped her lungs. "I will try."

My heart pounded in fear of what was ahead of us, but I meant every word that I said. I could break into a palace and rescue her, but only she could rescue our country. She had given me the confidence to become who I needed to be. Now, it was my turn to do the same for her.

We separated as Jonah and Alex approached, a curious look in their eyes. "What's the report?" Jonah asked.

Julia collected herself, shoving away her fear as ice returned to her eyes. She nodded towards the cop before replying, "Mother is here. We believe she is attempting to form an alliance with Premier Taggart against the Front, blaming the villa attack on them and coaxing Huron to respond."

"She stole our plan?" Alex said.

"Kinda, yes," I replied. "But if Julia can convince Taggart that Vera is lying, we can still end this."

Alex studied her sister. "Are you sure?"

"Yes." Julia glanced at me before returning her eyes to Alex. "Mother's schemes end now."

The cop returned, flanked by two of his partners. His hand shook as he removed his hat and bowed. "My apologies, m'lady. The Premier awaits your presence."

"Along with my guests," Julia replied, sweeping her arm towards us and the SUV.

He scowled. "As you wish."

I took her hand as Jonah waved for the rest of the group to follow, and together, we began our final march through the capital. The Axle was becoming visible now: a cylindrical glass-paned skyscraper so tall I had to squint to see the top of it. A voice in my head screamed for me to stop, to run away with Julia and never return, but there was no turning back now.

Julia whispered to me, her eyes fixed on the Axle, "I've been told that they built the city's streets so that from above they appear as the spokes of a wheel, with the Axle as, well, the axle of it. Even with Huron's poor management, the city is known for its stylish cars, as we've seen."

My mind flashed to the Minutemen car that now sat, destroyed back in Payne-Phalen. We both needed the distraction from the force we were about to face, but my chest ached. "I miss my car."

She furrowed her brow. "We can find you a new one after all of this."

"No. I'm gonna find it and fix it up. That car saved my life twice."

Alex appeared next to Julia. The look on her face was grim. "At least it can't be worse than the shitmobile."

Kaja replied from behind us, "Uh, it was pretty bad."

"Well, it's surely better than Huron's bureaucratic architecture. Seriously, who the hell would want *that* as their capitol building?" Alex quipped as she flung her arm towards the Axle.

"It's threatening. That's for sure," Manny replied as he gawked at it. "But the whole wheel thing is kinda cool, I think."

276

Tyler recoiled and signed something I didn't recognize. Alex noticed my confusion. "He said, 'They nuked people dumbass.'"

"Oh... right," Manny mumbled.

"Glad we're all in a good mood for the big face-off with the evil Queen," I said, trying to lighten the mood. In truth, I was scared out of my mind, and despite the joking distractions, so were they. I could see it in the way their eyes never left the Axle. This was far outside my comfort zone, and I'd spent the last nine or so months in the palace with the royals. For our new friends, this was unlike anything they'd ever faced. We were walking into the lion's den, and there was a real chance that we'd be eaten alive.

Grey bureaucrats gawked at us as we followed the cops down one of the spokes towards the Axle. *Why is it always grey? At least the UPF bothers to decorate a little.* From what I'd seen so far, Huron wasn't worried about hiding their brutality. Between Rockford and the outskirts of Detroit, people wore their toil. They didn't need tags to know they were slaves.

Even if we convinced Taggart of our plan, my stomach churned at the thought of working with Huron's elites. More likely than not, there were people just like me in Detroit, fighting for their lives. While they starved and died in combat, I strode with royalty to negotiate with their version of Bachton.

At the same time, I was fighting to protect the UPF from Vera's wrath. I would have hated myself for that a year ago. Now, I saw the little gives and takes, compromises and deals that would need to be made in the short run to save the country from bloodshed. I could swallow my pride if it meant saving the people I'd fought for my entire life.

As we approached the heart of the city, I felt every muscle in my body tense. In my mind, I fought off flashbacks of the bombing in front of our old capitol building and its bloody aftermath. Every time Delaware's broken, lifeless body appeared, my heart stopped. More than that, my body became numb as it faded into a void. That moment would never leave me, but I needed it to remind me to stay strong for her sake. She had sacrificed herself to stand against the monster that Vera and the UPF created. Even if this was Julia's fight to lead, I would make sure Delaware's loss was not in vain. I had new friends and adventures. It didn't feel right without her, though. *I miss you Del.*

The only thing keeping me sane was Julia by my side. I could feel her anxiety through our interlocked hands. I knew she could do it, but it felt wrong for the pressure to be on her. In life and death situations, it had always been me fighting to save those I loved. Not being the one leading the charge should have been a relief. Instead, I felt useless as Julia took the helm. If she failed, there was nothing I could do to protect us. *Do I fear losing control as much as Vera?*

Five golden doors marked the entrances to the Axle, one for each of the spokes. In front of it stood a statue of a man wielding a hammer alongside a car. At his feet was engraved, *When we build, we are free.* The grey-clad guards watched us closely, standing like statues as we approached.

After the cops handed us off, the guards gave each of us a pat-down. My fists clenched as they took my gun and knives. I hated the guard getting handsy with me enough, but when he started patting-down Julia, a fire lit inside me. I shoved him. "Back the hell up!"

"Ivan!" Julia shouted as the guards pulled their pistols.

Oh shit. There were at least a dozen guns pointed at my head. I felt each of them. Slowly, I raised my arms to show I wasn't a threat. It wasn't enough. The guard grabbed my shirt and threw me to the ground. I didn't resist, and a stabbing pain shot down my arm from my shoulder as I smacked into the pavement. I couldn't move it. *Screw these assholes.*

As much as I wanted to kick his ass, I couldn't risk Julia getting hurt. Tyler had more balls than me, though, and threw himself at the guard. They wrestled for a moment before Alex yanked him away, yelling for him to stop. He seethed as he looked from me to the guard. It was incredibly stupid, but I appreciated him fighting for me.

I could only watch from the ground as the guard spat out blood and put his gun to Tyler's temple. "Give me a reason not to kill you, boy." The gun didn't shake one bit.

Julia jumped between them, her eyes cold and sharp. "He cannot speak! Please, put the guns away. We mean you no harm, but is it necessary for two princesses to be searched so thoroughly? Are we not foreign dignitaries?"

It surprised me that she wouldn't accept the search for the sake of diplomacy. *Is she hiding something?* I struggled to my feet, gripping my shoulder. The guard wasn't messing around with that throw, and I could still barely raise my arm without screaming. My rage dulled the pain as I took my place next to Julia.

The guard's eyes flicked from Tyler to me and then to Julia. He swallowed, and for the first time, the gun wavered. *She beat him.*

After a few more seconds, he lowered the pistol. "Fine, but the rest must be searched."

Julia smiled. It wasn't her usual, sweet smile, but the cunning one of a victor. I liked her new bite. Her time trapped in the palace had ripped away much of her veil to reveal the witty and strong girl I knew. The guards finished their searches, and she turned to lead us through the doors. When her eyes met mine, a chill flew through my body. *Nothing can stop her now.*

Chapter 27

The only color inside the Axle came from the gold-rimmed portraits along the wall of the interior chamber, which also, unsurprisingly, was a circle. Each portrait framed one of the old premiers of Huron. Based on the number of them, their leaders tended not to last long. *Does the job kill them, or do their rivals?* The final portrait was of Nathanial Taggart himself. Compared to those before him, he was significantly younger, but it was hard to know if his quick rise to power was a good thing for him or not.

The windows allowed only a little natural light to creep into the otherwise dim building. Above us, dozens of identical floors stretched to the sky. With the boredom of the place, I began to wonder if the premiers didn't just kill themselves out of depression. I'd only been in the building for a minute, and I could feel it sucking away my soul.

Julia took a deep breath as a lanky man shuffled out of a wooden door across the inner circle from our entrance hall. *Vera is in there.* I clenched my fists as my heart pounded and heat rushed through my veins. *You can't kill her.*

The aide straightened his glasses before clearing his throat. "The Premier is currently in a meeting with a foreign diplomat. If you would not mind wait..."

"In fact, I would mind," Julia said before he could finish. She ran her hand along the railing in the center of the room. From behind her, I couldn't see expression, but he could, and fear crept across his face as she continued, "We have escaped captivity, traveled hundreds of miles across two countries, and survived an assault to meet with the Premier. If I remember correctly, he was quite eager for us to visit, and I can assure you that Premier Taggart will be intrigued by what I have to share with him."

The aide wrinkled his nose before letting out a deep sigh. "Very well. Please allow me one moment madam." He raced back across the inner circle and slid back into the room for only a few seconds before emerging again. As he paced back to us, he wiped the beads of sweat from his forehead with a handkerchief. "The Premier will see Princess Julia, Princess Alexandria, and er... Ivan Matelski now. The remaining members of your party will wait in our lounge."

Julia bowed her head. "Thank you, sir." She squeezed my hand before releasing it and gliding along the circle. Alex and I followed a few paces behind as my heart pounded like a drum in my chest.

Julia strode into the room ahead of us. When I entered behind Alex, the battle lines were drawn before a word was spoken. To my left, Vera paced like an impatient cat ready to pounce on its prey, her eyes fixed on Julia. The stares alone sent goosebumps down my arms. Hit with the gravity of the situation, I found my-self frozen not far beyond the door.

On the far end of the room, Nathanial Taggart sat at a simple wooden desk decorated with nothing but the scattered papers of an overworked government official. Behind him was a glass wall, revealing a view of the Detroit River and the tip of Canada. With the overcast sky, a shroud was cast over him.

Julia waved with her eyes for me to join her and Alex across from Vera. I forced my legs to move as Taggart pushed himself to his feet and surveyed the room. *What did Vera tell him?* After straightening his tie, he ran his hand through the Huron flag alongside his desk. "I would say it is a pleasure to see you all again, but under the circumstances, I cannot."

"I must apologize for our condition," Julia said as she looked down at her tattered clothes before meeting Taggart's gaze again. "Over the past few days, we have traveled quite a long way and survived several attacks."

Vera glared at me. "Trouble always seems to find you when Ivan is around."

I scoffed and replied, trying to hold in my anger, "We can handle trouble, just like we handled Demetri."

"He brags about murdering my chief of security, who I sent to ensure the safe return of my daughters after Ivan kidnapped them."

Julia stepped forward. "Ivan did not kidnap us, Mother. You did."

Alex followed suit. "And he didn't kill Demetri. I did."

"You did what?" Vera replied with a gasp.

"Enough!" Taggart's voice echoed through the room, stopping us all in our tracks. "What are you accusing the Queen of?"

Julia took a deep breath before replying, "Following the assault on the villa, that I am certain we are all aware of, Ivan attempted to bring my sister and me to safety in a St. Paul safehouse. Along the way, Mother's soldiers slammed a military vehicle into our truck, kidnapped us, and left Ivan to die. Luckily, he was found by a mutual friend who nursed him back to health. In the meantime, Mother detained us within the palace, cutting off our contact with the world outside and threatening the lives of those we cared about if we talked. A few days ago, Ivan rescued our friends and us from the palace. We believed that coming to you was the only way to prevent a war and expose the truth of who conducted the attack on the villa."

Vera fumed as Taggart drummed his fingers on his leg. After a few moments, he sighed. "Let me guess; you wish to accuse Queen Vera of causing the incident?"

"Precisely, in coordination with the People's Front to eliminate their rivals."

"Hmm. Yes, unfortunately, your mother has explained to me that she anticipated you coming to me with these wild accusations." Julia's eyes widened as he crossed his arms and continued, "It's cunning of a girl who wanted to be queen herself to defame the one person who stands in her way. I'm curious why you would protect the Front when you've spoken so provocatively against them."

A grin worked its way across Vera's face as she strode across the room and took Julia's hands in hers. "I do not know what your Red boyfriend has been telling you, but it was not I who kidnapped you. Ivan violated his orders when he decided to take the two of you to a location unknown to the royal guard. He placed your lives in danger. If it was not for the actions of my guardsmen, the Front's men could have captured you, or worse."

I clenched my fist. *Don't do it.*

Before Julia could reply, Alex lost her cool. "Liar! All you've done is endanger us all in your plots for the crown. Ivan saved us from *you*."

Vera's eyes dropped as she let out a sigh. "What have I done to you to earn your anger? I know it has been hard losing your father and Helena, but we are a family, and no matter what, we stick together."

"Do family members lie to one another and scheme beyond each other's backs?" Julia replied, ripping her hands from her mom's grasp and standing her ground. "From the beginning, it was never about family. We were nothing but pawns in your game, and I have had enough. I don't need your approval anymore."

Taggart cleared his throat. "As much as I enjoy watching your family drama, I have a country to run, and due to the Front's actions, a war to prepare for." He rounded his desk and took his seat once again. "Queen Vera, I look forward to our alliance bearing fruit over the coming months."

Shit. He didn't believe us, and if Julia couldn't change his mind fast, we were doomed. Vera paced over to the Premier's desk as Julia pulled a cell phone from her pocket. "I have proof that implicates my mother in the attack." She smirked. "Would you like to hear it?"

Hear what?

Vera spun back around, her eyes fierce. "Nonsense. She has nothing but fabricated lies and…"

Taggart's hand shot up to silence her. She didn't appreciate that, and her tongue clicked as he spoke to Julia, "Please, continue."

"Thank you," Julia replied with a nod of her head. "The following is a video of Demetri revealing both Mother and the Front's involvement in the plot while holding a gun to the head of our former head of security."

I resisted the urge to laugh as she turned the phone towards them and played the video. My voice came through first, "Why'd you do it? All those people at the villa… You helped kill them."

Demetri's chuckle sent a shiver down my spine. "No innocents died that night. The blood spilled was tainted with greed and corruption." Taggart's brow furrowed as Demetri's voice continued, "My job is to serve the Queen. She and the Front wished to purify the elites of the rot. The princesses would have been safe if you had not intervened."

"That's enough!" Taggart yelled, his jaw clenched as his face burned red.

I grinned in pride. From Julia's angle, Demetri hadn't seen her, and I had been too focused on the gun to Jonah's head to realize what she was doing. *Glad I asked that question. She's a genius.*

Shock covered Vera's face. "This changes nothing about our agreement."

Julia ignored her. "Sir, are you truly willing to ally with a woman who defamed your nation in the pursuit of personal power? If you cannot trust her to tell the truth about this, how can you trust her when the lives of your men and women in uniform are on the line?"

He wavered, drumming his fingers on the desk in thought. "I

am sorry, but the Queen is right. The People's Front still intends to attack us, and an alliance in the best way to ensure the security of Huron."

Oh come on! I rolled my eyes and huffed in frustration. We were wrong; Taggart was no better than the tyrants that ruled before him. Like Bachton and Timothy I, II, and III, he was afraid of losing the power he had. *Coward.* While Taggart was not the one who covered up the nuclear test in Rockford, he had no ideals. For the sake of political power, he would have done the same thing. Whatever Vera had offered him blinded him to the fact she would stab him in the back if he ever stood in her way.

"She promised Chicago to you, did she not?" Julia replied, raising an eyebrow. *She's onto something.*

"She did."

Vera scoffed. "Are you actually listening to her?"

"Do I have a reason not to? I made a promise to my people and my party that there would be changes, and as their leader, I am expected to hear all the facts before making a decision." *Maybe I was wrong about him.* He turned his head back towards Julia. "Do you have a better offer for me?"

Vera fumed. "My daughter is not in a position to make an offer. The royal army is under *my* command, and I am the Queen."

"Not for long," Alex quipped back.

"Alex..." Julia whispered with a nudge.

"The Royal Council has made their decision," Vera replied. "If you would like to challenge their authority, you will not do so as a member of my family."

Without hesitation, Alex flung her family ring at her mom's

feet. Metal rang against stone as it skidded across the floor. "Fine! Take my damn ring. It doesn't mean anything anymore. You destroyed our family."

If I didn't know better, I would have thought she stabbed Vera in the heart. The Queen recoiled and gawked at her rogue daughter. *How did she not see this coming?* Alex glared back, her breaths heavy and her shoulders hunched. With the burn still exposed on the side of her head and her temper flaring, she was the opposite of her mom: a powerful force that had just been unshackled.

Julia was not so rash. She froze, her fingers closing around her own ring. It was just a symbol, but it represented everything she had cared for her entire life. In my heart, I was afraid as she was. I never had a family, so I understood how hard it was for her to turn her back on hers. I put my hand on her shoulder. "You don't have to do it."

A shaky breath left her lips. "I'm sorry, Mother." She pulled the ring from her finger and dropped it. It clattered to the floor as Julia wiped a stray hair from her face. "I pray God forgives you for all you have done, but you cannot save our country."

Vera's voice cracked as she struggled to find a response. None came.

Julia stepped towards the Premier. "If you agree to assist us, I promise that you will have Chicago without bloodshed. There is no need for a war between Northern Mississippi and Huron for us to find a resolution."

"And how, exactly, do you intend to make that happen?" he replied.

"With my mother's key to the emergency broadcast network,

we will play this video and deliver a message to the people of our country. The Front will be unable to deny their involvement in the plot, and the Royal Council shall have no choice but to strip Mother of her crown. A new election will be held, one that I intend to win. With the royal army on our side and the people rising up against the Front's tyranny, we will remove them from power. Unlike my mother and the Front, I have no affiliations with the Chicago Union, and I have no intention of protecting a government that cooperated with her plot to kill Ivan."

She glanced back at me, her eyes soft for only a second before the determination returned. Somehow, it looked like she had outmaneuvered her mother at her own game, but Vera was not finished. "Every word she speaks is slander! Do you not see, Nicholas, that she wants the throne at any cost? If she is willing to cast her family aside, what will she do to you when you are the next dictator standing in her way?"

"Dictator?" Taggart asked, popping out of his seat. "Those are strong words for a woman with your reputation. Frankly, I don't care about either of your domestic policies. I see one plan that involves a massive and expensive war and another that doesn't. Unless there is anything else, your highness, I believe we are finished."

Vera gasped. "You will regret this decision."

She turned to leave but stopped as Julia spoke, "I have one more condition."

With a sigh, Taggart replied, "What is it?"

"I ask that you visit the city of Rockford. The western portion of the city has suffered for decades after your predecessors bombed it to cover up a nuclear weapons test that leaked radiation into the air. Nothing can rectify what happened there, but if you truly wish to prove that you are different, try. Stepping outside the royal walls opened my eyes to the reality of my country; I hope this can do the same for you."

He glanced at Vera before turning to gaze out the windows. "I have read about those tests, but I cannot reveal the mistakes of our country's past."

Julia stepped towards him. "I understand that your position does not allow you to do such a thing. All I ask is that you see it for yourself so that, perhaps in time, your people may heal."

"Very well," he replied, his eyes softening for a second. "It cannot hurt to visit the city."

"Thank you," Julia said.

With a scoff, Vera started towards the door again, but he interrupted her, "I believe you owe your daughter a key."

"I do not have it in my possession," Vera replied, her eyes fixed on her daughters. "How unfortunate."

Julia swiftly closed the distance between them and ripped the golden necklace from around Vera's neck. *What is she doing?* She threw the necklace on the ground and stomped on it before reaching down and picking up a flash drive from the shards. "The monarch always carries the key on their person in case of emergencies."

With her fists clenched, Vera spat, "This is not over," and stormed out of the room, leaving the four of us behind in silence.

Panic flooded through me. "You're just going to let her go?"

Taggart shook his head. "No."

290

Vera stumbled back into the room, flanked by two Huron guards. "Target has been apprehended, sir," one of them said.

"Take her to a holding cell until she can be returned to Minneapolis with her daughters," Taggart said.

"The Council will not tolerate this!" Vera yelled, fighting against the guards.

He sat behind his desk once again. "That is none of my concern. Guards, remove her."

She glared at us as the guards dragged her away, and I grinned as I watched them go. Julia's eyes remained fixed on the door before her eyes flicked to the drive. As she examined it, I couldn't help but smile. *She did it.*

Julia glanced over her shoulder at me before turning to face the Premier. As she bowed, she said, "I must apologize for burdening you with the conflicts within our family."

Taggart leaned forward against his desk. "No apology is needed as long as you deliver on your promise. What do you need from me to ensure this happens?"

She released a deep breath before moving to my side and slipping her hand into mine. Both of us trembled as we clung to each other for dear life. I could feel her pain as she mourned the loss of her family. Behind her face of stone, she wept. The purest woman I'd ever met lost her dad, her little sister, and now her mom. All she'd ever wanted to do was make them proud and be the perfect princess. Those dreams were gone now.

She pondered for a moment before replying, "All that will be required is a computer, a camera, a place to film, and a flight back to Minneapolis tonight."

"It will be done."

I squeezed her hand and took a deep breath, releasing the tension that had gripped my body. "Let the fun begin."

Chapter 28

Manny jumped to his feet when he saw us and nearly tripped over himself sprinting to us. "You're alive!"

I chuckled and glanced at Julia. A sense of calm had returned to her, but she hadn't released my hand since we'd left Taggart's office. I wasn't complaining. "You know Vera wasn't shooting at us, right?"

Alex huffed. "It felt like she was, but she didn't see Jules coming. When she played that video, oh, you guys should have seen the look on her face."

"Why didn't you tell me about it?" I asked Julia.

She shrugged. "The more people that knew, the more likely my phone was to be confiscated. Besides, I wasn't sure we needed it until the situation became desperate."

We turned our heads as Tyler struggled out of the lounge chair he'd been napping in to run and hug Alex. *Cute.* She blushed and returned it.

From down the hall, we'd already seen Jonah pacing back and forth across the room. During the commotion with the boys, he had been waiting patiently to speak. "What video?"

"The one Jules took while the brute had a gun to your head," Alex replied with her arm around Tyler. "It was the perfect distraction, so well done."

"Happy to help, I guess. How did the meeting go?"

Julia squeezed my hand, which I took as instructions to reply while she processed what had happened. "Julia was amazing! She convinced Taggart to work with us, and Vera ran away in tears." She rolled her eyes. "Fine, she wasn't crying, but she sure as hell knew we beat her."

"Impressive," he replied before flashing a smile at Julia.

She struggled to return it. "This may be a victory, but we're not finished yet."

"Wow, normally I'm the downer," Alex said with a huff.

I squeezed Julia's hand tighter. "Vera could have ruined everything, but you stopped her. The video will end this."

She let out a sigh. "We can only hope. The Premier is preparing the room for us now."

Jonah nodded. "Then we should make our way there. Do we all understand the plan?"

"Cut off our tags, say why, tell everyone to meet at the capitol building, and flip off the UPF," I said with a smirk. Even after Julia's encouragement, I was scared to remove my tag. My legs were weak just thinking about it, and my hands hadn't stopped sweating since we'd entered the building. It felt like I was about to amputate a limb, not remove an earring. My tag had defined me for my entire life, whether it was black or red, but it was time for me to move on. I took a deep breath. *If Julia could do that, you can do this.*

"Correct, as long as you don't do the last bit," Jonah replied.

Julia reached out her hand to Lillian. "Then we must prepare. Shall we inspect our studio?"

Lillian nodded, and they linked arms before leading the group through the halls. With Julia's hand no longer in mine, I felt alone. *Come back.*

Jonah hung back with me while the others marched ahead. "You alright?"

I faked a smile. "Yeah, I'll be fine."

"You are a terrible liar."

"I dunno. It's gotten me this far."

He chuckled and glanced ahead at the rest of the group. "You know, I don't want to do this either. I'm risking Christina's life on top of everything I've worked for, but it is the right thing."

Then why is this so hard? I watched Julia powering ahead, a train of followers behind her. If she wasn't before, she became a queen that day. She'd defeated her fears. I hid behind mine. "It feels wrong, but those assholes killed Delaware. I'd rip the damn thing out if it would end this."

"Don't do that. We need a halfway-decent looking king." He grinned. "I've believed in Julia ever since I joined the royal guard, but she can't do this alone. All of us will be there to support her, but you are going to be the one by her side. I hope you're ready for that."

I shook my head. "I doubt I'll ever be ready, but I'll do what I have to."

"Good. And remember that you are not alone either. We are here because of you just as much as her. Don't forget that."

He patted me on the shoulder and trudged ahead, leaving me behind to make a decision. *There's no choice. I'm not a Red. I'm not Ivan 1813715. I'm Ivan Matelski, and I won't let a color define me.* My tag felt cool against my fingers as I spun it. It was not part of me. It was a parasite that needed to be cut out.

My lungs struggled for air as I jogged to catch up to the rest of the group. I grasped Julia's hand, and we traded smiles. *Everything will be okay.* For the first time in forever, I actually believed that thought. After years of suffering and months of pain and loss, things were finally starting to look up. I had a girl better than I could have dreamed of, Vera was all but defeated, and we were approaching a position to challenge the UPF. We had lost so many people along the way, but their deaths were not in vain. Because of them, we could free our people from their chains. Soon, the colors would be gone. Julia and I would be able to live our lives and travel the world like she wanted. My anxieties faded with the thought of exploring with her.

"London," I whispered to her.

"What?"

"You said on the plane to Chicago that you want to travel the world. I never knew where before, but I think I'd want to go to London, as long as you came with me."

She bit her lip. "I would love that. I have never been to London, but Father always said that Buckingham Palace is beautiful. Visiting it with you would be a dream come true."

"Then it's a date," I replied with a smile.

Behind us, Kaja groaned. "Get a room."

I stuck my tongue out at her, and she did the same to me. Julia chuckled. "Behave children."

"Ouch," I said, rubbing my arm like she'd punched me.

She rolled her eyes and smiled as we reached the room that Taggart's people had prepared. Like the rest of the Axle, it was dull and grey. Two aides positioned a camera facing an empty wall. Behind them, another was seated at a wooden desk, typing away at a computer. *Not much, but it's all we need.*

I took a deep breath as Julia handed the key to the aide at the computer. That little flash drive would get us access to every screen in Northern Mississippi. There was nothing the UPF could do to silence us now. The aide's screens flicked for a moment before code flashed across the center monitor. A few seconds later, there was nothing but a black screen with text asking for the password.

What password? The key was supposed to be all we needed. My heart sank as I looked at Julia for an answer, but her eyes were wide. "I... I don't know. Alex?"

Alex groaned and shook her head. "Mom never told me anything about a password."

"Shit," I spat while I paced. *Nothing's easy.*

"I know it." We all sighed in relief as Jonah approached the computer and studied the screen. "It was partially my responsibility to send out an emergency royal message. I needed to know it in case the monarch became incapacitated. Hopefully, they haven't changed it."

He typed the password and hit enter. The monitors went blank. "Damn it!" Alex yelled. "Why does she ruin everything?"

Julia held up her hand. "Wait."

As if on command, the screens flickered back to life. I sprinted over and wrapped up Jonah in a hug. "I'm so glad you didn't die!"

"Thanks..." he replied, chuckling.

Alex crossed her arms. "Huh. Well done, Jonah."

"That's possibly the nicest thing you have ever said to me," he replied with a cheeky smile.

"Don't get used to it."

Julia held back a laugh and spoke to the aide, "Are we all set?"

He nodded. "We are ready to broadcast when you are."

I took a deep breath. "Here we go."

We lined up along the wall. Julia stood in the center with me to her right and Alex to her left. In her hands, she spun her family ring, but she'd done the hard part already. For her, this was just symbolic now. Before we started, one of the aides handed me a pair of clippers. *Last chance to back out.*

The aide signaled to his counterpart behind the camera. "When the red light turns on, you're live."

Julia nodded. "Thank you, sir."

"Ready?" I whispered to her.

"I feel as if everything has led to this moment," she replied with fire in her eyes. "I am ready. Thank you, Ivan, for everything."

I smiled as she wiped a stray hair from her face. She was about to be on every screen in the country without her usual makeup and fancy clothing, but she didn't need any of it. Julia was a queen, a leader. People followed her because of who she was, not how she appeared.

The aide behind the camera gave a thumbs up, and in a flash, the red light lit up. My chest instantly tightened. *Holy shit. Everyone can see us right now.* I took a deep breath. *Stay calm.*

Julia stood tall and spoke, looking directly at the camera, "Good morning. My name is Princess Julia Hughes, and I am here with my friends in Detroit, the capital of the People's Republic of Huron. In the past few days, we escaped from captivity in the palace and traveled across both Northern Mississippi and Huron to expose the truth of what happened at the Patterson villa. We have been lied to by the Queen and the General Secretary. They told us that Huron wished to eliminate the elites of our country and destabilize us from within, but instead, we discovered that the attack was a plot crafted by both my mother and the General Secretary to eliminate their political rivals and create an excuse for war."

She paused and nodded to the aide behind the computer before speaking again, "The following video was taken after Demetri, the Queen's head of security, along with multiple other royal guardsmen, attempted to kill my friends in an attempt to capture both my sister and myself."

The clip played, and I reached for Julia's hand while it did. For a moment, her fingers locked with mine. Then, the video ended, and she released them again. "This plot has been the culmination of their plan to eliminate those they consider their enemies within both the elite and Red populations. From my father's assassination to the rise of the Fracture: all of it was orchestrated to allow my mother to become queen and for the Front to purge anyone who dared to oppose them." She took a sharp breath. "It is time to end the corrupt system of lies that has enslaved us all. The Front has used the Prism to divide us, and now the Queen has assisted in their crimes against humanity. It ends now."

Julia slid her ring off her finger and examined it for a moment. "I refuse to be loyal to a system that divides us, allowing for the powerful and corrupt to remain in control while thousands starve and are slaughtered." She dropped the ring and waited to continue until it had clattered to the floor, sending a ringing echoing through the room. "Today, I renounce my loyalty to the royal Hughes family and declare my intention to take the White Crown, not as queen of the royals, but as queen of all the people of Northern Mississippi. It is time for the people to have a voice."

She glanced at her sister, who stepped forward and dropped her ring. "My name is Princess Alexandria Hughes, and I, too, renounce my loyalty to the Hughes family."

Julia's eyes switched to me. *My turn.* I stepped forward. My hand shook as I gripped the clippers. It took me a couple seconds to find my words, but I let out a raspy breath and stared into the camera. "My name is Ivan Matelski. The UPF and their Prism stole everything from me, and I've lived my life in chains like so many other Reds. I grew up as an orphaned slave, barely surviving every day. I've worked in the steel mills, burning my hands to get my rations. I've seen the horrors inside the work camps. I heard the screams of the innocent dying in front of the old capitol building. And I held my best friend's charred body after she killed the leader of the Fracture. Bachton and Vera are two sides of the same poisoned coin that I have fought against my entire life. They've held the shackles on all of us. Today, I declare independence."

My hand was numb as I held the clippers to my tag. Fire raced through my veins. I wasn't afraid. I was angry. All the pain I'd experienced flashed through my mind. I hated Vera. I hated Bachton. Finally, we were getting revenge.

I took a deep breath and squeezed. There was a *click,* and I watched my tag fall to the floor. It rattled for a moment before laying still. I stared down at it. *Ivan 181375. No.* I rubbed my heel into it and raised my head once again. "I am not a Red. I am not Ivan 181375. I am a free person, and I will never again be enslaved."

Julia gave me a closed-mouth smile, her eyes full of pride. All I wanted to do was feel my ear. The weight from the tag was gone, and it felt weird. The physical weight was small, but the emotional one was massive. *I'm free.*

Jonah took the clippers and stepped to my side. "My name is Jonah Clarke, former chief of the royal guard, and I am not a Blue." His tag dropped to the floor. "Ivan and I are equals, and the Prism cannot change that."

Julia nodded. "We are all equals."

He replied with a smile as our four friends repeated the process: saying their names before clipping their tags. In front of us was an array of colors. The symbols of our slavery were laid out before us. It was that simple.

When they were done, Julia spoke again, "This evening, we will meet at the steps of the old capitol building and show the Front that we will be trifled with no longer. Not more than a few weeks ago, we lost too many friends and loved ones at that spot, but tonight it will be where we make a new beginning. Together, we can save our country. God bless all of you, and I await our meeting tonight."

The light flicked off again, and in a flash, it was over. I grabbed my tag and ran my fingers along its numbers. It felt like I was staring my old life dead in the eyes, but it was hard to mourn it now that I was free.

When I looked up, Julia's eyes met mine. She smiled. "You did it."

I glanced around the room to see the whole group watching me, and I closed my hand around the tag before sliding it into my pocket. "We all did it."

"What now?" Tyler signed.

"We go back to St. Paul and rally the people," Julia replied. "Now that we need not worry about our phones being traced, I can contact the Royal Council along the way. They will provide transportation and security, our mother will be detained, and a new election will be held."

"And you will be queen," I said.

Julia blushed. "Perhaps if all goes well. Duke Bilgram cannot be underestimated, even after spending time in hiding from my mother."

Alex jumped forward and threw her arm around her sister. "Long live the queen!"

"Long live the queen!" we all shouted in reply as Julia couldn't hold back her smile. This was her time to shine, and she deserved it. There would be a clash between the UPF and the people when we returned, but they'd been exposed. For the first time, we would have the upper hand. *Time to go home.*

Chapter 29

My second time on a plane was better than the first. Taggart had extended us the "diplomatic courtesy" of flying us back home, and we were approaching the end of our short flight. While I stared out the window at the clouds passing by, Julia prepared a speech for the crowd in front of the old capitol. Her eyes were narrow and fixed on the sheet in front of her as she huffed.

"Want some help?" I asked her.

"No." She groaned. "Why is this so difficult?"

"Maybe you're forcing it?"

"What do you mean by that?"

"You didn't write out your speech in front of the cameras ahead of time, and that was awesome. Why would you do it now?"

She pursed her lips and stared at the seat in front of her. "Because this is different. There will be a crowd of people looking at me to inspire them—to be their leader. When the electors meet, I will become queen of the royals, but tonight I must become queen of the people."

I took her hand and kissed it. "You won't be alone up there. All the people want to hear is your honest call for their freedom. You have given them hope already."

Tears ran down her cheeks. "I miss my kitten," she said before chuckling and wiped them away. "Mother has probably treated

Hope terribly."

A *ding* rang through the plane before a voice came over the speaker telling us if we don't buckle up, we'll die on the runway or something like that.

"Hope will be fine," I said with a smile. "If anything can fight a black widow, it's a cat."

"I hope so."

Outside the window, St. Paul was in view, rubble and all. People were gathering in preparation for the speech, but the craters from the airstrikes were visible, still scarring the city. That day seemed like it was a year ago, not a few weeks. The mall in front of the old capitol was bare now, but I could still picture the bodies thrown across it and the screams of the injured piercing the air. I shuddered. That day would never leave me. Neither would the image of Delaware's burned corpse. I laid my head back against the seat. *I miss you Del.*

Less than a minute later, we were on the ground. *Thank God.* The ride may have been better than my first, but I still hated flying. The pressure in my ears, the noise, the constant rocking, I hated all of it. Julia noticed my discomfort and pulled me to my feet. "Let's get you to solid ground."

With the rest of the group, we shuffled our way through the plane. I was excited to be home, but when I stepped onto the stairs out of the plane, my heart pounded. Under the lights, UPF soldiers and jeeps lined the runway. A row of royal guardsmen on each side was the only thing keeping them from us. Shouting filled the air as soldiers and guardsmen ordered each other to move away. *We're on the brink of war.*

"We need to get to the car," I said, leading Julia down the stairs. With so much on the line, all I could do was move forward to avoid panicking. Huron gave me my weapons back after leaving the Axle, but I'd brought knives to a gunfight. The situation was ready to explode if we didn't hurry. Jonah and I shielded Julia as we raced through the pathway to a black convoy of SUVs waiting for us on the other end of the runway.

Soldiers yelled at us to stop, their faces red in anger, but we pushed forward. Blue-clad royal guardsmen pushed back the soldiers and raised their rifles as our aisle thinned. *Just keep moving.* I held onto Julia with everything I had. Someone fell into our path. A shot rang out. I covered Julia's head as a scream pierced my ears. Another shot followed. My veins burned. *We're so close.*

We jumped over a fallen guardsman and took off at a sprint, but a soldier grabbed onto Julia, ripping her off her feet. I pulled a knife and sliced at his arm. He cried out, and she slid from his grasp.

"C'mon!" I pulled her back to her feet. Chaos surrounded us. Flames burned my mind. *Go.* I gripped onto Julia and barged forward through the scrum. Soldiers tried to stop us. I threw them aside.

We reached the car, and I glanced back, my body trembling as Julia climbed inside. A guardsman and soldier both lay dead in a growing circle of crimson. Both sides wavered at the sight, unsure what to do now. No one knew. If this was the next civil war, they would be the first deaths.

The rest of the group reached us and climbed in behind me. "Go!" I shouted. The chauffeur floored it, and soon the scene was nothing but a scuffle in the rearview mirror. Behind us was a convoy of other SUVs, likely full of other guardsmen.

"That was too close," Jonah said with a shaky breath. "Did they actually shoot at a princess?"

I shook my head as my heart's pounding deafened me. "I don't know, but we're on the edge of a civil war. Bachton's vulnerable, and he knows it."

Kaja's mouth had been open since she'd gotten in the car, but she finally seemed to gain some awareness. "That was insane!"

Manny shuddered. "Some of us aren't so excited about getting shot at." He rubbed his stomach where the military shot him in our escape from the capitol.

"I am just happy everyone is alright," Julia replied with a raspy breath.

I sighed. "Not everyone. At least one guard and soldier are dead."

"Damn..." Alex muttered as she glanced back at the airport.

Julia's head dropped into her hands. "Did we fail already?"

"No," I replied. "We stopped one war; we can stop another. The pressure on the UPF is growing. They'll break soon."

Alex scoffed. "When tyrants break, they go down shooting."

I didn't have a response to that. *She's right.* The UPF had held onto power through fear and control. Why would they be any different in their final moments? Everything we'd done had been to avoid another war, but no matter what we did, it felt like we were sliding into one anyway. I reached for the tag in my pocket, and my rage kept burning. "If they start a war, then we have to finish it."

Julia swallowed, and that icy glare returned to her eyes. "I do not wish for war, but you are right. We must first attempt to break them with political pressure and diplomacy. We will use every means possible to avoid further conflict. If all else fails, though, we must be prepared to defend our people." She turned back to face Jonah. "We will need a dedicated leader of our army."

He nodded. "It would be an honor, your highness."

"Stop it," she replied with a smirk. "To all of you, I will always be Julia. No crown can change the friendships we have built."

I bowed my head. "Yes, my queen."

She jabbed my arm. "How did I know you would say that?"

"We hang out too much."

"You can say that again," Alex replied.

We pulled off the highway into downtown St. Paul, and when the crowd appeared, my jaw dropped. Thousands of people crowded not just the mall in front of the capitol, but also the surrounding streets throughout downtown. All we could do was watch in awe as their chants echoed through the city. *They came.*

The protestors weren't alone, though. Black-caps in riot gear and soldiers were everywhere, encircling the crowd and blocking our path. They clashed with the people on the outer rim, throwing them to the ground and raising their rifles.

I clenched my fists. "They're going to kill them."

"No, they won't," Jonah replied. "Look."

The rest of the convoy joined us, and blue-clad guardsmen poured out of each SUV, rushing to defend the crowd. I opened the door to follow them, but Julia grabbed my hand. "It's time."

I squeezed her hand, and we stepped outside. Everywhere I

looked, guardsmen and protestors fought with soldiers and police. Shouting and chanting cut through the night. I pulled a knife and held it up my sleeve. My muscles tensed, but for some reason, Julia was composed. Her eyes focused on the capitol building before she checked that the rest of the group was behind us.

"You okay?" I asked her.

She took a deep breath and ran her fingers along the bracelet I'd given her. "No matter what happens today, I love you, Ivan."

"I love you too."

"Let's go." She pushed forward, towards the crowd.

I ran to catch up with her while Jonah called from behind us, "Julia! We need to wait for the guardsmen to clear a path... Julia, stop!"

"There isn't time," she replied, still charging forward. Her hand slid into mine as we walked together into the chaos.

The rest of the group caught up, and Alex scowled at the guardsmen. "It's ironic how quick they go from imprisoning us to protecting us."

"The Council instructed them to do so. They are soldiers doing their duty," Julia said. "Loyalty is fickle."

"That's why I don't trust soldiers," I replied.

Jonah huffed. "Thanks."

"No problem."

As we approached, the crowd realized who we were, and with the guardsmen's help, they held open a pathway for us. We strode through the crowd as people shook our hands and cheered for Julia as we passed by. With no light to guide us but the moonlight and the flashlights on peoples' cell phones, I could still see the tags on peoples' ears. Reds, Oranges, Yellows, and even a few Greens and Blues were in the crowd, their eyes eager to see Julia. As I watched their faces, my hand drifted to my naked ear. I still saw the Reds as my people, but I wasn't a Red anymore. After tonight, neither would they.

The shouts of the soldiers faded as we crossed the mall. Instead of grass beneath our feet, there was ash from the Fracture's fires and the UPF's bombing. My breaths became weak as I remembered that day. Around us, the destruction was still everywhere. St. Paul, my city, looked like a post-apocalyptic hellscape, and that alone tore at my heart. People had abandoned it, but Julia brought them back. Life had returned to the forgotten twin.

We climbed the steps of the old capitol. I glanced up at the headless statue of Law, where I'd stood to stop Max's destruction. If the airstrike had been much closer, I would have died on that pedestal, but instead, I'd risen from the ashes of those flames.

We turned to face the crowd, and the flashbacks raced through my head. But instead of fire, I was greeted by the lights of the crowd's phones. They were taking videos. *Everyone will see this.* We marched on the same spot as the Fracture, but they sought to burn, we'd come to rebuild.

Julia glanced at me and then her sister with a smile. The shouts of the crowd died to a strained silence. In the moonlight, she almost seemed to glow as she spoke, "I am touched that so many of you answered our call this evening, for tonight marks a new beginning for our country. Tonight, we cast aside the divides that the Front has forced upon us for a hundred years and step forward into our future, where we are free to choose our own path.

In the American Declaration of Independence, Thomas Jefferson wrote 'that all men are created equal, that they are endowed by their Creator with certain unalienable Rights, that among these are Life, Liberty and the pursuit of Happiness.' Those that came before us and those that govern us now failed to uphold those words. I promise you that as your queen, I will protect the rights of all our people, no matter their color, their race, or their background. I may stand before you labeled as a princess, but being born to a royal family does not make me any better than any of you. Join us in removing the symbols of our enslavement to the Front's failed system. See that a color does not define who you are."

The crowd cheered as she paused and smiled. People pulled out scissors, knives, and clippers to cut off their tags, and cheers echoed through the mall each time another person removed theirs and held it up like a trophy. As I watched, I found my breaths becoming shorter as tears ran down my face. Where there had been Reds, Oranges, Yellows, Greens, and Blues before, there were now people—individuals not defined by the UPF's labels. It was the first time in my life that I saw a tagless crowd of non-royals, and it was one of the most beautiful things I'd ever seen.

When most of the crowd had removed their tags, I stepped forward and shouted, "Long live Queen Julia, queen of the free people!" before kneeling next to her.

That caught her off guard, and she gasped as Alex followed my lead. Soon, people in the crowd began echoing my call and kneeling themselves.

Julia said on the plane that tonight she had to become the people's queen, and I made sure that was a formal declaration. I was proud of her. The girl I met only eight months before would not have stood in front of a crowd, calling for revolution. In the time since then, she had become the leader Northern Mississippi needed. Her mom sought the crown to bolster her own pride, but Julia stood in front of a crowd dressed in tattered and torn clothing. She was already a greater queen than Vera could have ever been.

She reached down and pulled me to my feet. "Thank you, Ivan, but you should never kneel to me." She gazed at our entire group before speaking to the crowd. "None of you should kneel to me. Whether I wear a crown or not changes nothing. We are equals, and you will all be welcome into my palace as such."

The crowd rose as Julia turned to Alex. "Let's go home."

Chapter 30

With the speech finished, the crowd began to disperse. Lillian watched them anxiously. "How are we going to escape? The soldiers are everywhere."

I smirked. "It's dark, so if we hurry, we can use the crowd to blend in. Split up in pairs and meet back up at the SUV." I grabbed Julia's hand and met her eyes. "C'mon."

We bolted down the steps and merged into the mass of people. At first, they tried to make space for us, but I waved for them to come closer as we made our way back towards the convoy. Ahead of us, soldiers scuffled with the crowd as they tried to arrest as many people as possible. It was useless. There were thousands of us, and with the help of the royal guardsmen, the soldiers were overwhelmed by the crowd.

With Julia's hand in mine, we rushed through the soldiers' lines. One of them noticed us and tried to get in our way, but I lowered my shoulder and knocked him down. The SUV was just steps away. There was no way I'd let them stop us now.

Jonah, Manny, Kaja, and Lillian were already waiting for us in the SUV when we arrived. I ducked my head in and asked, "Where's Tyler and Alex?"

Jonah shrugged. *Shit.* Around us was nothing but the skirmish that had become downtown St. Paul. Blue-clad guardsmen fought with the green and black mesh of soldiers and police.

Shots rang out from across the mall, and all hell broke loose. The crowd's trickle turned into a flood as frantic men, women, and teenagers fled the chorus of gunfire. My heart raced as I scanned their frantic faces. *Where are they?*

"I'm going to find them," I said before starting towards the crowd.

"Ivan! Ivan!" Julia called after me. I turned back to her. In her eyes, I could see the fear I felt in my chest. "Come back to me."

"I promise," I replied before rushing into the chaos one last time.

The tide of the crowd was against me. I pushed forward, but each step went nowhere. It was impossible to see anyone in the madness. I yelled for them, but in the noise, there was no way they could hear me. I spun around, desperate to see them somewhere among the crowds. Nothing. "Alex! Tyler!"

Someone smacked into me, sending me to the pavement. I sputtered and rolled. Searing pain ran up my arms. I looked down to see the blood dripping from my forearms. *Can't I ever catch a break?* In front of me, a Green soldier raised his rifle and yelled something at me through the noise. I slid the last knife from my sleeve. *Not today.*

The soldier fired, but I was already moving. He spun as I danced through the crowd. They knocked him back, and I used the distraction to slide around him. By the time he could raise the gun again, I had his back with the knife to his throat. "Drop it!"

He groaned and dropped the gun. "What do you want?"

"Where is Princess Alexandria?"

He raised his arms in surrender. "I don't know! I swear!"

I kicked him hamstrings, sending him to his knees. "I don't believe you."

"They said something about her over the radio, but I don't know anything more than that."

They've got her. I slammed the butt of my knife into the side of his head, knocking him out. The crowd thinned as I sprinted back towards the SUV. Bodies of soldiers, guardsmen, cops, and now untagged people lay scattered across the pavement as those left fled. *What have we done?* Standing among the carnage was a familiar face. "Tyler? Tyler!"

His eyes rose to meet me before returning to the ground.

"She's gone, isn't she?" I asked.

He nodded.

I took a deep breath as my mind spun. "C'mon. We need to get back to the group."

He followed me to the SUV. I threw open the door but didn't get the chance to speak. Julia was bawling. She already knew. *But how?* I climbed in next to her and wrapped her in my arms. "I'm so sorry."

The car started moving as she cleared the tears from her eyes and showed me her phone. "Listen."

A message played. It was Bachton's voice. "Hello, Julia. It is passed time for you and I to speak. Come meet me at the Prism Center, and bring only Ivan with you. Both your sister and I would truly appreciate it."

"That asshole!" I groaned.

Tyler signed to Julia, "There were too many."

"This is not your fault," she replied. The look of determination had returned to her face. The dove was ready for war. "We will get her back."

"How?" Kaja replied, her voice shaking.

Julia's icy-eyes cooled the fire I felt in my heart. I sighed. "I hate to say it, but we need to negotiate."

"Ivan and I will attend the meeting with the General Secretary," Julia said with a nod. "Jonah, please inform the Royal Council of the situation and ensure that my mother is detained."

Manny crossed his arms. "Why can't we help?"

"I appreciate your willingness to help Manny, but Jonah will need all of your assistance in handling what is undoubtedly going to be a turbulent situation at the palace. Do you think you can do that?"

"Of course!"

She smiled. "Good. I appreciate your support. When I am queen, you all will have crucial positions in the monarchy, and that work begins now."

Lillian bowed her head. "It's our honor."

We soon reached the palace gates and dropped off the rest of the group. Lillian hugged Julia before leaving, while Jonah gave the formal salute of a soldier. Part of me felt lost as I watched them go. We'd spent days by each other's sides, and I missed having a team. I stared out the window at the palace. It was good to be back, but nothing would be the same. Vera would be in chains, and Julia would wear the crown. We were so close, but Bachton had Alex. There was no way Julia would rest until her sister was returned.

Her hand gripped mine so hard it hurt. I wanted to comfort her, to tell her it would be okay, but neither of us knew what would happen. Bachton could want anything from us, and even with the royal guard on our side now, we would be defenseless in the Prism Center, the UPF's capitol building. Alex was worth the risk.

The streets of Minneapolis were quiet compared to St. Paul. Even after our announcement, the loyalists in the capital followed the UPF's curfew orders. We had popular support at our backs, but they still had the power of fear. I stared out the window into the darkness, wondering what would come next. Fear and anger clashed in my chest. I wanted to kill Bachton for everything he'd done, but I knew it would solve nothing. We were closer than ever to defeating him. It didn't matter. He still ruled.

The Prism Center soon came into view, its black glass exterior reflecting the moonlight. I'd never seen it in person as it was in the heart of the city, surrounded by an excessive number of government buildings. The whole area was closed to the public, and since the Prism Center itself was only two stories, the taller buildings around it masked any view of it. Only Purples and the most elite Blues ever came near it—just like the UPF wanted.

Now, an untagged former Red and a princess who disavowed her family stood at the heart of the UPF's power. My fear faded as I gazed up at it. Instead, I felt only contempt. "We can do this."

"We have no choice. We must do this," Julia replied. "But there is no one I would rather have by my side."

A small smile forced its way to my face. "I love you, sweetheart."

"It is going to take time for me to adjust to you without your tag," she said with a grin.

I chuckled. "Me too."

A UPF guard in all black approached and gestured for us to follow. Julia and I traded glances before walking side by side into the building. As its name implied, the Prism Center was shaped like a triangle. We entered on the southern edge and headed down a hall adorned with various designs featuring the Prism. The narrow purple carpet covering the wooden floors dulled our steps as I studied the old maps and propaganda lining the walls. I wondered how much of the UPF's strategy had changed over the century they'd ruled, but I didn't have time to think much because we soon reached Bachton's office.

The guard patted me down before we entered. This time, I didn't attack him as he left Julia alone. He confiscated my knife, but it didn't matter anyway. I had no plans to kill Bachton. This was a rescue mission, nothing more. Cutting off the head of the hydra was not worth risking Julia and Alex's lives.

Bachton's office here was different than the one I'd seen after my release from prison. The room was at the point of the building, and the edges intersected behind his desk. Along the wood-paneled wall hung a steel Prism, its points touching each edge and the ceiling. The little light in the room crept through the windows far to Bachton's right and left. He sat in the shadows.

When we entered, Bachton pushed himself out of his chair and bowed his head for a moment before speaking, "I am pleased that you received my message. Please, sit." He pointed an open hand to one of the two leather couches in the center of the room. *Weirdly diplomatic.*

Julia's eyes narrowed. "Thank you for the offer, but we have had quite a long journey and would prefer to stand."

"Very well," he replied as he rounded his desk and sat on the couch opposed to the one he had gestured to. "I suppose you'd like me to tell you where your sister is."

Julia stepped closer to him. Her glare sent a chill down my spine. "This kidnapping violates the Treaty of Minneapolis. You will release Alex immediately."

Bachton reached for the wooden box sitting on the glass coffee table and pulled out a cigar. A guard paced across the room and provided a lighter for him. "Thank you, Roger." He took a puff before looking up at Julia. "I love a good cigar. It's consistent. You always know what you're going to get. You two, on the other hand, have been quite the opposite."

"Where is my sister?" Julia asked, crossing her arms and moving to the opposite end of the coffee table. She towered over Bachton, but he did not seem intimidated.

With another puff of smoke, he analyzed Julia for a moment before replying, his tone slow and condescending, "I remember when you were a little girl. At the time, I was nothing more than the Secretary of Unity, but I saw something in you from the beginning. Your father lacked the conviction to challenge me, your mother was choked by hubris, your eldest sister had little courage, and Alexandria was caught in directionless rebellion. But you... You were different. I saw you had passion, determination, bravery, humility, and a brain, which is a rare trait among the royalty."

He paused and glanced from the Prism in the corner to her.

"You must have barely been a teenager at the time, but you approached me and challenged me on government policy. A princess challenging a minister! Ha! But you were not foolish, and you bit your tongue at the right moments. At first, I believed that you would be a force to be reckoned with. But as you grew, I dismissed you as yet another quiet princess engaged in the pleasantries of royal society. Perhaps I should have trusted my first impression."

"You have yet to answer the question, General Secretary," she replied sternly.

He grinned. "That first impression is why I am surprised you were reckless enough to hold that rally in the heart of a military occupation. The tag cutting part was a cute touch that will only endanger your followers' lives. Is this Red ruining your potential?"

My cheeks were hot, and I spat, "Stop talking and answer the damn question."

His eyes moved to me. "Oh, he speaks. I wondered if you'd gone mute after Delaware's tragic death."

I leapt across the room and grabbed him before Julia could intervene. "I'd kill you if you didn't have Alex! You've taken everything from me, and I can't wait to do the same to you." My hands shook as I gripped his shirt. I hadn't even thought about it before I'd moved. Everything burned. *No.* I released him and stepped back.

His grin widened. "Has the princess leashed the attack dog?"

Julia's eyes were fixed on me. They were soft. "Ivan..."

I took a breath. "Insult me all you want, Bachton. It's all I've heard my entire life, but this isn't about me. Release Alex."

"So she has," he replied. "You see, the only reason I have not killed both of you is the political repercussions of that decision." He took another puff of his cigar and stood before circling back behind his desk and staring up at the Prism. "I do not believe either of us desires another civil war, Princess Julia, but your actions tonight risk a century's worth of work. The Treaty of Minneapolis will crumble if you follow your current path, and that is unfortunate. But perhaps it is an outdated document."

Where is he going with this?

Julia approached the desk. "What are you proposing?"

He turned to face her. "Perhaps we should find an alliance to lead us forward, something that would be beneficial to both of our interests. You can fulfill your potential as a legitimate and powerful queen if you agree to cooperate with me. Together, we can take the first step into the future."

"You're a tyrant!" I replied. "Why would we work with you?"

"Because it would be a shame if something happened to Princess Alexandria."

Julia leaned on the desk, glaring at him. "There were two things that you were correct about, sir: I will not cave like my father, and I am not a schemer like my mother. Unlike you, I believe what I say in public. Your threats are bluffs. If you harm my sister, you will face diplomatic backlash from even among your allies in the Fifth International, and the people will never forgive you. For now, you may have some loyalists on your side, but the murder of a princess will not go unpunished."

Bachton scowled and snuffed out his cigar on the desk. "That is an unfortunate decision and one that you will live to regret, young princess. But, you do indeed have a pulse on this flashpoint. I cannot execute your sister. That would convince your cowardly Council to finally act, but that does not mean that I must release her."

Julia stood straighter once again. "It is also true that the Treaty of Minneapolis is indeed outdated. I have no wish to ally with you, but if negotiation can provide a ceasefire, at least for the time being, then I will swallow my pride."

I clenched my fist. *Negotiate with the UPF? Is she right?* There weren't many options, but a new treaty could delay our progress or worse.

"Yet again, you surprise me, princess," he replied. "What would you have to offer?"

With her eyes narrowed and focused, Julia moved to the second couch and crossed her legs. I joined her as she pursed her lips. When she spoke again, her eyes were like daggers, "In return for the disbandment of the work camps, I am willing to grant royal funds to assist in rebuilding St. Paul and the Enclave to make them hospitable once again."

"What leads you to believe that we would need financial assistance in such measures?"

I scoffed. "We aren't blind. The riot was weeks ago, and there are no signs of new construction."

Julia nodded. "The Front's financial struggles are a poorly kept secret."

"Very well," Bachton replied with a wave of his cigar. "Now, I do have my own demand in return for the release of your sister."

"And what is that?"

"Your mother, the Queen. She betrayed the collective and plotted to begin a civil war. That cannot be forgiven."

For the first time, fear crossed Julia's face, but it was gone as quickly as it appeared. *Her mom for her sister. A hell of a trade.* She froze. For me, the choice was an easy one, but I wasn't the one being asked to hand over my mom to be executed. I decided for her. "You can take me instead."

"Ivan, no!" she grabbed my arm.

Bachton gave a single laugh. "I expected that from you, Ivan, but unfortunately, you are not as valuable as the Queen to me. There are factions within my own party that want nothing more than to see her dead, and the people must see we are dedicated to justice."

I scoffed. "Justice? What justice can a mass murderer provide?"

"Perception is a powerful thing. Your princess understands that." The smoke from his cigar obscured his face, but I could see his grin. He wanted to see us squirm, and he was getting it.

Julia folded her hands in her lap. For a few seconds, she looked down at them before glaring at her counterpart. "My mother is still a royal and therefore shall be tried as such under royal law. Following her sentencing, though, we could allow you to have a trial of your own. You may publicize it as you wish, but she shall not be executed. Custody of her shall be shared between your guards and ours."

He nodded almost too hastily. "Very well, as long as we can make a public announcement of her trial within the week, we have an agreement. Richard, please bring these two to Princess

Alexandria."

"Let peace reign for as long as possible," Julia replied as we stood. I could only glare at Bachton for a few seconds before we moved towards the door.

Before we could leave, though, he interrupted us, "And princess, I do hope this Red does not continue to ruin your great potential."

She didn't look back when she replied, "I pray that someday your pride no longer blinds you to the truth."

We left, and I could breathe for the first time since we'd entered the building. The agreement was not ideal, but the camps would be ended, St. Paul would be rebuilt, and Alex was coming home. Vera deserved to rot in a cell for the rest of her life, watching her daughter be a greater queen than she could have ever been. She would pay for her slaughter.

The guard opened the next door down the hall. Inside, Alex was tied to a chair and gagged. When she saw us, her eyes lit up, and she rocked back and forth in the chair. The guards flanking her untied her and took the gag from her mouth. They tried to force her to her feet, but she threw them off. "If you ever touch me again, you sons of bitches, I will kill you!"

I chuckled. "Glad you're okay. Not sure what we'd do without you."

Julia rushed past me and hugged her. They didn't exchange words, but they didn't need to. I knew how much Alex meant to her, and I couldn't imagine what would happen if we'd lost the rebel princess.

When they released one another, Alex scowled at the guards

and stormed out of the room. Julia and I traded smirks and fol-lowed in her wake. We emerged into the night once again, and as I held the SUV door open for the girls, I gazed at the night sky with a full heart. I'd been beaten down for so long, but as that long day drew to a close, a new dawn was coming.

Chapter 31

After we returned to the palace, the guardsmen took Julia and Alex directly to the room where the dethroned queen was being held. Once their excitement of being reunited had passed, both of their faces had turned stone cold. As we wound our way through the halls of the palace, I didn't say a word. Even if I knew what to say, it wasn't my place.

They weren't in the room very long. I had just enough time to close my eyes and lean my head against the marble wall outside when they emerged once again. It caught me off guard. "Everything okay?"

Julia ignored my comment and waved to the guardsmen. "I am finished with her."

They bowed and rushed inside to collect her. Julia's eyes were cold as I rubbed her back and asked, "What happened?"

"Nothing." She remained focused on the door.

After a minute, Vera emerged with the guards. Her head hung low, and she avoided eye contact with her daughters. I spat at her as she passed me. She shook her head, and rage cracked through her voice. "You have destroyed my family. You ruined everything, you fiend!"

"No, your highness. You did that yourself." I nodded to the

guards, and they dragged her away as she scowled at me.

Anger still flooded through my veins, but I was tired all of a sudden. Watching the guards take her away ahead of her trial was not a triumph. We'd beaten her at her own game, but it felt shallow. Getting revenge didn't bring Delaware back or fill the hole that was left in my heart. All it did was remind me how much of me was still missing, even as I worked to mend the wound. For now, though, I needed sleep. My little room in the servants' wing was calling my name.

We stood there for a long time in silence before Alex spoke, "Everything really has gone to shit."

Julia's eyes were heavy. I couldn't tell if it was from exhaustion, sorrow, or both. Like me, she was an orphan now. Alex and Natasha were the only family she had left, and I doubted Natasha would forgive her for what she'd done. It didn't matter that Julia had no choice; Natasha couldn't see the evil within her mom, and she would blame Julia for her life in prison.

"The danger of what is ahead has become all too real," Julia replied. "We knew from the beginning that we would have to sacrifice part of ourselves, yet I truly did not understand how much." She sniffled and looked from Alex to me. "I never wanted to be queen, especially not like this, but a ruler must make the hard decisions for the good of her people. I am blessed to have both of you by my side to help me make those."

Alex chuckled. "We're screwed if it's up to Red and me to save us all."

"Speak for yourself," I quipped back. "Julia, you'll be an amazing queen, and of course we will do everything we can. Bachton only got a taste tonight of what's coming for him."

"I hope you're right," Julia replied. "For now, though, you should rest, Ivan. Alex and I must speak with our sister." I nodded as she continued, "I have not forgotten my promise to have a funeral for Delaware, Lorelai, and the others who perished in the airstrike. We can reach out to Snapback and the remnants of the Militia tomorrow."

Alex and I traded sorrowful looks before I said, "Thank you."

"She deserves that at the very least. They all do," Julia said. "Go ahead and rest for now. I can see the exhaustion in your eyes."

"You sure?"

Alex replied for her, "We've got this, Red. Natasha is nothing we can't handle."

"Okay." I took a deep breath and pecked Julia on the cheek. "Love you, my princess. You were perfect today."

She blushed as her sister gagged. "I'm right here!"

"As if you lacked romance on our trip," Julia replied.

With a gasp, Alex quipped back, "Tyler likes me? I was unaware."

Julia rolled her eyes and hugged me before pulling her sister along. "Come. We should not delay this any longer."

I bowed. "Night, m'ladies."

Alex flashed a peace sign. "Later, Red."

"You can't call me that anymore," I replied with a chuckle.

Only her pointer finger dropped. *Still Alex.* With the girls gone, I meandered through the halls and back to my room. I knew I should check on the others, but my mind drifted. Nothing mattered at the moment but sleep. Apparently, they weren't on the same page.

"Ivan!" Manny popped off my bed, beaming. The others were all clumped in the closet-room with him.

"What the hell are you guys doing in my room?" I snapped. It was harsh, but I wasn't in the mood. Vera's imprisonment weighed on me more than it should've, and I was shaken by the fact I had to say goodbye to Delaware tomorrow. She was gone. The funeral was the final acceptance of that.

He stepped back. "Oh…"

Lillian patted his arm. "I'm sorry, Ivan, we just wanted to hear how things went."

They're your friends, remember that. I crossed my arms and leaned against the doorframe. "Julia reached a deal with Bachton to free Alex and end the work camps in return for the monarchy paying for the rebuilding of St. Paul and the Enclave."

Their eyes lit up. "That's terrific!" Lillian exclaimed. "I knew she could do it."

I sighed. "But we had to agree to joint custody of Vera in prison. She will be tried as a royal first, but then they can have their own public trial, accusing her of whatever they want. It was the only choice, but it seems wrong to let them deliver their crude justice."

"Let 'em ruin her," Kaja said as she lay on my bed, aggravating me even more. "Didn't she try to kill you?"

"Yes, but that's not the point."

Tyler signed, "What kind of justice would a quiet trial be?"

I shrugged. "What type of justice is lies? They'll blame all of it on her and attempt to wash their hands of their slaughter." That brought the room to silence before Lillian rose and hugged me. "What is that for?"

"I can see you're mourning."

My shoulder slumped, and I unclenched my fists. "Tomorrow we're having a funeral for Delaware and everyone else who died in the airstrikes."

Their heads dropped. *We all knew people.* It didn't matter what color you were that night; bombs don't discriminate.

"It doesn't matter how much we succeed. We can't forget the people we lost," I continued. "But all of us need to sleep first. We can talk more tomorrow."

Kaja chuckled. "You kickin' us out?"

I crossed my arms. "Maybe. Go to bed. You need it as much as me."

"Fine," she replied with a smirk before hopping off the bed and leading the rest of the group out.

Manny smiled up at me as he passed by. "Night, Ivan!"

I smiled back. "At least two of you are nice."

"Lillian is dangerous," Tyler signed.

She raised an eyebrow at him. "I am not!"

His mouth gaped open as he realized she was paying attention during my sign language lessons. I chuckled. "The only thing Lillian threatens is your ego. Night guys."

He flashed a peace sign at me and disappeared down the hall. I shut the door, flopped onto the bed, and fell asleep before I could even pull the covers over me.

Chapter 32

"Welcome home, man." Snapback lunged at me and lifted me off the ground.

I laughed as he set me down. "Missed this place."

He glanced over at Julia, standing at the front of the crowd that had formed along the Enclave riverfront. "She really do it?"

I followed his gaze to her. Dressed in a formal black dress, her golden hair like a crown in the warm light of the setting sun, she was a royal again. But something was different. She now held herself as a leader, a queen. Around her were tagless former Reds gawking at her or frantically asking her a hundred questions, and amid the scramble, her eyes met mine. They told a million stories: love, loss, and triumph. We'd been through too much, and the road ahead wasn't any easier. We both knew that. As we stared across the crowd at each other, though, all I could think of was how much I loved her. In a few minutes, we'd be remembering those we'd lost. She was all I had left. "Yeah. She did."

"Wow. Takes guts to throw your own mom in jail," Snap replied.

"It took compromise. Bachton wanted to kill her for tricking them." I sighed. "As much as it sucks, those deals are going to keep us alive until we can rebuild."

"What about the tagless?" He tugged at his ear. It was as weird seeing him without one as it was not wearing one myself. We'd worn them our entire lives: black then red. My mind had the phantom feeling it was still there.

"We have ideas, but the timing has to be right. I promise I'll let you know when we have a plan. Until then, the Militia is more important than ever." I surveyed the faces along the riverfront, some of which I recognized from our raid on the New Ulm camp. They no longer looked like ghosts, even if their road to recovery wasn't over. "Luckily, with the tagless and the end of the camps, we'll have plenty of new members. You ready?"

His head dropped. "Without Naomi? No."

I hugged him. Snapback wasn't going to cry in public, but I knew exactly how he felt. We were saying goodbye to my best friend, but he had fallen for Delaware years ago. Even if they hadn't been dating long, her death just a few months after losing his best friend, Blitzkrieg, had ripped his heart out. I had Julia, but all he had left was the Militia. Life was unfair.

When we released each other, I looked towards the crowd. Aaron stood among them, and he nodded when he noticed us. "You won't be alone," I said. "With royal support and the Minutemen, we'll build the Militia into a force stronger than it's ever been. I promise you we'll make Del proud."

"Damn right." He huffed. "I should head over to finish getting things ready. Let me know when you want to start."

"Thanks, Snap." I headed over to Aaron and met him with the Red handshake.

He smiled. "I thought you weren't a Red anymore."

"And I see you're not a Yellow now."

"It's a terrible color. Did not compliment my skin," he replied with a pat of his face.

I chuckled. "Thanks for everything you did. There's no way we could have pulled that off without you."

"Especially in the shape you were in." He nodded towards Julia. "The Minutemen put a lot into Operation Pridefall. Glad she, and you, didn't let us down."

"So what's next for the Minutemen? I assume you'll be helping us and the Militia…"

"White Crown is still our goal. With Julia as queen, we will have the leverage we need to finish the Front. Until that happens, we will support the Militia's reconstruction, of course. Snapback will need all the help he can get." His eyes found Snap in the crowd. "It's a risk leaving him in charge. He isn't prepared."

"It's our job to make sure he is." Before Aaron could protest, I made my way towards Julia and finished, "I think it's time to start."

He huffed, and I was giddy with my trick. There were fewer and fewer people I could trust every day, but Aaron would always be one of them. Behind his tough exterior was a guy that cared too much to give up on trouble makers like Snap and me. When I had reached rock bottom, he picked me up. We both would do the same for Snapback.

Julia's soft smile met me when I joined her along the riverfront. She'd dressed me in all black, and I felt invisible as the sun dipped below the trees in the west. Behind us, I could hear the flow of the Mississippi. Just a month ago, the noises of downtown St. Paul would have carried across the river, but now, it was an eerie quiet. It felt appropriate.

In the crowd, I noticed Alex hugging another girl. Tears streamed down both of their cheeks. "Is that Lorelai?" I asked Julia.

"It must be," she replied as Alex beamed at us.

My eyes drifted to my feet before I smiled back at her. Alex deserved that happiness, and it was a relief to know Lorelai had survived. To some, she would have been another name on the list of deaths, but each life mattered. Seeing the two of them reunited gave me hope.

We stood before the crowd, Snapback alongside me. For once, the Enclave looked alive compared to downtown St. Paul. People were everywhere, all coming to remember the lives lost to the UPF's brutality. The sight brought joyful tears to my ears and tore at my heart. For the first time, I was as at peace as I could be about Delaware's death as I scanned the faces of those she led. Everything we did and continued to do was in her memory, and we would finish the job for her. When the Enclave was abandoned and the Militia on the run, she was the one who stepped up. She'd kept these people alive, and because of her, they were home.

Julia spoke first, her voice mixing with the river, "Thank you all for gathering with us today to remember the lives of our friends and family lost the night of the Front's bombing. We may never have the opportunity to bury their bodies, but they cannot take from us the memories we hold. Candles are being distributed through the crowd. Each represents a life."

A tagless man handed each of us a candle. I nodded to him before staring down at mine and nervously picking at the wax. In my hands was the life of Delaware or a stranger who had stood against the rioters' tide of violence. That was jarring. None of us knew what would happen when we stepped in front of the Fracture, and none of us were prepared for what did.

Snapback stepped forward and pulled a lighter from his pocket. "We will never forget what they did for us. They were our friends, family, girlfriends…" He swallowed, and I could tell he was trying to hold back his emotions. "They were the bravest people, willing to sacrifice themselves so that we could hope to be free. Delaware… Naomi was the girl I loved. She couldn't stand to watch the suffering caused by Max, and she decided to end it."

He started crying, and I found myself struggling to hold back my own tears as he continued, "The UPF stole everything from her, but she made them regret it until her final moment. She was a strong-minded, funny, and adventurous girl. The Militia will never be the same without her, and I will never be the same without her."

The sun's light faded as he lit the candle. As I watched the flame dance in the dark, I began to cry myself. *I'll never see her again.* It was my turn to speak, but the words were caught in my throat. My eyes went to the sky. After a few seconds, I found the words. "Delaware loved the stars. From the moment I met her, I knew she was a fighter, but I found in time that she was a dreamer. She'd lost everything she had yet fought for a better world for others. In seconds, she would go from a sarcastic and joyful girl to an aggressive warrior, defending those she loved. And that's what she did until the very end."

My voice cracked as I tried to push through my tears. I wasn't thinking of what to say next. I was pouring my heart out, talking to her as much as the crowd. "I blamed her at first, for putting herself in danger. But I was wrong. Del was a hero, and I miss her every single day."

I lit my candle with Snapback's and whispered, "I miss you, Del."

Julia took a raspy breath. "The sacrifices of all our fathers and sisters, mothers and sons who we have lost will not be forgotten. All of those who stood against the Front's tyranny died as heroes. They will be remembered as such." She lit her candle with mine before passing it onto the crowd. Her hand slid into mine, grounding me to reality.

Still, my heart ached as the candlelight was passed through the crowd. Each new light was another person slaughtered by Bachton and the UPF. It was impossible not to feel some guilt. They marched because of my plan, but I got to live. That would never leave me. It would spur me forward to ensure no one suffered their fate again.

Soon, the whole crowd was illuminated by hundreds of flickering candles piercing the darkness. The lights showed the tears and sorrow of loss, but they also showed hope. So many people in the crowd were like me. They'd lost everything, and all that remained was hope that the future would be better than the past.

I saw that hope in their eyes, but my chest tightened as I realized they weren't staring only at Julia. Their hope rested in all three of us. That scared me, but with Julia's hand in mine and friends by my side, I knew we would be alright. We'd been through hell, but we'd pushed through. Ahead of us would be another election and our final fight against the Front, but no matter what happened now, we would succeed or fail together. White Crown had begun. *We're coming for you Bachton.*

END OF BOOK THREE

A Word From The Author

Thank you for taking the time to read the third book of The Prism Files! I hope you have enjoyed reading it as much as I have enjoyed writing it. If you did, please consider giving it an honest review online.

To stay updated on my writing for the series, receive more insights into the world of The Prism Files, and have the chance to win free books, sign-up to receive my newsletter at: www.Brendan-Noble.com